Archie AND Emma

A Novel Based on Actual People and Events

BRIAN MERCER

outskirtspress
DENVER, COLORADO

Archie and Emma
A Novel Based on Actual People and Events

v2.0

Outskirts Press, Inc.
http://www.outskirtspress.com

ISBN: 978-1-4787-4816-8

PRINTED IN THE UNITED STATES OF AMERICA

This is a work of fiction based on actual people and events. Many of the events and characters described herein are imaginary and are not intended to refer to specific places or living persons.

This book is dedicated to our grandchildren. I hope to live long enough to take you to ballgames someday, but if not, this book will have to serve as our time together. By the way, your dad wasn't really this lousy at baseball.

Part One

Prologue

I was a stranger, and ye took me in.

Richmond, Indiana, 1857

Jackie could feel his five-year-old legs turning to jelly as he ran faster than he could to keep up with the rest of his family. He tried his best to believe his father when he said, "Just one more clearing, Jack!" even though he'd said that at each of the last dozen rest stops.

Jackie at least had the satisfaction that his two older sisters weren't doing any better, as Mother had to constantly cajole them to keep going, and, after all, tonight had at least been easier than the last two nights. Not only was this stretch of Indiana flatter than the portion they had finished earlier in the week, but these fields didn't have as many holes or ruts. Jackie had lost his last shoe the night before when he stepped in a hole that just about broke his ankle.

"Derned gophers!" his father had muttered as he picked Jackie up and carried him the rest of the way.

Mother and Father were so proud of their "little man" when he announced he'd be able to run again tomorrow, but Jackie knew he wasn't really as brave as all that. He'd just much rather run all night than be carried like a sack of potatoes, every step making him feel like his ribs were about to explode as they smashed into his father's powerful shoulders.

Now that he was running shoeless he was even more thankful for the rest stop that each grove of trees or the occasional building afforded them. He took those opportunities to pick the little rocks he'd collected out of his bare feet and put them in his pockets as souvenirs. Unfortunately, Mother soon caught on to the secret rock collection and made him leave them behind - something about them weighing him down.

There was another challenge that made this run more dangerous than the others - a new, full moon. Tonight's moon was mesmerizing; one of "God's great wonders," as Jackie's Grandpa used to say. They could only hope it was so beautiful that it distracted the hunters long enough for them to get to the next station safely. If they got caught it would be easy to blame God for setting a giant flood light in the sky to illumine their every move. But God was on their side. He had to be.

Jackie's only goal, as the family dashed through each clearing, was to run fast enough that Father wouldn't feel compelled to take his hand. Being yanked along by one limb and having it partially ripped from its socket repeatedly was only slightly less painful than the rib-smashing. If only he was a little older and stronger, then he wouldn't need help and he could drag his sisters along by the hand.

As they dashed behind an old beech tree to catch their collective breath, Jackie began to be thankful for his dark skin. He couldn't think of another time that he'd been thankful for it, but for right now, it was helping him hide in the darkness, making him just a little bit safer. The reality was of course that his white shirt negated any camouflage effect his skin might have afforded him, but he'd take any help he could get.

The Jacksons were just about to dart out into the field and race for the next hiding place when Father heard a noise he didn't like and brought their progress to a halt. He pushed the group back behind the closest tree and placed a finger to his lips. Jackie and his sisters didn't need to be told what that meant or how important their silence was. Leaving the beloved family dog behind in Ohio was enough of a reminder.

Father snuck a peek around the tree and spotted the party responsible. Looking back at him was a set of glowing, yellowish eyes belonging to a raccoon that was scurrying his own family across the field to safety. Both fathers stood for a moment and stared at each other; there was a greeting between them, of sorts. Jackie's Father was almost embarrassed that he felt a kinship with this animal but...how could he not? Besides, no one else saw the exchange. Father waited for another moment just to be sure it was the raccoons that were responsible for the noise he'd heard and then he and his family dashed for the next tree.

John Jackson, Sr. was an impressive man, at least that's how he appeared to his son. When you're five years old your father is always a massive hulk of a man regardless of his relative size to other adult males, but for Jackie, John was a towering figure in every way. Sure, he stood about six feet tall and roughly two hundred pounds, but that wasn't so impressive. And, yes, he was the first Jackson they knew of to graduate from that era's version of high school, or to own his own business, or to have his name appear in the paper for some reason other than an obituary - or worse. But the things Jackie always admired him for were his courage, his refusal to take "No" for an answer, and his faith that pushed him to do things that defied rational sense - like this trip for instance.

The America of 1857 was far more dangerous for "Free Blacks" like the Jacksons than it had been even a few years earlier. Recent federal actions had brought national, anti-slavery tensions to the boiling point. The Kansas-Nebraska Act of 1854 followed by the Dred Scott decision of 1857 enraged northern abolitionists and set the nation on a sure path to civil war. But for the Jacksons, and so many like them, it was the Compromise of 1850 that permanently altered their lives.

In return for California's inclusion as a free state and assurances that the Union would remain intact, the compromise threw Southern Democrats a number of bones that promised to fortify slaveholder's rights; the most notorious of these provisions was the new Fugitive Slave Law.

What this meant to the average person was that southern slave hunters, sometimes known as slave catchers, were allowed to cross into northern states to pursue escaped slaves and then bring them back to their masters in the south. Prior to the new law, northern authorities openly hindered the slave catchers' work, but now they were under obligation to not only stop working against the bounty hunters but to aid them for fear of prosecution that could bring six months in jail and a one thousand dollar fine. This went for the private citizen too.

The slave catchers needed only to provide an affidavit to a commissioner declaring that the "escaped slave" was the property of someone else and the commissioner would bind the slave over for deportation. Those accused had no right to a trial since this was a property rights issue. Commissioners were paid $10 for a decision against the "slave" and only $5 for a decision to release them. As would be expected, such a payment, or bribe if you prefer, was very successful. As a result many free blacks whose families had not known slavery for several generations, if ever, were caught, bound over as escaped slaves and sent "back" to a southern state they had never before seen. The slave catcher would then sell the slave at auction or offer him to an owner whose escaped slave could not be found.

Opponents of slavery in the north were furious about the new law and with President Millard Fillmore for pushing it through Congress and signing it. Bands of abolitionist rebels freed detained blacks by force, even burning jails to the ground. Anti-slavery rhetoric intensified to the point that prominent Christian ministers publicly dared the government to prosecute them for harboring blacks. They were confident that the authorities could not beat back the crowds who would stop at nothing to set them free should they be jailed for their disobedience.

John Jackson had watched several of his Dayton, Ohio neighbors fraudulently hauled away as a result of this new law. Families were torn apart without warning, unlikely to ever be reunited. Due to his physical size and abilities he knew he was a prime target to be bound into slavery as well.

His entire life could be changed in an instant - and for what? A $10 paycheck for a slave hunter who had never done an honest day's work in his life? He was disgusted at himself for even entertaining the thought of giving in - to willingly give up all he had worked so hard for. But the more he thought about the prospect of being separated from his wife and children the more he realized that nothing was worth losing them, so he began to devise a plan to escape north of the border. Canada, still a British colony, had outlawed slavery in 1834 due to the tireless work of English abolitionists William Wilberforce, Thomas Clarkson, Granville Sharp, Hannah More and many others back across the pond, so she became a promising destination for blacks hoping to remain free.

Meanwhile, the rebellion against slavery and the Fugitive Slave Law only grew. The Underground Railroad, as it was called, continued chugging along. In Indiana, despite public sentiment against blacks that culminated in an 1851 state constitutional amendment forbidding black settlement in the state, the human smuggling operation was as strong as ever. The Richmond and Newport areas have since become legendary as the Grand Central Station of the Underground Railroad due to the efforts of one Levi Coffin.

Father whispered to the whole family, "There it is! The Coffin House! That's our stop for the night. Just one more field, Jack." Jackie believed his father this time - he had to, even if it was just enough to get him to the next rest stop.

John Jackson escorted his family at full speed across their final clearing of the night. The house they were heading for was a simple, one-story dwelling encased in shadow-casting elm trees that were a welcome sight after a clearing that seemed like it stretched for days. Mother and the children hid themselves in the bushes that lined the house as Father crept up to the door and rapped on it gently.

He had heard so many stories of the Coffin House and its proprietor, the so-called President of the Underground Railroad, that he had built this citadel up in his mind to so great a degree that no building could measure up to his fantasy. Still, this was very disappointing. What he didn't know was that he still hadn't found the Coffin House and never would. Levi Coffin and his wife, Catherine White Coffin, had sold the house and moved to Cincinnati back in '47, but their courage had inspired so many that others had carried on their work. The stories of the Coffins' heroics in Indiana only grew when the couple moved to Ohio and opened a free labor warehouse. John had heard the tales and for months had planned his route to pass through Richmond, not knowing that Mr. Coffin was already his neighbor in Ohio, or that the Coffins had actually lived ten miles north of Richmond in Newport.

John heard a knock from the inside that echoed his. Was this a password he didn't know about? He didn't know what to do so he knocked back in the exact same pattern. Almost immediately, the door opened a crack.

From inside the man's voice whispered, "How many are ye?"

"Five." John said equally as quiet.

"Quickly!" said the voice and the door opened.

John motioned to his wife and she scurried her brood in to safety. The man, who couldn't have been more than thirty years old, didn't say a word but motioned for them to follow him as he put his fingers to his lips. John liked him already.

The inside of the dwelling was just as modest as the outside. Even in the dark John could tell a lot about this man by what wasn't in his home. Everything in the front room told him that he valued function over style. The man took them to the center of the house and John saw over the fireplace the only words to be found in the house. The stitched sign read,

"For I was an hungred, and ye gave me meat: I was thirsty, and ye gave me drink: I was a stranger, and ye took me in."

That told John about all he needed to know.

The man led them to a back room and motioned for John to help him move a trunk. The trunk rested on a rug, and when that was pulled away it revealed a trap door that led to a secret room underneath the house.

The man said to John, "I'm sure your children are weary. Let us get them to rest."

John answered sincerely, "I can never repay your kindness, Mr. Coffin. May God pour heaven's riches on you."

"I'm not Mr. Coffin, sir," said the man.

"Then who is it my pleasure to thank for saving the lives of my family?"

"The Lord saved you. I am just His friend. My name is unimportant, as is yours. 'Tis safer we remain strangers. The sun will be up soon. Get your children to bed and we'll bring their breakfast in good time."

In the dimmed light, one of Jackie's sisters tripped on the rug and sent a wooden cup hurtling to the ground from a small table near the window. Immediately, as if on cue, a child's cry could be heard from the next room. John quickly picked up the cup, returned it to its place, and apologized profusely.

"Fret not," said the stranger, "'tis almost time for her feeding."

"How old is she, sir?"

"Fourteen months, nearly. She is a great blessing from God Almighty, but rare is the blessing that comes without trial."

"I have been so blessed myself," John responded.

"A curious thing," replied his benefactor, "a soul petitions Providence for great blessing and then objects when that petition is granted. Her mother fell gravely ill when she came, but the Lord heard my cry and spared me from anguish. Now we hear our blessing's cry on the hour."

The man's wife emerged from the back of the house with her daughter in her arms. She was an adorable red-headed child with green eyes that sparkled like the prairie on the first day of spring. Her mother was no more than a child herself and from a single glance at them together one could tell that years later they would be mistaken for sisters.

Jackie had seen many white children of course, yet he couldn't help but stare at this creature who was now reaching out her little hand to him. Her mother bent down so the two little ones could see eye to eye and urged Jackie to reach out his hand to her. Just as they were about to touch, the little girl burst into a squeal of delight that startled everyone in the room. The man of the house motioned to John that they should be moving along so they all made their way down the rope ladder into the cellar.

As they descended into the secret room they could neither see nor hear a thing, but Jackie smelled something that could only be described as foul-smelling flowers. They would discover in the morning that there was a truly foul smell in the room that just wouldn't go away. It had been left by many last minute house guests, but the proprietors had arranged dozens of flowers all over the room in an attempt to mask the offensive odors.

As the Jacksons settled into a spot along the western wall and quieted down the children, John could tell they weren't alone.

"Who's there?" He whispered. "We're the Jacksons, from Ohio."

"Watson, Missoura," a man's voice responded.

"A pleasure." John replied.

"Did you see the catchers tonight, Jackson?" Watson asked after a moment.

"No, but that doesn't mean they didn't see us. That moon sure was bright," John said with a twinge of complaint.

Watson confided, "We decided to stay here an extra night to wait it out. The children needed the rest." A pint-sized, "mm hmm" from his right validated his assertion.

"Reckon we could stay here for a week the food's so good," said a new voice from across the room.

Startled, John asked, "Who's that?"

"Robinson, Mississippi. Good to know ya."

"Likewise, how many more are we, Watson?" John wondered aloud.

The voices came from all over the room.

"Williams, Alabama."

"Atwood, Tennessee."

"Cummings, South Carolina."

"Banton, Virginia."

Jackie couldn't believe his ears. He always knew that his wasn't the only family that had to run every night but now he had proof. All of a sudden he didn't feel so alone. "Papa?"

"Yes, Jack?"

"Mr. Coffin is a good man, ain't he?"

"Isn't he," John said, correcting Jackie's English as he was wont to do. "That's right, Jack. He is a very good man. But this isn't Mr. Coffin."

"That makes two good men, don't it? Doesn't it?"

"There are many more than that, Jack." John turned to Watson's slowly appearing silhouette and asked, "Who is this man, Watson?"

Watson whispered, "Nobody knows his name. He's just calls himself a Friend."

"Yessir, that he is," John replied.

The Jackson clan began to drift off to sleep with visions of their new home in Canada filling their dreams. Though no reality could expect to match the hopes of a soul's God-breathed yearning for freedom,

Canada would be a welcomed sight when they finally arrived three months later. But like any of us might experience, the final destination is not always the greatest gift. Often each thing learned on the trip is worth a dozen glorious arrivals.

John said a silent prayer of thanks for another night of safe travel. Finally, his family was safely asleep and he was about to join them when Jackie stirred on his lap.

"Papa?"

"Time for sleep, Jack."

"Can I ask you a question?"

"One question."

"Our friend...is he a lot like Jesus?"

John tried to come up with an answer that would sum up the nuances of the situation so a five year old could understand, but in a moment of clarity he realized that his son might be more perceptive than he'd care to admit. He found the perfect answer. "Yes, son. That he is."

1
The the Angels Angels of the Angels

Glendora, California, Present Day

Taylor would never admit it but eating an eighty year old man's dust once a week was starting to get a little old, though not nearly as embarrassing as him singing at the top of his lungs in public. "Hold on Grandpa! Wait up!"

"*Take me out to the ballgame! Take me out to the crowd!* ...How's this for a spot, Taylor?"

"Whatever you want, Grandpa."

"Then this'll do."

Grandpa had picked out the same spot he'd picked out every week that season, behind the centerfield fence. That's where you sit when you're the proud grandparent of the centerfielder, or at least, the second-string centerfielder.

"*Buy me some peanuts and Cracker Jack...* Say, you aren't allergic to peanuts are you, Taylor?"

"No, I'm not Grandpa," came the terse reply.

"Good, we wouldn't want to see you go into anagalactic shock or anything."

"It's anaphylactic. And I'm no more allergic to nuts than I was the last three times you asked me."

"Oh, have I asked you that before?"

"Pretty much every week."

"Really, have I asked you that before?" Grandpa was the only one who thought that was humorous. He broke out into song again, stubbornly finishing the tune. "*I don't care if I ever get back!*"

Taylor was hoping that occupying him with practical concerns would distract him from his concert, which was drawing more annoyed glances from their neighbors with each refrain. Grandpa was carrying a lawn chair, a footrest, a small cooler and a bag of supplies. "Can I hold something for you, Grandpa?"

"I think that might be helpful, sweetheart." He loaded Taylor down with most of his belongings and made the descent into his lawn chair, singing all the way. He'd never intentionally let on that this was getting harder every week, but his groans gave him away this time.

John William Mercer, or Grandpa as he is affectionately known to his own grandchildren, other people's grandchildren and a vast assortment of complete strangers, is somewhat of a rarity. The energetic octogenarian is a native Californian for one thing, as was his father; he's been married to the same woman for over fifty years, held the same job since he left the Navy right after college, and doesn't have his therapist on speed dial. In fact, he doesn't even own a cell phone, though he has kept up with technology to some degree, dabbling with internet sales now that he's semi-retired, whatever that means.

After the Navy he joined the family retail company that had been in Los Angeles since 1887. Grandpa's great uncle John, for whom he was named, had come out from Indiana the year the railroad came through and set up shop selling poultry supplies when LA was still a sleepy cow town. The company moved dozens of times over the years and adapted their inventory to the changing city, finally ending up as the Natick Hotel Bookstore in 1901. Grandpa's dad, Archibald George Mercer, added collectible postage stamps to the mix when he joined the company in the 20's and Grandpa added his hobbies of model trains and planes when he started full-time in the 60's.

A history major in college and then a career selling historically-themed items at the store didn't reduce his natural tendency toward story-telling. Any opportunity he could take to regale an unsuspecting audience with tales of past glory that led to a significant, moral lesson was too tempting to pass up. Taylor was just such a target.

Grandpa had almost completed the arduous task of lowering his posterior into his chair when an impish voice piped up. "Can I get you anything else, Grandpa, maybe a crane?"

"When you get to be my age, let me know if you still find that funny," Grandpa huffed.

"Are you planning on being around that long?"

"You never know. I may just hang on for spite."

Taylor loved playing this game of verbal one-upmanship with Grandpa. She knew she was really no match for the master, that he could smite her with a mortal, verbal blow anytime he wanted, but they had been playing this game since she was a little girl and it had become their thing. Grandpa had developed a unique relationship with each of his grandchildren, trying to meet them where they were. Grandpa always said that Taylor had been "a little mouthy since before she could speak," so he thought their oral sparring sessions might help prepare her for a life in politics, or some other profession that required one to be articulate while saying nothing of significance.

Grandpa wasn't Taylor's biological grandfather; he was technically her great uncle, though that hardly mattered. Taylor's grandparents on her father's side both passed on while her dad was in high school, just about Taylor's age now. He had come to live with Grandpa and Grandma and raised his girls to consider them their grandparents, an arrangement that made Grandpa very happy. Grandpa had a total of eight "grandchildren" plus one biological grandchild, Nick, the second-string centerfielder.

Grandpa finally lowered his carcass into his chair with a thud and Taylor followed suit, groaning and all, which triggered the desired disgusted glance from Grandpa.

"So who's Nick's team playing today? Here's your stuff." Taylor handed him the rest of his belongings and he began to set up his miniature baseball-watching kingdom.

"Thank you, honey." He pulled his scorebook out of his bag. "They're playing the Cubs today."

"Are they any good?" Taylor asked.

"First place, if I remember." Grandpa made it sound as though he hadn't made it his responsibility to have the standings memorized at all times.

Sensing the answer, Taylor cautiously asked, "How's Nick's team doing?"

Grandpa answered in his patented deadpan, "Their next win will be their first."

"Oh my, this is gonna be a long day isn't it?"

"Now, winning isn't everything, sweetheart. Baseball is about tradition. Fathers and sons playing catch on the front lawn, the smell of the grass, the feel of a fresh ball in your favorite glove..." They exchanged a glance and he continued without skipping a beat, loud enough for everyone to hear. "But it sure wouldn't hurt to win one once in a while!"

"Will Nick get to play today, Grandpa?"

"Of course, everyone has to get at least one at bat and play three defensive outs."

"Good thing they have that rule," she said with a smile.

In his best Oliver Hardy impersonation, complete with head bob, Grandpa replied, "It certainly is."

Taylor asked, "Why does he keep playing, Grandpa? I mean maybe he should spend his time doing something he's good at."

"Well, first off, I don't believe it's mandatory to have your entire life mapped out at twelve, but, more importantly, I think he still enjoys it. It's hard to stop when it's in your blood."

Nick's team ran out onto the field for pregame warm-ups and

Grandpa started his own pregame ritual of waving conspicuously to Nick with a goofy grin on his face to get his attention. Nick did his best not to be rude to his grandfather and yet not let anyone on the team see – because that would be uncool. Not nearly as uncool as dropping every third ball thrown or hit to you, but you do what you can. Nick's coach often quipped that hitting fly balls to his team was a Catch 22. "You hit 'em a hundred and they'll catch twenty-two."

Taylor kept the conversation going at least in part to protect her cousin. "You're all big baseball fans on your side of the family, aren't ya?"

Grandpa knew an invitation for a story when he heard one. "It's something we've just passed down through the years. My father worked a lot, so to spend time with me uninterrupted he'd take me to ball games. My granddad was a pretty good player. I remember my uncle John telling me about..."

Unbeknownst to Grandpa, Taylor's cell phone had rung right after she asked the question and she was no longer listening. Her phone conversation, try as she might to disguise it, was more interesting than Grandpa.

"I'm sorry. I'll just be a little while. I'm at my cousin's baseball game... I told you that..."

The voice on the other end was dominating the conversation.

"No, of course I'd rather be with you..."

Grandpa muttered something undistinguishable and Taylor realized that she'd said that too loud. She stood and moved a couple steps away to have a more private moment.

"I'll call you when I'm done...I don't know, a couple of hours? ... I'm not mad, Carter... Carter?" The caller hung up, much to Taylor's dismay and Grandpa's delight.

"When did you get one of those things?"

Still distracted, Taylor grunted, "What?"

Grandpa pointed to the infernal contraption. "That leash. When did you get a leash?"

Taylor realized his meaning. "Oh, my phone? I've had it for years. Well, not this one, this one is pretty new. You like it?"

"Lovely," Grandpa said succinctly, "Who was yanking your chain?"

"Oh, that was just Carter," she said with a smile.

"Boyfriend?" Grandpa asked. Taylor nodded in the affirmative and Grandpa continued, "How long?"

With just a little bit of pride she answered, "It'll be two months tomorrow."

"Oh, a long-term relationship! Do you know him from school?"

The phone rang again and Taylor practically sprinted to her previous, private location out of Grandpa's earshot.

"Hi. Okay, I know. You too. I'll call you later." Her walk back to the chair had a little spring in it this time.

"He's pretty persistent," Grandpa sighed.

Knowing that the subject would change immediately if she could get him focused back on telling his story, Taylor asked, "What were you saying about your father? He taught you to play baseball?"

Grandpa was predictably distracted. "He taught me to appreciate it. He took me to my first professional game."

"The Dodgers?" Taylor asked. One could forgive Taylor for jumping to conclusions since Grandpa was wearing a Dodgers windbreaker and ball cap, though the cap was covered with pins from each of the thirty-nine ballparks he and Grandma had visited, making the team logo barely visible.

He overlooked her lack of historical baseball knowledge. "No, the Dodgers didn't get here until '58. My team was the Angels."

Taylor was puzzled. "The Los Angeles Angels of Anaheim? I thought they were new."

He said with a twinge of antipathy, "No, the Los Angeles Angels of Los Angeles. Which translated from the Spanish, I suppose, is The The Angels Angels of The Angels. They were part of the old Pacific Coast League."

"And your grandpa went with you too?"

With a laugh he replied, "Oh no, I never got to meet my grandpa Archie, but my uncle John said that he was quite the ballplayer."

"Was your grandpa in the majors?"

Grandpa thought for a moment of how great that would have been and then answered, "No, he grew up when professional baseball was just starting out. He never turned pro but they say he could have. Say, didn't your Dad ever tell you the story?"

"What story?"

"THE story!"

"I don't know what story you mean."

Grandpa stared at her aghast for a moment. "My grandparent's story!" Grandpa almost yelled.

Taylor cowered just a little bit. "Sorry."

Grandpa was incredulous. "You mean to tell me that you've never heard the story of your great-great-grandparents? Your dad has three girls; I'd think he'd have worn himself out telling that at bedtime every night."

"Maybe he doesn't know it," she said with a shrug.

"He named your sister after her, you know," he said.

"After who?"

"My grandmother, Emma Williams Mercer. Why it's only the greatest love story ever told." Realizing that he might have ventured into a bit of hyperbole bordering on heresy he looked to the sky and made the sign of the cross on his chest. "Okay, maybe the second greatest."

"So?"

"So, what?" Now it was Grandpa's turn to be a little clueless.

She asked semi-politely, "Are you gonna tell me the story?"

"Right now? You'll miss the game."

Clearly Taylor wasn't there for her love of baseball. "I'll survive."

"Well, okay, I suppose we have a while. Do you want the Reader's Digest version?" Realizing he had forgotten the generation Taylor belonged to, he backtracked. "Do you want me to condense it for you?"

Taylor asked, "How many innings do they play?" Grandpa showed her his scorebook all prepared for a six inning game. "You'd better tell me the whole thing."

"That thing isn't going to ring, is it?"

Nodding, she replied, "Probably, but I can ignore it."

Grandpa straightened himself, made several silly warming up gestures with his hands and began. "Once upon a time…"

He didn't get far. "Grandpa, please!"

Grandpa leaned over conspiratorially and whispered, "J.K." He was surprised that Taylor didn't recognize such a common cultural reference so he felt the compulsion to explain. "Just Kidding."

Taylor knew what he meant, of course. It was just sacrilege coming from him. "Seriously, Grandpa? Are you gonna pretend to be cool all day?"

Head hung, he said, "Yes, and fail miserably."

2

Shame on Your Teachers!

Grandpa began, "My grandparents, Archie and Emma, grew up about two blocks from each other in Cambridge City, Indiana in the 1860's. Emma's parents came from a long line of Quakers that came to America in the sixteen hundreds. In fact, one of her grandfathers came over with William Penn and helped found Philadelphia. Emma's great-grandfather was a famous Quaker preacher so it was a very traditional household. Emma had an older brother and two little sisters..."

Taylor wasn't sure she was really interested in the history lesson, but it beat watching the coaches rake the field.

"My grandfather's side has been here even longer. We traced my great-times-four grandfather, Colonel Oliver Smith, all the way back to Betsy Ross." Grandpa got a mischievous look on his face and went in for the kill. "In fact, his wife traced him back there several times."

Taylor would have none of it. "Oh, Grandpa, that joke's even older than you are. Just tell the story."

"Okay, but he was a colonel in the Continental Army, and we can trace our family back to five different passengers on the Mayflower."

Taylor was pretty sure that was a big deal but tried to play it cool. "So doesn't pretty much every family have someone who rode on the Mayflower?"

"Well, I suppose it doesn't exactly make us unique, but it is interesting. We have a lot of interesting people in our history. Our great times something uncle, General Hugh Mercer, was a good friend of George Washington. He crossed the Delaware with him - some even say it was his idea - and bought Ferry Farm, which was Washington's boyhood home, which is of course where he cut down the cherry tree, that is if that story's not just a legend, which it probably is. Actually, that story was first told in a biography written by a guy named Weems in 1800.... Wait a minute. What story was I telling again?"

"Does it matter?"

"Oh, my grandparents, right. My grandpa Archie's family was from New London, Connecticut but he was born after they moved to Buffalo, New York. Then when he was about six his father moved the family again to Cambridge City to start a new company called the Car Shops. They made railroad cars, reapers and other farm equipment. Grandpa had three younger brothers and two younger sisters. He and his oldest brother, William, worked in the factory when they were young. Now, you're studying American history aren't you?"

"More or less." Evidently the two questions, 1) was Taylor's class studying American History and 2) was Taylor studying American History, had two different answers.

"Okay, then stop me if there's something you don't understand. Wayne County, Indiana was settled in the early 19th century by The Quakers, otherwise known as The Society of Friends.

As much as she hated to admit that she didn't understand the first thing he said, though he had first lost her way back at William Penn, Taylor started to sheepishly raise her hand. "Uh, Quakers?'

Grandpa sighed, "Let's just say they were Christians who took their faith very seriously. One of the things they believed in strongly was that slavery was in direct opposition to Christianity. In fact, most of the clans that came to Eastern Indiana moved from Tennessee and North Carolina because they didn't want to live in slave states. Now, from your studies, what did they call people who opposed slavery back then?"

Taylor felt like she could finally contribute. "Oh, we just studied this.... umm... absolutionalists?"

"Well, that's close, I suppose. They were called *abolition*ists, because they wanted to *abolish* slavery."

"Ah, right."

"And you've heard of the Underground Railroad?"

"More or less?"

"Shame on your teachers! The railroad was a secret network of safe houses and safe routes that allowed slaves to escape from the south and into the north, and then usually into Canada. Abolitionists of all kinds, including Quakers and Presbyterians among many others, formed an underground resistance movement. Eastern Indiana was a Quaker stronghold so it became an important station on the railroad."

"And what does any of that have to do with your grandparents?"

"Nothing." Grandpa said brusquely. "So, back then the Republican Party was the party of Lincoln and the Abolitionists. They were so popular in that part of Indiana they didn't even bother coming through town on their campaigns because everyone was gonna vote their way anyway. So when there was a political rally it was more of a big celebration than anything else. In 1872, Republican President Ulysses S. Grant would run for re-election so the year before was fund-raising time. The Republicans threw a big party in town in his honor."

Taylor was hopeful. "And that's where they met, right?"

"Well, no. Remember I told you they grew up two blocks from each other."

Taylor almost yelled at him. "So, what was all that history for?"

"Background. It'll be important later. Remember, you can never know where you are until you know where you've been."

"I'm gonna have that put on your tombstone."

"Well, what you need to know right now is that my grandpa had just come back into town. He was twenty in 1871 and his parents had sent him to a military school when he was eighteen, but now he was back. Emma was five years younger so when last he saw her she was still just a little girl. Let's just say things had changed a bit."

February, 1871

"Don't look now, Archie, but I think we've attracted some attention." Though trying to be nonchalant, William nearly threw his back out trying to gesture towards the girls with his shoulders. Naturally, Archie began to turn to see what was jerking William's head around like that.

"Archie, I said *don't* look now!" William scolded.

"Well, what is it that I'm not looking at then?" Archie said with a twinge of frustration.

"Three of the most beautiful women I have ever laid eyes on!"

The Masonic Opera House was all decked out in red, white and blue bunting for the night's soiree, though Opera House was a misnomer. It was really the Opera floor. When Archie's father built the Car Shops in 1858 he built a three story structure directly across Church Street from the family home. The factory was on the ground level and the top two floors were the Masonic Temple and Opera House. Cambridge City was right at the intersection of old Highway 40 and the Whitewater Canal which brought all sorts of folks upstream from Cincinnati. The Opera House was the perfect place for a fundraiser, assuming your donors didn't mind walking through a factory to get there, and an even better place for young people to hang out and see who's who and what's what. Think of it as the 1870's version of the suburban shopping mall. It also gave you an excuse to put on your best suit or dress and pretend to be an adult, even if you were only fifteen. Evidently, there were funds raised at these things as well.

Archie attended the night's festivities with his brother William, and Jack, his Negro friend from his days at the military academy. They were an odd trio because, frankly, Jack was much more like a brother to Archie, despite his race, and William was the one who belonged in military school. In fact, the military ended up being his life's work.

After graduating from Yale, William saw action out west throughout the 1880's and early 90's against various Indian tribes, including a significant battle with Geronimo where he was involved in the legendary chief's capture. During those days he befriended Buffalo Bill Cody and nearly became the business manager for Cody's Wild West Show. Instead, he decided to take an offer to serve as the superintendent of the Carlisle Indian School where he hired legendary football coach Pop Warner and was at the reigns when Jim Thorpe set the gridiron world on fire. He met both President McKinley and Teddy Roosevelt and became a lifelong friend of the latter. He even held public office late in life.

Unlike his semi-famous brother, Archie was not destined to hobnob with heads of state, Wild West icons or football stars, and that suited him just fine.

William was smaller in stature than Archie but still an impressive specimen. When he reached his prime he would stand six foot two inches tall and tip the beams at over two hundred pounds, but for now he looked like a little boy standing next to Archie. Everyone did.

In chimed Jack, "Mr. William has done gone and misplaced his spectacles again."

Archie laughed. "So, Jack, in your estimation has my brother exaggerated the beauty of these ladies, or has he simply counted poorly?"

"No, his mathematics is fine, but his eyesight is all catawampus."

"I'm afraid my brother's vanity requires that he go out in public as a blind man rather than wear his spectacles. I'm afraid to turn around lest I behold three heads of livestock rather than the rapturous creatures he describes."

Whether William heard any of that we'll never know, as his gaze never left the girls, especially the one in peach.

Emma was there that night with her brother George and their cousins Susan and Luna Baldwin. Emma's uncle, Merchant Baldwin, was making the fifteen mile trip into Cambridge from Richmond for business and Susan convinced him to let her and her sister tag along. Susan would find any excuse to see Emma. She was technically Emma's aunt though they were born just days apart in February, 1856. Because of the distance they didn't get to see each other nearly enough. During the summers they had a tradition of spending a week each at the other's house, but during the school year their visits were months in between. Now that they were growing up and boys were the only topic of conversation, missing each other had turned to desperation. Like Emma, Susan had grown into a lovely young woman. Her long, dark hair and dazzling, dark brown eyes had made many a Richmond boy's knees buckle, as had her somewhat salty tongue. Her acerbic wit was a consequence of the trials she'd experienced growing up the youngest of eight children in a pioneer family, but mostly it was due to trying to cope daily with her sister.

Luna was a year older and the proverbial third wheel - the squeaky, lop-sided, slightly dense third wheel (okay not so slightly). She, like William, was very intent on being seen that night but nothing she could do would distract potential suitors from her more…er… noticeable companions.

"Ladies, my faith has been restored in the Indiana male!" This pronouncement was too loud by half to remain confidential. Even for Luna this was a tad on the indiscrete.

"Luna, why don't you step on to the stage and try again. I'm sure someone in the room didn't hear you." Susan had no qualms about letting her older sister have it in front of Emma. This generally caused Emma to play the peacemaker.

"Had you lost your faith, Luna?" Emma asked.

"Only temporarily."

"And what restored it for you, cousin?"

"Unless I miss my guess, I believe it would be the three striking young gentlemen directly behind you, Emma," Susan piped in.

"Ah, I see. Or, I don't see, truth be told." Emma had her back to the boys, and Susan gestured for her to stay put.

Luna countered, "Susan's vision is slightly impaired. I see only two such gentlemen."

"Emma, my dear sister apparently still believes that Negro men are not suitable for admiration."

Always the adult in the room, Emma chided, "Shame on you, Luna! What would Grandmother say?"

Luna defended herself. "She'd say that young women should only be interested in men who are good marriage material. Many conventions have changed, I agree, but there are still laws against such things."

Emma tried to take a peek at who it was behind her. "Well, I'm sure he's still a very attractive man. And I would like to verify that. Can I turn around yet, Susan?"

Susan noticed that William was looking right their way. "No, you may not."

Archie was beginning to be embarrassed by his brother's cross-room flirtations and decided to press the issue. "We are men of action, are we not, William? Go introduce yourself."

"You doubt I will?"

"You will as soon as I dare you. Consider yourself dared."

"Very well." William quickly ran his hands through his wavy blond hair, straightened his tie and casually began his trek across the room. He soon realized that Archie and Jack were not right behind him as he had assumed and covertly circled back around to them. William whined, "Are you not coming with me?"

Archie quipped, "When observing a natural disaster it's best to do so from a safe distance, wouldn't you say Jack?"

"I say, Ohio." Jack appreciated how often Archie allowed him to have the punch line.

William straightened his back and raised his chin. "If you stay here how will you verify that I actually introduced myself? I could just ask for the time and you'd be none the wiser."

Archie put his hand on his shoulder. "Brother, if you walk all the way over there to ask the time of three ladies who are standing in front of a six-foot diameter clock, their laughter will give you away; and likely bring down the wallpaper."

Jack tried his best to hide his amusement. "You know, now that you mention it Archie, watching your brother go up in flames in a crowded room may be the most entertainment we get this month. Maybe we should take a peek."

"All right Jack, you win. We'll watch him go up in flames from the center of the inferno. Why don't we bring a bucket of water with us?"

William was not amused. "Very funny, gentlemen. You should take that act on the road. Now let me do the talking." William started on his quest again, this time with Archie and Jack in tow.

Luna could see what was happening and squealed like it was feeding time on the farm. Startled more than usual, Susan jumped straight up in the air, her long peach dress jerking up above her ankles. If the whole room hadn't been looking at them, it was now.

"Composure girls, here they come," Luna whispered.

"Luna, I'm not in the mood for this. Are you, Susan?" Emma asked, knowing it wouldn't matter.

Susan replied, "Not especially, but it beats spending the evening with a stuck pig."

Luna deflected Susan by focusing on Emma. "Now Emma, why did you get all dolled up tonight if you didn't want to meet some boys? Let me do the talking, ladies. And remember, we're all eighteen."

Being Luna's sister was exhausting on many levels, and Susan had had enough for one evening. "If you want to fib your way through life be my guest but don't drag me into it again. My life is hard enough."

Emma warned, "Luna, you forget how small Cambridge is; I

probably know them." As the boys approached, Emma took a look back for the first time and saw that she was correct, she did know them, but before she could say anything they had arrived.

William began searching for just the right words to break the ice. He failed. "Ladies, please allow my to introduce meself..." All but Luna spent the next couple of moments watching William twist in the wind and biting their lips to keep from giggling. After what seemed like weeks, William finally spit it out. "My name is... Milliam... William... Wercer... Mercer..." And then, head hung in shame, he pointed to Archie and said, "This is my brother Archibald Mercer."

Archie and Jack had lost the battle to keep their laughter to themselves. Archie stepped in as he tried to compose himself. "Please, call me Archie. And this is our friend John Jackson."

"Please, call me Jack."

Emma shook Susan discreetly and gestured in Archie's direction as if to say to her, "*That's him.*"

"It is a pleasure to meet you gentlemen. My name is Luna Hall Baldwin. I was given that marvelous name because I was born under a full moon."

"And out in the hall," Susan wisecracked so only Emma could hear.

Each of the men greeted her individually as apparently Luna believed there should be a receiving line.

"And this is my sister, Susan Baldwin."

Susan was now obliged to walk the gauntlet herself. "I was born in the middle of the day. I didn't receive such a 'marvelous' name."

William just couldn't help himself. "Susan is a lovely name for a lovely woman." Normally, complimenting a woman on her appearance would be considered good form, even polite, but William could make the noblest gesture sound inappropriate.

Unfortunately, it was Jack who beat Archie to the punch trying to rescue him. "Well, just be thankful you weren't born during a cyclone. They coulda named you Gail." At least Jack thought that was funny.

"And this is our cousin, Emma Williams."

As Emma started her walk down the line, Archie finally put it together. He knew she looked familiar.

"You're Emma Williams?"

"Yes, sir."

"Little Emma Williams? My, you've uh... well, that is...you've..."

Susan rescued him. "Yes, she has."

Emma said, "A pleasure to meet you, sir," as she offered him her hand.

Archie cleared his throat a bit and responded with obvious admiration, "The pleasure is all mine."

Emma certainly had... well... you know. She had always been a gangly child and Momma had wondered out loud if she'd ever grow into her ears, but her fears were all for naught. Her face would never grace the cover of a fashion magazine, either in her day or ours, but when she turned thirteen she began an incredibly rapid ascent from awkward, freckled-face school girl to eye-catching, grown woman. That metamorphosis was virtually complete by now. Her mop of flaming red hair had transformed seemingly overnight into a crown of strawberry blond that was the envy of all and would one day result in a bidding war by the town's competing wigmakers. She had taken recently to wearing a green bow in her hair to accent her sea green eyes that always seemed to be on the verge of happy tears.

Archie wasn't the only young man whose head was snapped around when she walked down the street. Some of the neighborhood boys had recently been converted to secret admirers and had given her the code name Christmas, enamored as they were with red and green. When she came within range their nervous, reverential giggles in her direction and quips about the holiday season being their favorite time of the year were still interpreted by Emma as taunts. In her own mind she would always be that gawky preteen that the boys would never give the time of day.

In the moment that their eyes met, Emma felt for the first time what it was like to be worshipped, for lack of a better word, by a man.

Archie couldn't believe his eyes. The little girl from down the street who tagged along with her older brother George more often than Archie would have liked had become a stunning young woman. Archie could scarcely tear away his gaze. For her part, Emma had been gazing for far longer.

The Mercers were seen by many as the first family of Cambridge. In its heyday the Car Shops was not just the biggest employer in town, it employed a third of its working men. Mr. Mercer had played a significant role in building the factory as well as the Presbyterian Church, which was located down beyond the Mercer house further west on Church Street. His industry had quite literally put the town on the map. Archie was the oldest son and the heir to the throne, so to speak, but none of that caused Emma to fall in love with him when she was just old enough to read.

As children, the Whitewater canal had separated Church Street exactly halfway between the Mercer and Williams houses. The railroad had soon made the canal superfluous and it was gradually shut down, but as children, anytime the Mercers wanted to travel east to the river or the center of town they would have to pass over the Church Street Bridge and right by Emma's house. Archie, the oldest and the leader of the pack, would stop by most days and ask if George wanted to come on whatever adventure was currently sparking their collective interest. Emma learned if she were sitting on the porch playing when they came by that Archie would talk to her. She always loved how kind he was and how, even though he was always the biggest and strongest, he never bullied the smaller kids but saw it as his duty to be their protector.

Once when she was eight and he was thirteen the lot of them had traveled up to Lackey's Hill, a man made embankment created for the new railroad that was rock throwing distance from Emma's front door. While they were up there they heard a strange noise as if a large animal was rustling in the bushes. Archie instinctively grabbed Emma, his kid brother John, who was about five, and John's little friend Tommy Enyeart and put himself between the children and the danger. He whispered to hold on to him and not let go. Emma was happy to comply. When the danger turned out to be a deer everyone relaxed, save Emma, who was still dutifully holding on to Archie's leg. She knew right then and there that holding onto Archie would likely be a life's journey.

Archie had been away at school the last couple of years and that had nearly broken Emma's heart. When Archie left for school at eighteen he was still a boy, though a striking specimen at about six foot three inches and 180 pounds or so. His blond hair spilled into his eyes and flopped around on his head like meadow grass in the afternoon breeze. But now that he had returned any hint of his boyhood was a distant memory. His hair was short and businesslike and he had grown a fine mustache for a young man. He'd gained forty pounds of muscle and another inch, if not two. He was literally a giant in a day when a man of six feet was unusual. Emma was all of five foot two and when he took her hand in greeting it disappeared, as did any hope that she could regain her composure.

The music had picked up and William thought this a wonderful time to further break the ice. He also had grown tired of staring at Archie and Emma staring at each other. "Would you ladies care to dance?"

Luna, who was having a little difficulty taking her eyes off Archie herself, spoke for the girls. "We would love to!" Emma's excitement at the prospect was balanced by Susan's dread that she would get paired with William, a fear that was well-founded.

"We should choose partners democratically then," William said, referring to the red, white and blue bunting right behind them.

The problem with democracy is that it requires rules that are figured out in advance. Luna couldn't be bothered by rules. "Great idea! I know! We'll choose by age. Who is the oldest?" Luna asked, much to Emma's dissatisfaction.

Jack chimed in, "To know that we'd hafta to know how old you ladies are."

"I think she meant between us," Archie confided under his breath.

Luna would have none of that. "A woman should never reveal her age. It's bad luck."

"P'shaw!" Emma said, trying to beat Luna to the punch. "That's a silly old wives' tale. Luna is..."

"...the oldest..." Luna interrupted, "but we're all of age."

Emma, despite being quite accustomed to Luna's habit of stretching the truth till it snapped, was still shocked at her lie.

Archie, of course, knew that wasn't true, as did William, but there was no need to call her out on it. "Well, that's good. We'd hate to have your fathers upset at us. I'm twenty, Jack is nineteen..."

"I thinks. Ain't got no paperwork so I can't be certain." There were times when Jack's honesty was refreshing. This wasn't one of those times.

Archie, giving Jack a look that should have resulted in silence for the rest of the evening added, "And William here is sixteen."

Quite pleased with the results of her gambit, Luna proceeded to split up the teams. "That will work out just fine. I'm the eldest, so I'll be with Archie and then Emma with Jack and Susan with William."

William was over the moon about the results. "That did work out quite nicely, didn't it Susan? Do you like the arrangements?"

She bit her tongue and edited herself. "Of all of the ways that could have worked out this is certainly one of them."That made William feel very good about his situation. If only there were a better connection between his ears and the rest of his head.

The caller was just beginning the next dance so they grabbed a fourth couple and prepared for the quadrille. Archie's mother had been quite the society girl in her day and she insisted on teaching her boys how to keep up in polite company. Although the young men had not yet found much opportunity to benefit from her numerous dance lessons, the many hours of instruction in the front room came back to them rather easily. For a moment it even crossed their minds that she might know a thing or two after all. The girls hadn't been so blessed but they had learned on their own hoping that it would pay off on a night like this. Jack, unfortunately, had never even seen festivities like these and was a little lost at first. He liked to think of himself as something of an athlete and somewhat light on his feet. Emma was just hoping he wouldn't be heavy on hers.

As the music began to ring out, everyone had their own agenda of sorts. Jack was desperately trying to figure out how to get Emma to lead. William spent his time trying to sneak glances at Susan to see if she was sneaking glances at him while Susan was doing everything she could to avoid making eye contact. Luna was trying to capture Archie's attention but she might as well have been invisible. Archie and Emma couldn't keep their eyes off each other and they had no qualms about the other one knowing it. Their heads whipped around to retain eye contact as they danced as if somehow there was a fetter connecting their noses. They were so distracted that they caused several near misses that threatened to derail the dance altogether.

In one particular move the couples traveled in two circles, the women clockwise and the men counter, and grabbed hands as they passed creating a circular slalom course, for lack of a better description. This required significant concentration and Archie and Emma managed to stay on task the first two times that their routes brought them together. On the third, unfortunately, one of them, they never figured out who, forgot to release the other's hand and instead of continuing on their circuitous route around the group they circled each other. This caused an eight-dancer pileup that sent everyone flying about the room.

William's elbow inadvertently caught the gentleman from the fourth couple right in the ear which sent him sprawling, clipping Luna's legs out from under her in the process. Susan was launched into the neighboring quadrille with disastrous results. Arms and legs flailing, a shoe was dislodged from one of the women and landed with a thud on the stage. The band members stopped playing one by one only to discover that half the room was laying on the floor, moaning in pain and trying to deflect blame - except for one couple in the center of the floor who weren't aware that anything or anyone else was there.

"I'm sorry, Grandpa. I'll get rid of him." The cell phone had picked a fine time to go off again and Grandpa stared at it with murderous intent. Taylor bolted out of her chair and stepped over to her private spot. "Hi Carter... The same place I was the last time you called... It hasn't started yet... I don't know. It's baseball, they don't use a clock... My grandpa's telling me a story... Yes, for real!" She put her hand over the phone and turned back to Grandpa. "He wants to know if you have any cookies and milk for him too."

Taylor went back to her conversation while Grandpa muttered something that sounded like, "*Oh, I have something for him.*"

"Okay... yes... all right... bye." She closed the phone and said, "Sorry Grandpa. Okay, you can keep going."

"Doesn't he have a life?"

"I think I'm it right now. Basketball season is over and he doesn't know what to do."

"Does he play?"

Trying to be kind, Taylor hemmed and hawed a bit and then found the perfect description. "Kinda like Nick." That said it all. She tried to change the subject. "So did they get to dance together?

Grandpa answered, "Nope."

"Well, are you gonna keep going or do I have to beat it out of you?"

"I suppose I'd better keep going."

3

The Smartest Woman Alive

Archie had to figure out a way of slipping away from Luna, but that wasn't going to be easy. Even after the dance had run aground she was still attached to him like barnacles on a boat. But now what? The "couples" looked to each other, waiting for someone to suggest the next course of action.

William was the first to open his mouth as usual. "Susan says she's thirsty!"

Susan declared, "I'm not thirsty, I'm bleeding."

"Well then, I stand corrected. Susan's bleeding and I'm thirsty so we're off to the tables." William yanked Susan toward the back of the room where the refreshments were served. The look on Susan's face would have stopped a raging bull in its tracks; unfortunately, William wasn't bull-headed enough to notice.

That left just the four of them and Archie was hoping that his friend Jack could follow his lead. "So, Jack... Were you going to ask about...that...thing?

"What thing?" Jack had an annoying habit of thinking out loud. "Oh! That thing! Oh, that thing, of course. Yes. Say, Miss Luna, would you mind showing me that thing?"

This was one of the rare times when Luna had every reason to be confused. "What thing?"

"Well, I have no idea, but I'm told it's over this-a-way." Jack pointed over toward the tables. Luna cocked her head to the left and squinted at the "thing off that way" but couldn't find it. There was an impasse that only lasted about ten seconds but felt like minutes as they just looked at each other. Jack thought of a lot of things during those seconds, mostly the various ways he had coaxed the family dog to come when he called as a small boy back in Ohio, but none of those seemed appropriate, or most importantly, effective.

Finally, after a session of throat clearing coming from Archie's direction, Jack simply grabbed her hand and whisked her away.

"I suppose that just leaves the two of us, then doesn't it?" Archie said with relief in his voice.

"Yes, I suppose it does," Emma replied with a furtive smile she couldn't hold back completely.

We'll never know what would have happened next because right on cue another couple came to greet them. "Emma, I didn't know you knew Archie," the woman said.

"Well, yes, Mrs. McClave. We've known each other since we were children."

Mrs. McClave gestured to Emma. "Emma Williams, this is my husband, Chester."

Chester and Mattie McClave moved to Cambridge a couple of years earlier. Chester worked for Archie's father on the interior design and decor for the train cars and Mattie was one of the town's schoolteachers.

"Howdy do," Chester grunted.

"Emma, Chester works for Archie's father," his proud wife announced.

"Oh, I didn't know that," Emma responded politely, appearing to be interested. "I don't believe our paths have crossed."

"Well, that's most likely because Chester doesn't work downstairs in the factory very often."

Emma found an opening to talk to Archie while speaking to Mattie. "Does the Car Shops have another location in town? If it does it certainly is hidden well."

"No, just this one location." Archie hoped to draw Emma out. "Do you get out about town a lot?"

"Oh, I am just famous for my walking. Can't say a week goes by when I haven't circled the entire town. I find it good for the health."

Mrs. McClave just couldn't leave well alone and began to fill in missing information for Archie. "Archie, I'm Emma's schooltea…."

Emma burst into a horrifying coughing fit so Mattie couldn't finish her sentence. Why it was so important to not remind Archie of how young she was we'll never know but the distraction was effective.

"Child, are you well?" Mattie said with motherly concern.

"I must be coming down with something."

Chester smiled at Archie and quipped, "Looks like she needs to take a few more walks across town."

Mattie offered to fetch Emma a sip of water, an idea that Emma thought was inspired. "I'll be right back, Emma," and Mattie trotted off to the tables.

Emma kept coughing until Chester got the hint. "I suppose I'd better see if I can help her. Mattie!" Miraculously the coughing fit dissipated just as Chester left.

Archie was fully aware of what had just happened but thought it bad form to comment on it, no matter how entertained he was. He tried to initiate conversation but came up blank. Fortunately, he was saved by an all too familiar voice.

"Archie! There you are! We've been looking all over for you."

Archie was almost relieved. "Hello, Father, Mother. Are you having a good time?"

Eleanor said begrudgingly, "Archie, I believe your father has succeeded in bringing a smidgeon of culture to Cambridge after all."

Archie's parents, William and Eleanor, grew up together in New London, Connecticut. William's father was a prominent physician in town and Eleanor's families had been in the area since the middle of the seventeenth century and were direct descendants of governors, war heroes and Mayflower passengers. She was not pleased when William dragged her and their young family first to Buffalo and then out "into the sticks" of Indiana. She subtly reminded William of this regularly so that his life became a steady stream of inadvertent apologies.

Archie's father was very proud of his creation. "Yes, so, Archie, what do you think of the old girl? I think she gussies up quite nicely."

With an eyebrow raised Eleanor asked, "William, should I assume you are referring to the Opera House and not your wife?"

He fumbled over himself a bit. "Well, of course, dear. I would never refer to you in such a manner."

"My outfit is not to your liking then?"

"You do look splendid, dear. I was just saying that I would never refer to you as the 'old girl.' But you do look splendid. Would you not agree, Archie?"

"I am afraid there's only room for one foot in your mouth, Father," Archie said with a smile.

As Mr. Mercer tried to change the subject he noticed Emma standing there. "Now who's this pretty little thing?"

Archie jumped in, "Oh, excuse my manners. Mother and Father, this is Emma Williams."

Mrs. Mercer greeted her, "I hardly recognize you, Child."

"Yes, Mother, I had the same experience."

Archie's father hadn't seen her in some time either but shouldn't have tried to express that out loud. "My, you certainly have... well... that is you've...uh..."

Archie rescued him. "Yes, she has."

Emma was still learning how to engage adults in conversation but outperformed her more experienced counterparts. "How do you do, Mr. and Mrs. Mercer? I don't know when I've enjoyed myself at an event like this more."

Mr. Mercer took all of the credit. "You see Eleanor; even our younger guests are enjoying themselves."

Archie looked right at Eleanor with a look only a mother and son could understand and replied, "Yes, quite."

She immediately searched for an excuse to leave the young people alone. "I believe I am developing a headache, William."

"How coincidental," Mr. Mercer replied under his breath.

"Perhaps we should leave these two young people alone and visit your other guests," she said.

"Yes, certainly, it was good to meet you Miss Williams. Please remember me to your father. Come along, Eleanor."

Archie didn't waste a moment to get to the point for fear they would be interrupted again. "Would you like to take a walk with me, Miss Williams?"

"Mr. Mercer, I thought you'd never ask."

Archie's fears were well founded as Luna bounded back in with Jack in hot pursuit. "Emma! My father wants to leave."

"How soon?" Emma asked.

"Immediately."

Jack whispered to Archie, "Sorry, I tried. Found the wrong thing."

Susan and William Jr.'s trip to the refreshment tables had not gone well, at least that was the inescapable conclusion from Susan's face and posture as she returned to the group. It would be fair to describe her gait as having the attitude of a trudge but the speed of a gallop. William, even with his long legs, could barely keep up. She barked orders as she drew near. "Time to go Emma!"

"Yes, I heard," Emma grunted in frustration.

Archie was not to be thwarted entirely. He pulled Emma aside and said in muffled tones, "It has been a privilege to see you, Miss Williams. I hope that we will have the occasion to do so again soon."

This was not exactly a proposal of marriage but it did give Emma the opening to push the issue a bit. "I would like that very much, Mr. Mercer. Perhaps we could take that walk sometime. As you know, I enjoy walking." Then an idea occurred to her. She leaned back toward her cousins and without taking her eyes off Archie she said in a voice loud enough for all to hear, "Don't I, Luna?"

Luna had no idea what she was talking about. "Don't you, what?"

"Oh, I was just saying to Mr. Mercer here that I enjoy walking. Wouldn't you say that's true?"

"Oh, yes, she sure enjoys walking."

"How much do I enjoy it, Luna?"

"Well, I suppose she'd walk in her sleep if she could. She sure does enjoy walking."

It was clear from looking at Archie that he understood what she was trying to do but he didn't know how to help. Fortunately, help came from an unlikely source - Jack.

"Where does she like to walk?" The whole room seemingly looked at Jack puzzled. "I ask because where a person walks can tell you a lot about 'em."

Now one by one they began to understand the game. William piped in, "I've always said the same thing."

Then Susan caught on, "I'm beginning to see the wisdom in that."

Then Luna. "What?"

Okay, not everyone got it but Susan thought Luna being in the dark as usual might prove helpful. "Where does she like to walk, Luna?"

"Up to the top of Lackey's Hill," Luna said.

Susan continued, "Can you see the hill from here, Luna?"

The term "Duh" had not yet been coined but it was what was in Luna's heart. "Of course not, we're inside."

Susan tried to be kind, "If we were outside, could you see it from here?"

"Of course, it's right over..." she spun around a couple of times trying to figure out which direction was which. "There... down Church Street by the Lackey farm. It's the only hill in town. Why are you asking me all of these silly questions?"

Susan hoped to get one more out of her. "And why does she go up there?"

"You know that!" This was getting ridiculous, even for Luna.

"Well, you know me and my memory," Susan smiled sweetly.

"Susan, you have one of the best memories I know."

"Sometimes it's faulty!" Susan didn't mean to yell at her sister in public, but everything we say out loud has to first be a thought and every one of Susan's thoughts about Luna sounded like a yell in her head. This meant they all needed to be translated into a culturally acceptable tone; sometimes the translator wasn't up to the task. Susan caught herself and then said calmly, "Now why does she go up there?"

Luna was accustomed to being yelled at so she answered without so much as a blink. "Because it's the only place in town she can see her grandpa's star." Luna had grown tired of the third degree so she decided she would now ask the questions. "What time does she go up there? Answer me that."

Susan was glad to accommodate. "Thank you, Luna. I will. Eight o'clock sharp. And she stays up there for exactly fifty-seven minutes every night of the year. She hasn't missed a day since her grandmother died three years ago."

"Your memory almost has a mind of its own." Sometimes Luna said things that just made you scratch your head. If anyone else had said such a thing you would assume it was an attempt at humor but that wasn't a likely assumption in Luna's case.

Before things got out of hand Emma thought she'd try to divert attention from Luna's potential meltdown. "Excepting when we're getting snow. That is, I don't miss a day excepting when we're getting snow."

Taking Emma's cue, Susan tried her best to wrap up the conversation. "Thank you, Luna. That's all the questions we have..." but Emma's not so subtle throat clearing and motioning with her shoulders toward the clock were all Susan needed to send the final piece of Emma's telepathic communication to Archie. "...except to say that because the night is still young she'll likely be up there tonight."

Now that all of the necessary messages had been sent and received,

Emma was in a hurry to leave. "Good night, Mr. Mercer. It has been a pleasure."

A little stunned, but very impressed, Archie said with great admiration, "It certainly has, Miss Williams."

"Let's be off ladies. We don't want to be late. Good night gentlemen."

Emma and Susan, for dissimilar reasons, rushed off after the obligatory good-byes and well wishes, and left Luna in their dust wondering out loud what had just happened. Realizing she was muttering to herself within earshot of the men she trotted off to catch the girls.

It was all Jack and William could do to refrain from giving Emma and Susan a round of applause. "I think you just stumbled onto the smartest woman alive." Jack said with reverence in his tone.

"That was fantastic," William said, "She just flirted with you in public, set up a meeting in a clandestine location in front of four witnesses and walked away with her reputation intact because she never said a word!"

Jack agreed. "She's tricky. You got to like that in a woman."

"You boys will have to go on without me. I have a hill to climb." After a few steps Archie returned with further instructions. "William, compliment Mother on her outfit, would you? Oh, and Jack, beware of schoolteachers bearing liquid refreshment."

4
Stargazing

Grandpa, I think I like her."

"Well, now don't commit yourself too much there, darling. We wouldn't want you to get too excited."

"I will not let your sarcasm ruin my mood. I like her. You may continue."

This was a cue that they were about to begin one of Taylor's favorite games. Grandpa dutifully did his part.

"Thank you, Your Majesty. May I inquire on whom your Majesty's favor rests presently and why?"

"You may."

There was silence for a little while as it took Grandpa a moment to realize it was his line again. "Ah, well then, very good, on whom does Your Majesty's favor rest presently and why?"

In her best stuffy British accent Taylor answered, "Jeeves, my favor rests on my great-great-grandmother Emma because she seems to have been a modern woman."

"Jeeves? I was demoted from the Queen's Steward to the Butler?"

"Names, names, we don't have time to trifle with names - such trivialities."

Grandpa appreciated the aristocratic air Taylor just gave to her smack talk, though every once in a while even he had to acknowledge that he had created a monster. They had a lot of fun with these little role playing games of theirs. Taylor thought they were her idea, but these games were just another way for Grandpa to impress upon Taylor how valuable she was to him; you see, she always got to play the royalty and he the servant. They could drop in and out of these little games in no time flat. "So, what about her makes her seem modern to you? Is it cuz she's a little mouthy?"

Taylor replied, "Well, I can't say I missed that but, no, I think it's just the way she goes about getting what she wants."

"This is still the 1870's and things were very different back then. But, I think you're right. From everything I know about her she was way ahead of her time."

"Okay, so what happens when he gets up to her hill?"

"Now, who's telling this thing?"

Emma's hill – now there's a story.

We all have sacred places in our lives. Maybe it's our grammar school playground where we met our best friend for life, or the little league field where we were finally the hero one day, or maybe it's a place where something horrible happened that has become a reminder of what might have been. Perhaps that's where we get the term "took place." When something significant happens in life it's as if that event captures the place where it occurs and owns it forever - it takes that place.

Most of the places we consider sacred, or holy, are somewhere else. They tend to be far-off places that exist more in our mind than in physical space and time. We don't visit them every day. Often, we return to them years later only to find that they are so much smaller than we remembered or less colorful. Or maybe they aren't even there anymore. Maybe they've been paved over and made into a parking lot much as the place where Jesus of Nazareth was likely crucified outside the old city of Jerusalem is now a bus terminal.

These holy places can bring us back in an instant to the way things used to be and remind us who we once were. Most times the thought of that is repulsive - after all, who wants to go back and be that person again? We've put so much effort into making ourselves better and smarter that the thought of being that person way back there again makes us shudder - except when it doesn't. Except when we realize that the person we hardly remember had it pretty good. Sure, we still wouldn't want to go back and relive our childhood, but wouldn't it be great if life were that simple again?

Emma had found a way to make that sacred place of fond, childhood memories a daily part of her life. Just south of her house the railroad had constructed a four block long hill about fifty feet high and forty feet deep with the left over dirt from the digging of the Whitewater Canal. The east end of the hill ended abruptly at the Whitewater River just a stone's throw from the Williams home while the west end tapered down after it passed the Car Shops and the Mercer house. Before it was built you could have seen Lackey's Horse Farm to the south from Emma's house, but in Emma's day to see the horses you'd either have to walk through the underpass on Plum St. or climb to the top of the hill.

Emma loved horses and always wished she could have one of her own. That wasn't likely to happen, so she learned to become content with admiring other people's animals. The Lackeys were some of the first settlers of Cambridge and would go on to breed harness racing horses including one of the most successful racers of all time, "Single G."

Emma found a spot up on the east end of the hill where she could see the Lackey's horses to the south, the river just below her to the east and, most importantly, her house to the northwest. That was important because it was the price for allowing her to go out that far on her own when she was younger. Momma could always see her and wave a dishtowel to let her know she needed to come home.

The hill made for a nice vantage point, but it was nothing special to look at itself. In fact, it was downright pitiful. When the trains rumbled through you were sure the whole thing was gonna come down around you. With the flying rocks and debris there was no way to keep anything nice. Emma tried to plant some things over the years but the only living things that could take hold were weeds. Still, it was her sacred place. Not because anything had ever really happened there of note, at least not yet, but because it was all she had left of her grandmother, Rebecca.

Rebecca Baldwin was married to Hezekiah Williams in October of 1814 in the meeting house at Lost Creek, Tennessee in what is now the town of New Market just west of Jefferson City. Rebecca was the oldest of eight children, including her brother Merchant - Luna and Susan's father. Hezekiah was the second son of the famous itinerant Quaker preacher William Williams Jr. who was the first citizen of Richmond, Indiana and built the first home there.

The majority of the Williams clan wanted to leave Tennessee for a free state and while William was on one of his many Gospel journeys he fell in love with the Whitewater River area in Wayne County, Indiana. He dreamed of building a Quaker community there that could break down many of the spiritual and racial barriers of his day.

Rebecca and her husband set out for their new Indiana home in a covered wagon, carrying all their earthly possessions. The land Hezekiah's father had reserved for them in the north of the county was an untouched wilderness, so they built a cabin and cleared enough land for a farm. Of course by "they" we mean just the two of them. Like all frontier women, Rebecca was no stranger to hard, physical labor. A lumberman's saw took two pair of hands to operate and hers were the only other pair around. They made that wilderness their home until the town of Richmond was founded nearby and they decided to move into town.

The last few decades of the eighteenth century were difficult days for the Society of Friends as their most cherished values came into direct conflict. Many of the Quakers who immigrated to Tennessee came from Guilford, North Carolina. Guilford is about eighty miles northwest of Raleigh and about 250 miles east of Lost Creek as the crow flies, but on the other side of the Great Smoky Mountains.

When the United States were established in 1789 with the ratification of the Constitution, the Quakers had a dilemma. They believed strongly in obeying the civil authorities and thus opposing the government, even in respect to an unjust law, was a violation of their core principles. However, North American Quakers had recognized the evils of slavery by then, largely due to the influence of John Woolman, and by 1772 it was considered unacceptable for a Quaker to hold slaves. This put them way ahead of nearly everyone else as William Wilberforce was only a schoolboy at the time. By 1787 it is believed that every slave once owned by Friends had been released.

The new United States continued legal slavery in North Carolina, but the government was now "by the people" and that meant that the people were ultimately responsible for the laws. Many Quakers could not justify living in a state in which their mere presence validated that evil practice, so they began to leave the Carolinas and move to the Territory of Tennessee, which in the late 1780's was not yet a state.

North Carolinian John Mills bought a plot of land near Lost Creek and began to organize the other Quaker families who had moved there, including the Beals, Haworths, Thornburgs and Swains. The Williams and Baldwin clans would arrive in the early 1790's and add to the Lost Creek Meeting. That small group of families and others that joined them intermarried to so great a degree that virtually everyone in the new town was related by marriage.

It took a number of years for the Lost Creek Meeting to become officially recognized by the North Carolina Yearly Meeting because the organization was very concerned that Quakers not occupy lands stolen from Native American tribes. It took Mills some time to verify to the governing body's satisfaction that the three acres of land he had deeded to the meeting were legally purchased, so the meeting wasn't officially recognized until May of 1796. Ironically, Tennessee joined the union one month later.

The regularly remodeled version of the meeting house they built still stands and holds meetings to this day, but the future of the congregation was very much in doubt in the first years of the nineteenth century. With Tennessee gaining statehood and legalizing slavery, the Society was back in the same position it found itself in North Carolina. Which one of their cherished beliefs should they abandon?

The freeing of slaves had become a great social concern for the meeting and in early 1815 the Tennessee Manumission Society was organized at the Lost Creek Church under the leadership of Elihu Swain. This was a very controversial step to take for the Society and it is believed that the church lost four to five hundred members to Indiana and Ohio over a twenty year stretch. Some left for the same reasons they had left North Carolina, some because they felt the church was wrong for opposing the government, and others just left for greener pastures, but those who stayed vowed to fight for their principles. Rumor has it that Jefferson County, not coincidently, became a station on the eastern branch of the Underground Railroad, which in addition to smuggling African Americans seeking freedom, also hid conscientious objectors travelling north to avoid being drafted into the Confederate Army.

Rebecca was as adamant as anyone else that by staying in Tennessee the Society of Friends was approving of the detestable institution of slavery with their collective presence, but she still ached for the Smoky Mountains that had been her home all of her life. After five years in Indiana she convinced Hezekiah (or Josiah as she called him when she was happy with him) to take her back home. They tried to make a go of it again in Tennessee but the home and community they had remembered were long gone, so shortly they returned to Indiana.

Emma's love for her grandmother was fueled by a tremendous respect for a woman who had endured hardship we can't even imagine. In addition to the back-breaking work that was a staple of frontier life, Rebecca gave Josiah seven children in their first eighteen years of marriage; Melinda in 1816, Milton in 1818, Alfred in 1820, Aseneth in 1822, Emma's father William in 1827, Eliza in 1830 and finally Martha in 1834.

In 1823 a fever spread through Richmond and daughter Aseneth took ill while Hezekiah was exploring land in the western part of the state. He made the following note in his journal on that trip.

> "1st of the 6th month, this day we traveled 25 miles. This night me thought I saw my little baby lying breathless on her mother's lap, whose countenance to me bespoke deep grief indeed, which took such hold on my mind that I could not forget it, but often times as I was on my way home, oftener than the sun did rise, I set the language of my spirit, 'oh Lord, if thou hast taken our baby from us into thy most glorious bosom, oh gracious Lord be pleased to be with its tender mother & enable her to bear up under her hard trial'. This and the like of this was the prayer and supplication of my heart, until I came nearly home it was realized to me by a friend verbally telling me it was the case."

This was only the beginning of Rebecca's heartache. The winter of 1835 was one of the harshest anyone could remember. Sub-zero temperatures stretched for weeks on end. All of Rebecca's children caught cold and her family of eight became a family of five in less than two months. Nineteen-year-old Melinda, who had been invaluable in helping Rebecca care for her brothers and sisters, passed on February 4th. Rebecca's baby, one-year-old Martha, succumbed on March 6th and then five-year-old Eliza followed her on March 30th. How does a mother survive a trauma so unspeakable? How does she carry on after losing all four of her little girls? She cares for those that remain.

With an indomitable spirit and complete reliance on her Lord, Rebecca nursed little William back to health after months of illness. But in '47 she lost her beloved husband to illness and then two years later twenty-nine-year-old Milton was killed in a hunting accident. By the age of fifty-seven, Rebecca had buried her husband and five of her seven children, including all of her girls. Alfred would move his family to Cincinnati so Rebecca came to live with William's family in Richmond and then in Cambridge.

Emma became a daughter to Rebecca and to say they were "close" was to render that term meaningless. Understanding why Emma meant so much to Rebecca in her old age was easy; Emma helped to mend a mother's broken heart. But their relationship was more than that. They really were kindred spirits, dreamers; one was looking back to what should have been, and the other was looking forward to so many possibilities.

Many were the days that Rebecca would sit little Emma on her knee and regale her with stories about her Tennessee home. They pretended together, whether they were in Richmond or Cambridge, that any tiny hill they saw was the Smoky Mountains. As Emma got older the tales became more personal and even strayed into Rebecca's whirlwind romance with "Josiah." Emma never met her grandfather but to her he was nothing less than a prince. That's what happens when all you know of a man comes from a woman still deeply in love with him. She vowed to her grandma that she would never settle for less, even if it meant a life of solitude because a man worthy of her never materialized.

When Rebecca died in June of 1868, at age seventy-six, Emma was inconsolable. She had lost more than her best friend; it was as if she had also lost her journal because she had told Rebecca everything.

Her mother was helpless to provide her any comfort. She tried week after week to distract her with projects like sewing a memory quilt, but nothing worked until she told her an old tale that her mother had told her about a sad little boy.

The boy had lost his dog so he went out on a hill one night and hung the memories of his dog on a star. She then added that to this day they call it the Dog Star in honor of him. Okay, so even Emma knew that Momma had gone too far, but it piqued her imagination. So she found a spot on her hill and, well, the rest is history.

That private place had become a useful tool to heal all of Emma's hurts, but tonight it would become associated with a new memory, never to be the same again. When Emma would finally leave Cambridge for good a couple of years later her most difficult good-bye would be with her hill. It had become her best friend.

As soon as the Baldwin clan stepped out of the Opera House, Emma made up an excuse for her uncle about getting home quickly and made a beeline up the street to her house. She fixed her hair and dress, grabbed a stool and a warmer coat and headed for her hill. Typically, she was not particularly interested in how she climbed the hill or what she looked like when she was done but this time for some reason she thought it might be important so she took her time.

When she reached the top she pulled her usual stool out of the bushes and set it in its place overlooking the horses. Then she spent the next few moments trying to decide precisely where to set the second stool she'd brought. If she set it right next to hers someone might be inclined to move it further away, which might prove problematic. If she set it a distance away it might send a message she did not intend to convey. She decided to place it a little more than an arm's length from hers figuring that someone else's arms might be a bit longer.

After a few minutes she began to get a bit worried that she had misinterpreted Archie's interest or his understanding of her signals. After all, his long legs could surely get there faster than hers. She walked to the north edge of the hill to take a peek only to discover that he was bounding up the hill right then and there. She ran back and sat down, fixed her dress and hair and did her best impression of someone who was busy with other things.

"Why Miss Williams, fancy meeting you all the way up here." Archie was quite out of breath and began to wonder how such a petite little thing could get up there without help, much less looking like she hadn't broken a sweat.

"Hello Mr. Mercer. Have you lost your way?" Emma had decided that she'd best keep up the ruse of formality. Not only was it the custom of the day but she thought it amusing. She was delighted that Archie was willing to play her little game. He was quite good at it.

"I was told that this hill was a lovely place for walking. What I didn't know was that it was an even better place for catching one's breath. Do you mind if I sit?"

"Not at all," Emma said with as much indifference as she could manufacture.

Archie began to sit and noticed that the stool was just the perfect distance away. The only question was whether that was calculated or accidental. He looked a little silly on the tiny stool. For Emma, the stool was tall enough for her to sit with perfect posture, feet on the ground and upper legs parallel with the ground. Archie's knees were in his chest. For the rest of the evening he struggled to get comfortable without letting on how painful this was.

There was a silence between them that lasted only a few moments but it seemed like an eternity as they desperately searched for the perfect conversation starter. It would come as no surprise that Emma beat Archie to it.

"You have wonderful timing, Mr. Mercer. I felt the Lord prompting me this very evening to bring up an extra chair, in case some weary traveler needed a respite. That must have been you."

"It is good to hear that the Almighty still has His ear inclined to my distress."

"Have you been in distress much before, Mr. Mercer?"

Emma was so good at this game that Archie wasn't precisely sure she was playing. He was growing weary of the ceremonial tone so he looked her in the eye and said, "Please, call me Archie."

Emma nodded. "Archie."

"And may I call you Emma?"

"By all means."

Eye contact is a strange and glorious thing when two people are new to each other. This exchange had nothing to do with the names that were to be used from now on but everything about each of them finding a resting place; a place, maybe the first place, they had ever truly felt at home. When the words were finished the communication was only beginning as a moment of loud silence took their place. It was anything but an awkward pause, but still somebody had to end it so their words could catch up to their eyes.

"Emma, I didn't mean to slip into melodrama, that's just a scripture my mother regularly misquotes. It's become a source of family humor."

Emma saw an opening to make Archie talk about himself. "Was she motivated by a great deal of distress?"

"I had a sister die when I was three and a brother when I was seven, from the cold. That's why we moved here."

"So, you weren't born here?"

"Buffalo, New York. We moved here in '57."

Emma's plan was working to perfection. "Did I hear that you were off at school the last few years?"

"Ah, yes - an ill-fated attempt by my father to turn me into a military man. We have a number of famous soldiers in our family history, I'm afraid." In addition to Gen. Hugh Mercer who died at the Battle of Princeton, that side of the Mercer clan also boasted two Civil War generals and eventually George S. Patton.

After the Civil War, the pacifist sentiment that had defined the Quakers for centuries had begun to wane to the extent that Emma was almost unaware that it had ever been a staple of theological thought amongst the Friends. But Archie was certainly aware, in fact, it would take decades before those outside the movement no longer saw anti-war sentiment as the main thrust of the separation between the Quakers and other groups. Archie was concerned that Emma would think less of him for studying at a military academy so he made sure that she knew that his sentiments were much like hers.

"I kept telling Father that the military life suited my brother William more than me, but when you're a Mercer... Just because God made us strong doesn't necessarily mean He made us given to violence. I understand the necessity... but I just couldn't do it."

"Was Jack a classmate of yours?"

"No, the academy doesn't accept Negroes. We had met casually but we became friends when I had to defend him against a few of my classmates - eight to be exact. That was the last straw for me. Jack had taken work that led him to New York but wanted to move west so I invited him to come home with me. He remembered Indiana fondly from some travels during his childhood so we moved back here and my father put us both to work."

Emma was already in love. Yes, she had been in love with him since she was a little girl, but now in a couple of moments she had fallen in love with the man sitting arm's length from her, not just the one in her memory. He was a huge, powerfully built man's man on the outside but as gentle and kind as anyone she'd ever met on the inside. She loved that he was a friend to the friendless, not out of duty but on a deeper, maybe even spiritual, level. She sensed that he had let her inside his heart in a way he had not allowed anyone in before. She was right.

It struck Archie just then that he had not spoken that much to one person at one time in... well, maybe ever. Emma made him feel so comfortable in his own skin that he'd just rambled on. As good as that felt, he had grown very tired of hearing himself speak. "And now for you. How long has your family been here?"

"My great-grandpa was a traveling minister and one of the earliest settlers of the county."

"It must be nice to have that kind of history in a place."

"It has its advantages, but I've always dreamed of seeing the world. I'd like to see all the stars that I can't see from this hill."

Emma's gaze into the night spoke of someone who wished she were anywhere on earth but there. Archie thought he'd tuck that into his mental notebook and investigate it later, but for now he was interested in why the stars meant so much to her.

"Do you really come out here every night to look at the stars?"

"Not just the stars. I look at the moon some too."

"What brought on your interest in stargazing?

"They help me remember. My grandma died when I was twelve. We were very close. I came out here one night and named a star for her and ever since I've felt like she was still here, that I could visit her. Since then I've named one for everyone who's passed on."

"Why do you stay out exactly fifty-seven minutes each night?"

"That's how many years my grandfather lived. At least that's what I tell everyone. It also allows me to get home in an hour and my parents..." Emma stopped herself abruptly. She knew Archie was aware of their relative ages but there seemed no reason to remind him. "Well, that is... I like to get home in an hour."

She wasn't going to get that one passed Archie, but he didn't care at this point so he pretended to not notice and pressed on. "Which one is his star?"

Emma pointed up and to her left. "That one right there is Hezekiah."

Now, if you grew up in Southern California, as Grandpa and Taylor had, you wouldn't find that statement odd. In Glendora, folks are now known for gazing up in the sky, on what passes for a clear night, and remarking about the beauty of the stars (both of them). Pointing one of them out doesn't pose any problems. But in Indiana in 1871 there were thousands of stars visible pretty much every night of the year. To point to the sky and say, "that one" bordered on the ridiculous.

"Which one?" Archie tried not to laugh.

Emma realized how silly that was and tried to help. "Follow my hand."

Archie scooted his chair to the left near hers so he could bend down and look up where she was pointing. Emma pointed with her left hand, which meant that Archie had to get very close to see. Pretty soon no one was thinking about the stars.

"Do you see it?"

Archie was still a bit lost. "Well, there's a clump of three and then a real bright one just to their left. Is that it?"

Emma had never been so close to a man before except when her older brother wrestled with her, but that hardly counted. She even loved the way Archie smelled, which was odd since he had just been running up a hill. She replied, "No, go to that bright one and then go a little further left." It didn't occur to her what that would cause Archie to do.

Archie dutifully brought his stool further left until it practically touched hers. Now his face was just inches from hers. "There are two together standing on top of each other. Is it one of them?"

Emma could hardly breathe. It was all she could do to keep her hands and feet from bouncing up and down. She mustered just enough air to utter words she would remember for the rest of her life with equal amounts of pleasure and regret. "Now, just a little further left." And she closed her eyes waiting to see what would happen.

Archie, a little on the anxious side himself, leaned in slowly until the side of his face gently caressed hers. Emma yelped. She wasn't sure if it was just the excitement or the way that his moustache tickled her but she was certain that it wasn't audible. Archie was fairly certain it was. He answered her yelp, "Did I find it?"

"Yes, you did. You're very good at this." Again, they had to keep talking because everything else was way ahead of their words.

"Stargazing?"

Emma didn't know quite how to answer that so she just verbally shrugged her shoulders. "Mm-hmm."

Try as they might to do anything other than soak in this moment, they sat there and let time stand still. Finally, Archie came to. Trying to sound practical he asked, "Are there any other stars we should look at while we're here?"

Emma wasn't going to let this end but didn't fully realize the implications of her next answer - "There is one directly to your left" - until it had escaped her lips.

Archie slowly turned his head toward her and she followed his lead. If they each hadn't covertly backed up a bit their noses would have touched. Archie could see from the startled/horrified look on Emma's face, as clearly as he could see it being so close up, that she had no intention of asking him to do what her directions had implied. Instead he responded, "You're right. It's the most beautiful star in the sky. I don't know why I never noticed it before."

All of a sudden he realized that all of this had gone way too far way too fast so, as he backed up to a safe distance, he said in a confidential tone, "In fact, it shines so brightly I'm afraid it might blind me."

Archie was mortified at his own behavior. Here he was with a beautiful, but very young, woman at night on a hill in full view of her house and the rest of the town making advances that would seem horribly inappropriate to anyone looking in from the outside. In fact, they began to seem pretty inappropriate to him right about then. Now the reality is that no one could possibly see them way up there in the dark, but Archie's conscience didn't operate based on whether he'd get caught or not. Having said that, it did feel like God was watching them from above through thousands of tiny, sparkling eyes.

Emma hadn't taken a breath since she last spoke and let it out in a giant exhale that she couldn't conceal. It was so obvious that she had no choice but to giggle a little at herself. That tiny outburst was enough to break the tension and set everything right. She tried to begin the conversation in words again.

"I was going to show you the other stars, wasn't I?" Again, a little giggle broke through the pretense. "That one just to the left of the one you found is named Rebecca for my grandmother. And the two next to her are William and Rachel for my great- grandparents. Why don't you pick out two for your brother and sister?"

Archie found himself staring at her again. He just couldn't help it. The only words he could find were, "Anything you want."

5

Moving Back Home

Taylor was hoping that Grandpa would tell her she was wrong, but knew it wasn't likely. "So, this is the part where something goes bad, isn't it?"

"Nope, this is the part where the ballgame starts."

"You're gonna keep telling the story, aren't you?"

Grandpa shrugged, "Well, I don't know how to do that and keep score at the same time."

"You keep score of every game?"Taylor said with a raised eyebrow.

"Haven't missed one."

"I thought we weren't supposed to keep a record of wrongs."

Grandpa turned to her. "Oh, stop. If he ever gets a hit, or even gets on base, I want to make sure there is official documentation."

"If I help you, can you keep going?"

"Well, I can see this means a lot to you so I'll try to multi-do." Grandpa said while throwing up air quotes.

Taylor had to think for a moment. "Do you mean multi-task?"

Grandpa leaned in confidentially. "Is that what I mean?"

"We can hope."Taylor said with a grin.

Grandpa had developed a talent for ignoring her little zingers. If he acknowledged them all it would only encourage her. "Now, how did you know something went wrong here?"

"You said it was a great love story. Something has to go wrong. If they just met, fell in love and lived happily ever after there's no story."

"I beg your pardon. That's how it was for your grandma and me."

"That's boring."

"We've been married fifty-seven years!"

"Congratulations. Can we get back to the story now?"

"Well, I'm gratified that your father raised such a romantic. Okay, yes, something does go wrong. Archie's father died suddenly a couple months after that. He was only fifty and the family had to figure out what to do."

William Mercer, Sr. was descended from a long line of influential and even famous men. He was the third of the eight children of Dr. Archibald and Harriet Wheat Mercer. His father studied medicine at Princeton and then moved his practice to New London, Connecticut where he lived a noteworthy life and has a park and a street named for him to this day. His decision to study at Princeton was natural since *his* father, another Dr. Archibald Mercer, was its treasurer back when it was still the College of New Jersey under the leadership of the Rev. John Witherspoon, signer of the Declaration of Independence. *His* father Dr. William Mercer was also a medical doctor who came to America in 1747 with his brother Hugh, of Revolutionary War fame, who was a fugitive of the war between "Bonnie Prince Charlie" Stuart and George I of Scotland, and needed to escape to the new world.

As a young boy, Archie's father would regale him with stories about all of the famous Mercer men throughout history and how he was descended from many famous soldiers including Charlemagne, William the Conqueror and Robert the Bruce among many others. He also had a tendency to exaggerate his grandfather Archibald's own heroics during the Revolution, though technically in order for something to be an exaggeration there must first be some truth to it.

For his part, it was the most Archie could do to just keep all the names straight. The Mercer men in Archie's line going back for fourteen generations shared only four first names; William, John, Archibald and Thomas. As it happened, those were also the names of the first four boys in Archie's family.

Archie's father didn't go to college, but instead as a very young man created a dry goods business back in New London. After he married Eleanor they moved it to Buffalo and then sold it and created the Car Shops, among other companies, in Indiana.

He had taken ill in the winter of 1869-70 and had spent a good portion of it in the hospital up at Indianapolis. Dad was always invincible in Archie's eyes so when his mother wrote to tell him that his father had taken ill it was the final excuse he needed to return from the academy. Father had recovered enough to go home, return to work and convince everyone, including his family, that everything was fine. But he knew better.

The winter of 1870-71 had been balmy by Indiana standards. It was warm enough that Emma and Archie could still sneak away to her hill most evenings. They had decided to keep their new romance under wraps until they could work out some of the details. They were concerned about how their age difference would strike her parents. Actually, they were concerned about how any of it would strike her parents.

As sneaky as Archie thought he was being around the house, his parents were fully aware of what was going on. Father was concerned that Archie was setting himself up for a great heartache, but Mother was over the moon that Archie had found a girl that wouldn't take him away from Indiana. She was very thankful that he had come home and didn't want to see that change.

In April, William Sr. made an excuse to travel back to Indianapolis "on business" so he could again visit his doctor, but it was too late. A couple of days after he arrived, he was admitted to the hospital with chest pains and passed that very evening.

Eleanor received a telegram on April 23rd informing her of William's passing the previous day, but the news had gotten to Archie a few minutes earlier. He ran home to witness one of his former school chums, Charles Galt, who was working for the postal service, leaving the house after delivering the news. In small town Cambridge City, word of something like this spread so fast that Eleanor was literally one of the last to know. She collapsed into William Jr.'s arms and he and Archie dragged her into the parlour and laid her on the sofa.

The rest of the Mercer children including; John (12), Ellen, whom everyone called Nellie (10), Harriet (8) and Frederick (5) came running from their various Sunday afternoon play places and immediately looked to Archie for what to do, think and say. This was new territory and he had no more answers than they did.

Emma didn't know precisely what this meant for her and Archie but she could tell that he was backing away from her somehow. She asked him, in her usual causally blunt manner, but couldn't get an answer other than that Archie "had a plan." No matter how he tried to conceal it she could tell that he didn't like the plan one bit.

Archie wanted to tell Emma everything. In addition to their romance, she had become his best friend and his journal, but he couldn't justify talking to Emma about his plans before speaking with his mother first.

By early May the mood had lightened enough around the house that Archie and William felt it was time to broach the subject of "what now?" with their mother and the rest of the family.

Sunday dinners had always been a treasured tradition in the Mercer household. All of the family would make it a priority to be there and all of the household help were invited to eat in the main dining room. April 23rd's dinner had been missed for obvious reasons. The 30th had been an hour-long silence, except for Frederick, as the entire household was exhausted from the previous day's funeral and memorial and from the hundreds of well-wishers who greeted them at church that morning. There had been enough forced smiles and meaningless small talk for one day.

May 7th seemed like the perfect time to start the discussion of the next chapter in the Mercer story, so Archie and William conspired to keep the conversation light-hearted at dinner and then planned to bring up the future at the end of the evening. By then the members of the extended household would set off to do their chores and retire to their quarters behind the main house. Eleanor, however, had other plans.

Just as dessert was served, Eleanor cleared her throat and in her best impression of someone who was in charge of the household said, “Archie, I have been doing a great deal of thinking and I would like you to take charge of your father’s company. He would have wanted it that way.”

Archie was a little stunned that she had brought it up first, but thankful because he still didn’t know how he was going to do it. Still, now he was on the defensive. “I know he would have, Mother, but I’m not sure that I’m proficient enough with numbers and finances to run the company without him.”

Twelve-year-old John piped up, “Archie’s good with people and with his hands, but he can’t count to twenty without taking off his shoes and stockings.”

Archie didn’t appreciate the help. “Thank you, John. But it’s not as bleak as all that.”

Little Frederick then lightened the mood for everyone by blurting out; “His feet smell!” William, John and Frederick thought that was very funny, but Eleanor’s glare told them that this was not the time.

Nellie and Harriet were almost angered by the amusement on everyone’s face. Neither had allowed themselves to smile yet. Nellie said with just a touch of sarcasm, “I miss Father,” to which Harriet added a faint, “Me too.”

Eleanor, though she consciously tried not to snap at her, did anyway. “I know you do, Nellie darling, but Father would want you to be brave.”

Alice, the nanny, tried to throw herself in front of the proverbial train. "Miss Eleanor, maybe I should take the children to their rooms?"

Archie stepped in just before Mother could respond. "Thank you, Alice, but they need to hear this. I am sure they can be quiet and listen as we talk. But why don't you and Harold go on home now. I can put the children to bed when we're finished." Alice and Harold, Irish immigrants, rose and grabbed their plates. Horace the gardener and Betty the maid also rose on Archie's nod and began clearing the table. They closed the dining room door as they disappeared into the kitchen. Archie had taken the floor and wasn't about to relinquish it.

"I don't know the first thing about bankruptcy law, Mother, nor do I have any inclination or aptitude to learn. I am afraid our only option is to leave the proceedings up to Mr. Moore." Fortunately, Mr. Mercer had taken on a partner for the Car Shops venture, so the family was not alone in this.

John didn't quite understand that the "be quiet and listen" part was for him. "I don't understand how a flood in Oregon can make our company go under."

Eleanor looked at Archie and without saying anything communicated that she didn't understand it either, so he explained it as simply as he could.

"It's all very complicated, but as best I understand it the railroad company in Oregon bought two thousand train cars from Father on credit at $500 apiece, then Father turned around and bought the materials to build the cars on credit. When the floods destroyed the tracks in Oregon that company went under and couldn't pay for the cars after they had already shipped, which meant Father couldn't pay for the materials or to get the cars back to Indiana. I haven't heard but our suppliers are probably in trouble as well."

Nellie asked, "What does 'on credit' mean?"

John knew the answer. "It's what people do when they ain't got enough money to pay for what they want but they want it anyway."

"I suppose that's as good an explanation as any," Archie said.

After a moment of twisting her head back and forth Harriet asked, "Isn't that dishonest?"

The adults in the room contemplated how they would explain the unexplainable to a child. This resulted in an uncomfortable silence until Eleanor had enough. "If we go out of business, what will all the men at the factory do? Your father is the biggest employer in town."

None of them knew at this point how devastating a loss the factory would be to the town or to their reputation. The Mercer name was about to take a sizable hit.

Archie replied, "Part of the process will be selling the factory and getting those cars back to pay off the debts. Mr. Moore already has a buyer lined up who plans to take on our men, but it could be months before that happens."

That Eleanor had not always seen eye to eye with her husband in his business dealings had always been kept from the children, but it was becoming more obvious every moment. "Father spent most of our savings on building the opera house and the church. I don't know *where* our money is, or *if* it is. How will we put food on the table?"

"God will provide, Mother."

"Yes, thank you Nellie." Archie said with a real sense of respect for his little sister. "Mother, William and I should be able to find work fairly quickly in Richmond until the factory is back in business."

John and Nellie responded quickly, leaping to their feet, "I can work!" "Me too!"

Eleanor beat Archie to it. "There will be no children working in this family."

William was desperate to turn the conversation towards their original agenda. "There is another way."

"There is, William?" Eleanor asked.

"Yes... tell her Archie."

Here it goes. "We know you've never really felt at home here,

Mother. If we were to sell this house and Father's other properties in town we think you would have enough to buy a big house back in Buffalo and rent out rooms like you did before we came."

John could never keep his mouth shut. "But it's too cold in Buffalo. Isn't that how Mary and Thomas died?"

Archie answered his question, if only to end the interruption. "Yes, but they were very little. Harriet and Frederick are almost nine and six. We'll all be fine."

Eleanor straightened herself. "Archie, we can tell them the truth now."

"What truth is that, Mother?"

She explained, "Children, your brother and sister didn't die from the cold. Your father told you that so you wouldn't worry yourselves. They were just sickly. It was only by God's grace that Mary lived as long as she did and Thomas died when we got to Indiana."

Archie thought, *and I've been retelling this fabrication for how long?*

"How old would Thomas be now, Mother?" William asked.

"He would have turned fifteen last month and Mary would turn twenty-two come August. Do you remember Mary at all, Archie?"

"I suppose. Probably only what you've told me. When I think of her I only remember how sad you were for so long."

"That's all I remember of Thomas, Mother," William said, "that and the little cup in the cabinet."

"Oh, I'd almost forgotten about that." Eleanor got up, went to the china cabinet, and pulled out a small pewter cup about four inches high. Inscribed was:

Thomas Allen Mercer
-from-
Uncle Thomas
April 19, 1858

"My brother Thomas gave this to his namesake for his christening. Our Thomas didn't live to see his first birthday so I suppose this is the only birthday present he ever received." The room got quiet as Eleanor shined up the little cup with a napkin and replaced it in the cabinet. "I suppose I should pass it down. I know, I'll give this as a birthday gift to our first grandchild... *my* first grandchild."

Archie received a knowing glance and an elbow in the ribs from William, but he wasn't paying much attention.

Watching his mother, he began to remember just a bit of how long her sadness had lasted after Mary and Thomas had died and wondered if her sadness was all Frederick would one day remember of his father. He also sensed for the first time that her sadness might have been connected to being moved a thousand miles from her family and everyone and everything she knew. It had been nearly fifteen years since they moved from Buffalo to Indiana and another ten since they had left Connecticut, but still she missed her home. She tried valiantly to put up a brave face for her husband's sake but every once in a while it slipped out.

"We moved to Indiana because your father believed it would be better for his business. But, you are right, John, Buffalo is too cold and it isn't our home. If we are going to leave Indiana then we should really go home... to New London."

"Connecticut?" William asked. This wasn't part of the plan.

"I know none of you have ever been there but that's where both of our families are and it has so many good colleges - and the ocean. You'd get to meet your uncles Thomas and Frederick and Aunt Harriet and Aunt Jane ... why they all have children just your ages."

The children were very excited that they had aunts and uncles named after them and there was much commotion about meeting their cousins. Archie stepped back and saw joy in his mother's eyes that he had never seen before and could imagine for a moment the gorgeous creature that his father had always bragged about stealing away from all of the better men in town. How could he refuse her? "If that is what would make you happy Mother, then I'm sure all of us will adjust."

A cheer resounded through the house as the little ones ran to their rooms to pack. Eleanor was nearly as excited as they were. "Then look into that, Archie. I've been homesick for twenty-five years."

Archie hadn't planned to tell her about Emma but now he felt as if didn't have a choice. "I can take us back east but I won't be able to stay there just yet. I can't leave Indiana for good right now."

"Why not just bring Emma with us?" Eleanor asked with a smile.

"How do you know about Emma, Mother?"

She waved him off. "Oh, Archie, a mother always knows."

Archie looked right at William with a glare that would have been frightening even if he wasn't a giant.

Backpedaling, William yelped, "And someone has a big mouth."

"We're not that far along yet, Mother. I haven't even met her parents, and I don't know if she would accept me."

William raised his hand. "I do."

"And how do you know that, William?" Archie asked with keen interest.

William shrugged. "Susan has a big mouth?"

Eleanor got up from the table with purpose for the first time in a long while. "Well then, Archie, it appears you have much work to do."

William opened his mouth again before he thought. "All he has to do is convince Emma's father to let her marry a man who is unemployed, bankrupt and moving a thousand miles away. How hard could that be?"

Nellie quipped, "Someone has a big mouth."

6

They Didn't Care None Anyway.

Taylor caught Grandpa up on what happened while he was lost in his story. "Then number seventeen struck out and number three popped up to the shortstop. See, this isn't so hard."

"Not for you. You still have all of your synapses firing."

"You're 'multi-doing' just fine. So, did they move in the spring?"

Grandpa's head was spinning a little going back and forth between the game and the story. "No, but Archie had to find work to get his family through the summer while the finances were being worked out."

Archie brought Jack along this time to their eight o'clock rendezvous on the hill. Since there were only two stools stowed in the bushes, Archie sat on the ground in front of Emma, which was very convenient if you wanted a neck rub.

Emma looked even more like a little girl as she rubbed Archie's massive shoulders. "If I knew you were coming, Jack, I would have brought up another chair."

"Miss Williams, I don't mean to get in the way. Mr. Archie said I should come cuz it concerned me too."

Emma smiled. "I'm glad you're here, Jack. You're always welcome."

Jack hung his head a little. "I hate to invade your private place."

"It's called Lackey's Hill and my name isn't Lackey so you have just as much a right to it as I do."

Archie chimed in, "I'm sure one day they'll call it Emma's Hill."

Emma upped the ante. "How about Archie and Emma's Hill?"

Jack was beginning to get uncomfortable. "Next thing you know you two will be picking out burial plots."

"Emma, what do you think about being laid to rest right here?" Archie said with a grin and one eye on Jack.

"It does have a wonderful view and I certainly feel at home here."

Ever the one to point out the flaw in a plan, Jack just had to break the mood. "I hope you feel comfortable at the bottom of the hill too cuz I'm not coming all the way up here to visit you."

Archie teased him. "Now what makes you think you're gonna out live us both?"

"Well, firstly cuz I'm more likely to avoid getting struck by a train. I imagine you have plenty of close calls sitting up here every night."

Archie said, "The trains only run in the daytime so she's perfectly safe up here - except for the wildlife that is."

"But I have you to protect me from the deer and the raccoons." With a big smile Emma asked Archie, "Do you remember that?"

"Of course, I do. I most remember you not lettin' go of my leg the rest of the day." Archie said with a smile.

Emma put her arms around his neck from behind and rested her chin on his shoulder.

This made Jack even more uncomfortable. "I'm still here. Remember?"

Emma changed the subject. "You know, I have been up here when a train came through."

"What was that like?" Archie asked.

"It was a little scary. I hid behind a bush but I still got a dirt bath. And the whole hill shook like it was gonna slide down into the street. I wouldn't recommend the experience to anyone I cared about."

Whenever they talked it was if no one else was there, which was really annoying if you were the one that was there with them. Jack was about done being the third wheel. "It won't matter where you're buried then, you'll still end up at the bottom of the hill where I can visit you."

They all had a good laugh and there was quiet for a moment. Their minds went a myriad of places, including how it was possible for death to be so funny. Then Jack asked, "What're we gonna do, Mr. Archie?"

Archie had let it go the first time but this needed to stop. "Now, would you stop calling me that, Jack? It's embarrassing. I understand why you think you need to do it in public, but please, not when we're alone."

Emma, always the revolutionary, scolded him reflexively. "When you talk like that it tells people that you think you're beneath 'em. We're trying to put an end to that, not encourage it."

Jack's eyes got big. "Your woman sure can speak her mind."

Archie patted Emma's hand. "Yes, one of the many things I love about her."

Emma rang in, "His woman's name is Emma. Don't forget it."

Jack put his hands up in defense. "Emma. I got it."

"So enough sittin' here, where are you boys gonna look for work?"

Archie answered, "It'll have to be in Richmond. My father didn't put anybody out of work there." Archie's back tightened up at the thought of the fifteen-mile ride to Richmond each way becoming a regular occurrence.

Jack said, "There's always the bank. I hear they're trying to finish it by summer."

Archie said, "They're all full up, Jack. I asked. And anyway, they won't hire Negroes."

"You got a family to feed now; you can't be turning down work for me."

Archie and Emma both had a revolutionary streak in them, and this time it was Archie's turn. "Look, we've already discussed this. I'm not going to work for somebody who won't hire you because of the shade of your skin. Why would I want to work for stupid people?"

"They aren't stupid, they just ign'ant." Jack was used to flipping from perfect English to slang at the drop of a hat depending on who was present at the moment, but with Archie, and now Emma, he took great joy in using it for comedic effect.

Jack's father had worked hard to educate his children and insisted they spoke properly. Growing up in Canada hearing the Queen's English regularly hadn't hurt any either. Still, Jack had learned that most white folks were intimidated by articulate black men so he had learned to dumb down his language a bit when he first met folks, especially in areas so close to southern states.

John Jackson, Sr. desperately wanted his son to grow up in a world that saw him as a human being made in the image of God, not the son of slaves.

John Jackson and William Mercer couldn't have been more different in their upbringing, class, status and race, but they shared at least one thing in common: the desire to make the world a better place for their children.

Mr. Mercer was eighteen years old in September of 1839 when La Amistad was towed into New London harbor. The Spanish-made ship was carrying fifty-three Africans sailing from Havana, Cuba to be sold as slaves on another part of the island. The kidnapped Africans - of the Mende tribe from what is now Sierra Leone - revolted, killing the captain and a cook, and commandeered the ship. They tried to sail the ship back to Africa but were captured by the USS Washington off the coast of Long Island, New York and were harbored in New London to await the disposition of their case. Ultimately, the surviving Africans won their case and were set free, but not without more than two years of legal wrangling that culminated in former president John Quincy Adams pleading their case before the Supreme Court.

New London was awash in abolitionist sentiment already and this development only heightened the tension in a town where, before the United States were established, one tenth of the population had been enslaved blacks. The plight of the passengers of La Amistad was all anyone in New London talked about during those years.

The "peculiar institution", as slavery was referred to in those days, had been a hot topic of conversation around the dinner table in the Mercer house long before La Amistad arrived. William's father, Dr. Archibald Mercer, had been married before he married William's mother. His first wife, Abigail Starr, died five years before William was born but had left Archibald two daughters. He married William's mother, Harriet Wheat, immediately afterwards. William's half-sisters, Charlotte and Sarah, had adopted their mother's strong anti-slavery sentiments as most of the Starr clan had, but Archibald had grown up in New Jersey, a slave state. His recollection of slavery was much more benign than it might have been if he had grown up deeper in the south. This made for interesting debates.

When William was eleven, Charlotte had covertly brought home an edition of William Lloyd Garrison's controversial abolitionist newspaper, *The Liberator*. She set it out intentionally where her little brother would find it and William read things he had never heard before. For the first time he began to reconsider his opinion on the subject. He had always taken his father's side in everything but Garrison's no holds barred approach caused him to think for himself:

> "I will be as harsh as truth, and as uncompromising as justice. On this subject, I do not wish to think, or speak, or write, with moderation. No! No! Tell a man whose house is on fire, to give a moderate alarm; tell him to moderately rescue his wife from the hands of the ravisher; tell the mother to gradually extricate her babe from the fire into which it has fallen;—but urge me not to use moderation in a like cause like the present. I am in earnest—I will not equivocate—I will not excuse—I will not retreat a single inch—AND I WILL BE HEARD."

When the Amistad arrived William was ready to be his own man and stand up for what he now believed: that the enslavement of Africans was America's great birth defect. It was an unspeakable evil that needed to be spoken of at every opportunity - except around his father.

He never joined the American Anti-Slavery Society, largely due to their pacifism, but vowed to teach his own children to love freedom. He backed it up later in life by hiring blacks in his factories even though Indiana had outlawed black immigration. Those seeds of rebellion were planted with Archie as his father spent hours with him reading the newspaper accounts of the Civil War. He made sure Archie as a young teen understood that the blood spilled in that great conflict was, as President Lincoln implied in his second inaugural address, a judgment from God Almighty to pay for the two hundred and fifty years of the slaver's lash.

And yet when Archie brought Jack home from New York, William struggled mightily in his heart with his own prejudice. He knew that if he ever wanted to enjoy the respect of his son he had better keep his mouth shut, and he did.

Emma wasn't about to let them change the subject. "What about Starr piano, Archie?"

"They don't need anybody." Archie said with a shrug, "I hear the fire department is starting to pay its folks now but you have to be a volunteer first to get in."

Jack had a brainstorm. "I hear they're paying their baseball players now up in Fort Wayne and down in Cincinnati!"

Archie gazed into the sky. "Wouldn't that be fine? Makin' a living playin' ball?"

Emma could see the two boys getting lost in their little dream worlds and felt the need to interrupt. "I think you'd have to be pretty good first."

Jack looked at Archie with his mouth wide open. "She doesn't know?"

Archie had intentionally not told Emma of his baseball playing prowess because ball players in those days didn't exactly have a sterling reputation. He tried to wave Jack off but to no avail.

"Why, Archie is the best striker I have ever seen. Nobody can hit it farther. The fellas don't even want him to play anymore cuz he keeps on losing the ball. And he plays a near perfect third sack too."

Emma leaned over and tried to look Archie in the eye. "Really? How come I didn't know that?"

Archie shrugged. "Jack exaggerates. He's the ballplayer. He's the fastest runner there is."

Jack laughed. "That's just cuz I got so much practice getting chased as a child."

"You shoulda just let those girls catch you," Emma said wryly.

Jack snickered. "Girls! It was them slave hunters that were chasing us. Dern near chased us all the way to Canada."

Emma was wide-eyed. "You were a runaway slave?"

"No, but without papers nobody could tell the difference. They didn't care none anyway."

She was too curious to let him off the hook. "Did you escape on the Railroad?"

"Yep. I was real little but my Momma tells me we traveled through here on our way north. Canada was nice and all but after the war it was safe to come home so I went down south where it was a little warmer. When Archie invited me to come home with him I figured, 'why not?' Momma said there were some nice people in these parts; too cold in New York anyway."

"Did you ever find any of those nice people?" Archie was trying to be funny, but Jack took him seriously.

"Not yet. It's been nearly fifteen years and I don't remember much of it, just glimpses really, but it sure would be nice to meet some of the people we stayed with and thank them. Don't suppose I ever will." Little did he know.

Archie went back to the original subject. "You know, Jack, I did see a posting in a place right here in Cambridge down on Main past the river that was looking for people."

Emma nervously asked, "Really? What kind of place?"

"The Marble Works," Archie answered.

Emma did her best to be nonchalant, but she was a horrible liar. "That old place? You wouldn't want to work there."

Archie asked, "Emma, is something wrong?"

Emma, knowing she had been caught, turned to Jack and hemmed and hawed a bit. "Jack? Remember that thing?"

"What thing?" Jack hadn't known Emma long but anyone could read her "please get lost" face. "Oh...that... thing at the bottom of the hill? Yeah, I'll go get it. How long will it take me?"

Archie saw Emma's look too and knew they were about to have a talk. "Quite a while, Jack."

"Well, then I'd better get started."

As Jack made his way down the hill out of earshot, Archie braced himself. "What's the matter, Emma?"

Emma took a deep breath. "If I told you about something I did that was wrong would you still love me?"

"How could you even entertain such an idea? I will always love you."

She stared at the ground for a moment and then asked, "Even if you found out that I lied?"

Ah, that makes sense, he thought. *She's still concerned about our re-introduction. Well, let's fix that right now.* "You're fifteen I'm not the best with mathematics, but I at least knew that. And you never actually lied. It was Luna that lied. You just allowed me to believe something that wasn't true. I'm a Presbyterian, that isn't a sin for us."

Emma wasn't sure she should laugh at that or not but couldn't help it. "No, not that, but I am sorry about that too."

Archie chased her to make eye contact. "Well, what is it then?"

Emma sighed. "I may not have told my parents the whole truth about you."

Now it all made sense. "That's why you won't let me meet them. I was beginning to wonder if you even had parents anymore."

Emma shook her head. "No, I want you to meet them, I do, but my father is very… traditional."

Archie chuckled. "Whose isn't?" Then he sobered up and asked, "Wait, do you think he wouldn't approve of me?"

Emma took his hand and reassured him. "No, he'll love you. So will my mother."

Now he was a little confused. "Well, then what's the worst that can happen? If he doesn't give his consent we'll just wait until you're eighteen. That's not so far away I suppose."

Emma smiled. "I suppose I've run out of excuses."

"Emma, if we're going to be together he has to be told, one way or another. We might as well get it over with. Trust me."

"I trust you. But let me tell them about you first and soften the blow."

7
A Mother Always Knows

The last Cubs batter of the inning struck out swinging but Taylor hardly noticed. "So the marriage age was eighteen?" She was deep in thought and oblivious to Grandpa's plight in trying to keep up with the ballgame.

He recapped the inning with her to be sure he got it right. "So there was a grounder to first, a walk, a pop out to second, two wild pitches and a strike out, right? Did I miss anything?"

Taylor wasn't really listening. "What was the big deal about her age? Didn't everybody get married young?"

Forced to multi-do again, Grandpa came back to the story. "Well, no, not everyone, sweetheart. But you always got your father's permission and if he didn't give it, you were out of luck. Among the Quakers it was even more important."

Emma's father, William Baldwin Williams, would certainly be considered "ultra-traditional" today, but then again he was born in 1824. In his time, however, and especially among the Friends, he wasn't as old-fashioned as Emma might have thought. And really, "ultra-traditional" often gets an unwarranted, bad reputation.

While it is currently stylish to ascribe to a postmodern, anything goes philosophy in theory, in practice no one really lives that way. Though we may not always want it for others, we still want our own right to life, liberty and property protected. Whether or not we say we believe in the Ten Commandments for ourselves, and what could be more ultra-traditional than the Ten Commandments, we still believe that thou shalt not murder, bear false witness, steal or covet another man's wife should at least still apply to the other guy. When threatened with the loss of our inalienable rights, even the most progressive amongst us can suddenly become ultra-traditional.

Given that, it may not be wise to judge a Quaker father living in 1871 by today's standards. Like any father, W.B. Williams wanted the best for his eldest daughter. The lens that he viewed "the best" through, however, was certainly different than how most view things today and even different from many of his contemporaries.

W.B.'s house was certainly not the house of a wealthy man. The cozy, single floor structure was well kept, but furnished simply and without flair. It had three small bedrooms, one of which Emma shared with her two younger sisters, one for her brother George, and one for Mother and Father.

Mr. Williams was not a terribly impressive man when compared to a man like William Mercer. Starting out his career as a farmer, he changed professions multiple times in his life, but most of his career he was involved in some type of sales. In fact, during Emma's formative years he was on the road more often than he was home, selling this or that for a company based in Richmond. In the late sixties, during Emma's grade school years, he was gone so much there were whispers that Mrs. Williams was a widow, or worse.

It wasn't until 1870, while Archie was off at the academy, that W.B. found a regular job that allowed him to stay home with his family. He was now the manager of the showroom for a Cambridge City marble concern and managed the day-to-day store operation while his employer was away for months at a time.

W.B. was a man of few words, and even fewer friends. His premature gray hair, his beard that reached nearly to his belt, and his steel blue eyes that seemed to look right through you, painted a picture of a lonely, unhappy, and maybe even belligerent old man. Men like this often have their opinions on the topics of the day decided upon by others without ever being heard themselves. W.B. was no exception. He must've been exactly as he seemed.

Emma's mother, Susannah Rich Williams, on the other hand, couldn't have been more charming. She was the quintessential prairie version of the "belle of the ball." Always willing to engage strangers in conversation, she was a joiner, whether it was social clubs or other folks' conversations without invitation. If there were ever a woman who belonged in another age it was Susannah. It's not that she didn't find significance in her life with her family, she certainly did, but she yearned for more - not more independence, respect or even significance, she just wanted to understand. She wanted to know things she didn't know, see things she hadn't seen, read what she hadn't read. In short, she wanted to be fully human.

The time had come to mention Archie to her parents, but Emma wanted nothing of it. She could imagine so many things going wrong.

What if Father met him already and doesn't like him? What if they don't approve of his family? What if Mrs. Mercer and Momma have had a run in? Or worse, what if Archie's mother doesn't approve of me? I'm not exactly high society material. She's Town Mouse and I'm Country Mouse. What if she doesn't like our family?

Nightmares are always worse when you're asleep. Often the best thing to do to make them go away is to get out of bed.

When Emma got up that day she feared the worst but as the day went on she concocted various scenarios and figured out how she could control the outcome. The most important parts of the strategy were 1) to put the focus on her parents' courtship initially to disarm them and, 2) to start the conversation just before it was time to go off to her hill so she could end it abruptly to limit the damage. Now that the plan was set, it was all left to the execution.

At the dinner table that night the conversation had centered on her youngest sister Lily's troubles with an older girl at school. Middle sister Mary Ina was more than willing to step in. "I'll teach her a lesson for you, Lily."

Big brother George said facetiously, "Now Ina, Friends don't fight."

Lily interjected, "That's all right, we aren't friends."

Emma was thankful that the dinner banter had been light and that Father was in a relatively good mood. When the little ones were finished with supper they dutifully cleaned their plates in the kitchen and then went off to their room to play. George had an appointment with a friend down the street and rushed off when he was finished, so only Emma and her parents remained. Momma was flitting in and out between the kitchen and the dining room and Father was reading the Cambridge City Tribune, as was his custom. As Momma came in and out, she tried to sneak a peek at the paper whenever she could.

Emma figured that this was her time. *Here we go.* "Momma?"

"Yes, dear?" Momma answered as she scurried back into the kitchen.

"How old were you when you married Father?" Emma already knew the answer but she crossed her fingers hoping that this foray into the past would bring about the desired results.

"Seventeen," came the answer from the kitchen.

"Oh, really? My." Now that her gambit had begun, she focused on her intended target. If only he would come out from behind that paper so she could see his reaction. She continued questioning her mother. "And how old was your mother?"

Momma was on her way in to grab some plates and answered, "Fifteen, I believe."

"Hmmm," Emma mumbled in a feigned surprised tone. *Now let's draw him in.* "Father, how old was your grandmother, Rachel?"

After a moment or two had passed, a faint, "Fourteen," came from behind the paper.

Now I have him. "Didn't she have four children before she was twenty?"

The paper came down gradually and she felt her father's eyes bore through her skull. "Child, I am noticing an alarming trend in your questions. For the record, my mother was twenty-two and her mother was twenty-one."

Fiddles. Never let the witness answer a question you didn't ask.

Momma stood with her hand on her hip. "Are you going to tell us about him, dear?"

Trying to act casual, Emma replied with a distracted, "Tell us about whom?"

That wouldn't work on Momma. "Why, the boy you're in love with, of course."

Emma lost her pretense. "How did you know that?"

Susannah smiled. "A mother always knows, and I was a girl once too. You come home from your hill beaming like you just saw the heavenly gates themselves. That's the way my mother said I looked when I first met your father."

Father was interested now and came out from behind his paper. "You never told me that," he said with a gleam in his eye.

"I didn't want it to go to your head."

Father folded his newspaper and placed it down on the table. This worried Emma a bit. "Well this is all news to me. So tell us about this beau of yours. Where is he from? Do we know him?"

"Well, you might, Father. He's from Buffalo, New York, but he moved here when he was seven."

Father went on a bit of a fishing expedition himself. "And how long ago was that?"

Oh, here we go. I can already hear him say Archie's too old for me. She didn't want to take the bait quite yet so she just tugged on the line a little. "Before we came here from New Garden."

He pressed her, "And what year was that?"

Momma could see that the young man's age might be a tender spot for Emma so she tried to intervene. "Don't you remember, Father? It was in '64. I remember because it was the year before Mr. Lincoln's Train came through town."

He was accustomed to being two-teamed. "I am well aware of when we arrived in Cambridge. I believe I was involved."

Sensing the inevitable, Emma gave up the pertinent information. "He's twenty-one, Father."

Momma forgot whose side she was on for a moment and exclaimed, "This is no boyfriend. This is a man-friend!" She then gave Emma an odd look that evidently meant she was proud of her.

Father smiled, "Ah, I see. You're afraid that I won't give you my consent because of your age, aren't you? Well, if this is God's man for you, then your age is immaterial, as is his. What does he do?"

"He's working on selling his family business at the moment." *Yes, that was a good way to put it. Now escape before anything happens!*

Father wasn't finished. "Well, he sounds industrious, Emma. What's the name of his…"

No sooner did Father's words escape his lips than Emma was up like a shot and out the back door. "Oh my, look at the time, it's almost eight o'clock! I can't be late. I'll be back soon."

Momma ran to the door and yelled, "Your stars can't wait a few minutes?" But it was too late. The rear door had already banged shut and Emma was off, just in time.

Fathers can be fairly obtuse when it comes to their daughters. "That child and her imagination! Hopefully something will come from this stargazing business someday, though I can't imagine what."

Momma tried not to sound patronizing. "I don't think she's been rushing out to see the stars the last few months."

"Do you think she's been meeting with this man…? We didn't even get his name."

Susannah smiled. "I believe his name is Archie."

W.B. was a little hurt. "Now, how do you know that?"

"Oh, I've overheard her up in her room several times practicing how to accept his proposal. She's come a long way."

Now Father was alarmed. "This is serious then. I hope the Society finds him acceptable."

Susannah sat. "William, what if he isn't from the Society? I don't remember there being a Friends settlement near Buffalo."

He waved her off. "You needn't worry yourself. Emma could never love a man out of society. She has been raised far too well for that."

"I hope so, for her sake. Remember all we had to go through."

He patted her hand on the table. "Yes, I certainly do."

8
God's Man for Me

Robby, the shortstop and the closest thing Nick's team had to an All Star, shouldered his bat.

"C'mon, Robby! You can do it!"

"Why are you so excited, Grandpa?"

Grandpa had risen to his feet to cheer on the boys, waving his scorecard all about. "When we get a man on base it's a big deal. It may not happen again."

Robbie let fly with a mighty swing and the ball went hurtling toward left field.

"Oh, he hit it! That-a-way, boy!" Grandpa bellowed.

"And they caught it. Better luck next time, Grandpa."

It was a line drive in the box score, but in reality it was little more than a pop fly that didn't require the left fielder to move his feet. If he hadn't put his glove in the way it would've hit him in the chest.

"Nice try, Robby! You'll get 'em next time!"

"Well, that was exciting for a moment! Wasn't it, Grandpa?"

"I suppose." All of a sudden Grandpa became aware that he was standing up and didn't remember doing it. "How did I get to my feet?"

Taylor laughed at him. "You jumped up like someone put a tack on your chair. Can we go back to the story now?"

Grandpa was thankful for any burst of energy. "Adrenaline is a wonderful thing." He started the descent into his chair again and went back to his story.

Susan and Luna were in Cambridge City again that week and Emma ran right over the next morning to their room at the Vinton House to share her news. Standing out on Main Street in front of the hotel the girls literally jumped up and down together in celebration - adrenaline indeed.

After a good minute or two of hugs and cheers Susan said, "That's such good news! We're so happy for you!"

Then Luna shouted, "Congratulations!" She was so loud the entire street stopped for a moment to see if a crime was in progress. As usual, she didn't quit while she was behind and with a quizzical look on her face she asked, "What are we celebrating?"

Susan was in too good a mood to let Luna ruin it. In an almost polite tone she responded, "Emma's father just gave his consent."

Luna cheered again, then calmed down and asked, "For what?"

Susan tried to hold back her frustration and calmly said, "For Emma to marry Archie."

Now fully apprised of what they were celebrating, Luna jumped up and down again trying to get the girls to join her once more in the celebration dance and yelled, "Congratulations!"

Emma and Susan tried to ignore her and began to talk about the details. "So the meeting went well, I suppose. Did your mother like him too?" Susan asked.

"Who?" Asked Luna.

"Archie!" Susan barked at her like a drill sergeant and then calmly turned back to Emma.

Emma confided, "She hasn't met him yet. Neither has Father."

Susan was a bit perplexed. "He gave his consent sight unseen?"

Emma tilted her head and scrunched her nose. "Well, he didn't really give his consent yet, he just said he would."

Susan had to admit, "Now I'm confused."

Luna tapped on Susan's shoulder and asked, "See what it's like?"

Emma saved Luna for the moment. "He said that my age wouldn't matter if Archie was God's man for me, which we all know he is. I know they'll love him just as much as I do when they meet him."

Susan had never seen Emma so happy. "No one could love him as much as you do. I am very jealous."

Luna was aghast, "Are you in love with Archie too? That's shameful, you and Emma are cousins. You shouldn't fight over the same man."

Susan pulled Emma away just a bit. "What am I going to do if you move to Connecticut? Please don't leave me alone." But it wasn't enough away.

"I'll still be here!" Luna broke out her ear to ear grin that looked like she was having dental work done - which she badly needed, by the way.

Susan took a look at her sister and with tears in her eyes said to Emma, "Please don't leave me alone."

"She's setting herself up for disappointment, isn't she, Grandpa?"

Grandpa had expected that Taylor would get involved in the story, like everyone else he had ever told it to, but never had he had someone think so deeply while he was telling it. "How did you become such a pessimist?" He asked.

"I'm not a pessimist," she huffed, "I'm a realist."

Grandpa chuckled. "That seems to be a razor thin distinction."

Taylor wagged a finger at him. "No, no. A pessimist sees the glass as half empty. An optimist sees it as half full. The realist says, 'Why didn't you use a smaller glass?'"

"So I suppose then you're the type that reads the end of the book first?" Grandpa asked.

"Is that such a terrible thing?"

"I suppose not. Should I just tell you how it ends and be done with it?"

"I know how it ends." Taylor harrumphed, "They live happily ever after or we wouldn't be having this conversation. And I know it must go horribly wrong for a while or it wouldn't be the 'greatest love story of all time.'"

Grandpa interjected, "The second."

Taylor agreed, "Okay, the second, but look how bad that one went for a while. No, it's how you get there that makes the story good."

Grandpa sat back and enjoyed his granddaughter thinking grown-up thoughts for a moment and then continued. "Well, okay then, it does start to go horribly wrong. Archie and Jack went to the marble shop to see if they could get work."

9

Forces? What Forces?

The economic chaos that ensues in a community when its largest employer goes under can't be summed up by statistics alone. Yes, the Cambridge City unemployment rate, if they kept track of such things, would have increased by over 5,000% overnight, resulting in three hundred men sitting idle or looking for work to tide them over until the company was reopened, but even that didn't tell the whole story. With so many men out of work there was a tremendous pressure on the other businesses in town to extend credit to their neighbors who were hit by the closure, which, of course, caused a ripple effect throughout the town's economy.

The only businesses in town that were booming were the saloons. When that many men have nothing to do day after day it didn't portend toward social health for a community any more in that day than it does in our own. Consequently, families and businesses started to leave Cambridge City and head back to wherever they came from regardless of whether they had steady work or not. The businesses that stayed didn't want to hire men from the Car Shops because they couldn't afford to train them only to lose them when the factory got going again in a few months.

What ensued was a general pall that lay over the town as if a dark cloud had found its way into the airspace over the community and stubbornly refused to leave. Cambridge City had briefly lost its way of life.

Many of the town's residents had come to Cambridge to help supply the Car Shops with materials and finished goods for their railroad cars. Mills, iron works, furniture makers and many other businesses depended on Mr. Mercer and his company for their livelihood. Some businesses in town, however, weren't entirely dependent on the Car Shops because they had other customers. The Marble Works, owned by James W. Carpenter, found itself in just that situation.

Carpenter married Ezelpha Tyner in 1854 when they were both nineteen. Ezelpha's father was one of the founders of Cambridge City and the couple settled there for good in 1857, the same year the Mercers came to town. Carpenter started his business with $200 worth of unwrought marble (which he borrowed) and by the early 70's had turned it into the most successful marble business in the country. The secret to his success was importing Scottish granite. The costs were lower but the lesser quality wasn't noticeable which allowed him to undercut his competitors. Soon he had taken half ownership of the Scottish quarry and became both wholesaler and retailer.

By the time W.B. Williams' sales job in Richmond had dried up, Carpenter's business was booming and he needed help. He was traveling back and forth to Scotland regularly to tend to the import business so the storefront in Cambridge, which dealt predominantly in tombstones and other monuments, didn't get much of his attention. His partners, J.J. McCarthy and Barney McMahon hired W.B. to handle several accounts and tend the store from time to time. This allowed him to be home most of the year and keep to a regular schedule.

As Archie and Jack searched for work, they found themselves in an interesting position. While they were put out of a job due to the closure of the Car Shops like everyone else, they had no intention of going back when it re-opened, so that was an advantage. Of course, they also planned to leave in less than a year, but that didn't need to be public knowledge. However, when your father's bankruptcy almost brings a whole town down with it, your reputation tends to get sullied as well, regardless of whether you had anything to do with it.

On one hand, they had a lot going for them. They were both imposing physical specimens and bright and well educated for the time.

On the other, they had two glaring liabilities: Jack's skin color, and Archie's last name. There was nothing they could do about the former but maybe they could conceal the latter problem.

Archie and Jack stopped a half a block west of the Marble Works to get their strategy straight. Archie would do all the talking and Jack would smile a lot and look smart. Then Archie had a brilliant idea. "Jack, I think it best if we don't use my real last name. These folks could be one of my father's old suppliers."

Jack looked down his nose at him. "So we're gonna lie?"

Archie waved him off. "No, no, nothing like that. Just follow my lead."

Jack yielded. "I suppose. Just don't go saying something I'm gonna regret."

They walked down in front of the store and saw the employment notice in the window. "See there," Archie said in frustration, "I knew it. They're looking for three men. We shoulda brought William after all. I shoulda caught that."

They opened the front door, removed their hats, and rang the bell on the front table. Jack whispered, "Archie, what's the proprietor's name?"

Archie replied in the same hushed tone, "I didn't catch that either, I'm afraid."

"Well, for the best ballplayer in the county you sure don't catch good." Jack loved it when Archie tossed him a soft ball.

"Oh, no wait. There it is on wall - Carpenter."

W.B. Williams entered from the back room. "Can I help you gentlemen?"

Neither Archie nor Jack recognized Mr. Williams. Jack had only seen him once in the dark fifteen years ago. Archie hadn't seen him since his beard had turned gray and had never really noticed him anyway.

"How do you do sir? My name is... Archibald and this is Mr. Jackson. We are here to enquire about your sign for employment in the front window."

This was both welcome and unwelcome news for W.B. Both McCarthy and McMahon were out of town on business and they had left him in charge of the retail operation and replacing some men who had left Cambridge City. This wasn't the first time he had been on this side of a job search but he didn't relish what was to come. "I see," he said nervously.

There was a bit of an awkward pause as the three men hoped someone else would get the ball rolling. Finally Archie stepped forward. "What are the positions you have available?"

W.B. smiled in apology. "Oh, yes, we need a salesman, a craftsman and a monument installer. Have you had any experience in selling, Mr. Archibald?"

Archie was a little taken aback by the use of his name in that fashion, but it served the intended purpose. "Most of my experience has been in management, but I'm sure that I could pick up sales rather quickly, and Mr. Jackson here is a fine craftsman, in fact, he worked at a quarry back home. Isn't that right, Mr. Jackson?"

Jack wasn't sure about what management experience Archie was referring to unless he just meant following his father around, but at least he didn't fabricate Jack's experience. "Yes, sir I did. Of course it was limestone rather than granite."

W.B. wanted to see if they might be stretching the truth a bit. "Where was that, now? Over in Bedford?" The Bedford Indiana area was famous for its limestone quarries.

Jack spoke up, "No, sir. Ontario, Canada. I don't think I've ever been over to Bedford."

Jack was telling the absolute truth but W.B. had never heard of Canadian limestone. Then again, he hadn't heard there wasn't any. That's what happens when you go from selling farm equipment to selling marble overnight.

Archie decided to jump in. "Yes, sir, Mr. Jackson here grew up in the Great Lakes area of Canada. He's strong as an ox..."

Unfortunately Jack tried a joke. "... and twice as smart!" There was again an uncomfortable silence as W.B. didn't quite understand Jack's wordplay and Archie tried to figure out how to again navigate the awkwardness. Finally, Jack blurted out, "That was a joke." He and Archie started to laugh hoping that W.B. would join them, to no avail.

Archie tried one more time, "He's smart, witty..." and then looking directly at Jack, "on occasion..." then back to W.B. "...and the fastest man in the county. Why, if you had a holdup he could chase down the thief even if he was on horseback."

W.B. was amused. "It is not often that thieves try to run off with slabs of granite but I will keep that in mind."

Archie tried to change the subject. "Oh, and my brother William would be quite suitable for the installer position. He's just sixteen but he's eager to learn."

W.B. might have been a bit confused still about Jack's attempts at humor, but he did recognize a fellow salesman when he heard one. "I do agree that sales will most likely come easy for you, Mr... Archibald."

Archie replied, "Thank you very much, sir."

Archie's comment stopped W.B. in his tracks. He was sure that he had seen Archie before but he couldn't place it, but now that phrase just made him scratch his head. He knew that he had heard that awkward way of saying "Thank you very much" before. It was spoken so oddly, like the speaker was not familiar with English, that he KNEW it belonged to someone he'd encountered; still he couldn't place it. "Have we met? You sound very familiar."

Archie could see in Mr. Williams' eyes that he had just heard the voice of his father.

Archie's great-grandmother had emigrated from Sweden and Archie's grandfather had grown up hearing her broken English in his boyhood home. Several of her butchered English phrases had made their way into the family lexicon. That particular one was an overused family joke that had become so natural to all of them that Archie didn't even realize when he said it. The hair on the back of his neck stood at attention as he tried to misdirect Mr. Williams. "Well, we've only been in town a few months. We came here from New York." And that was technically true.

W.B. was satisfied. Having met so many people in his travels over the years he was often mistaken about names and faces; this was probably no different. "I'd be willing to give you a chance to prove yourself. When can you start?"

This was good news. Archie enthusiastically responded, "I'm available immediately, as is Mr. Jackson."

W.B. nodded, "Very good. You can begin on Monday then, fifteen dollars a week to start. I hope some occasional travel will be acceptable."

Archie agreed, "Oh, of course, yes sir, and how about Mr. Jackson?"

W.B. took a deep breath. He knew this was inevitable but hoped somehow he could avoid it. "I am afraid I don't have a position for Mr. Jackson at the moment."

Archie tried to remain calm. "Did the other two positions get filled, very recently?"

"We will see you at eight sharp on Monday morning, Mr. Archibald. Good day." W.B. nervously poked at a couple of objects on the table hoping to appear busy.

Jack was no stranger to this kind of treatment. It was just the reality of life. But as common as it might have been, he never got used to it.

Archie, on the other hand, had only experienced it through Jack, and then only when someone was stupid enough to pick on "the nigger with the pet giant," as Archie's classmates had derisively called them just before he sent six of the eight to the infirmary. The anger that had consumed Archie on that fateful evening would haunt him the rest of his days.

The first two or three would-be assailants he had rebuffed with verbal warnings but then the leader, who like his friends had clearly consumed too much whiskey, threw a nearby wooden chair at Jack and it was on.

Archie went after him with fire in his eyes and laid out three of his protectors with the chair. When a fourth and fifth came after him he knocked them cold with one blow each, teeth and blood flying everywhere. The two that hadn't yet been involved took one look at the crumpled figures of their mates and ran away as fast they could in opposite directions. When Archie caught up to the leader he beat him so savagely, so relentlessly, that Jack had to intervene for fear that Archie would be responsible for the man's death.

Archie and Jack told everyone that they moved back to Indiana for a variety of reasons; Mr. Mercer's health, the weather, Archie's disillusionment with the military… and those were certainly important considerations. But, truth be told, they didn't so much return to Indiana as they fled New York. There was an arrest warrant issued for a "nigger" who had assaulted and nearly killed a group of students who were minding their own business. They knew if they stayed and answered the charges that several "eyewitnesses" would come forward to testify that Jack had attacked the boys without provocation and it wouldn't matter what they had to say. They got out of there fast and limped home.

Archie never recovered from that evening. You would think he'd have mixed emotions, simultaneously being proud of himself for protecting a friend and feeling guilt for taking it too far, but all of his recollections were nightmarish. He had witnessed the wild beast inside of him and he was ashamed. Jack had seen it too and it scared him to death.

Archie was beginning to see red. "I suppose you might have a position for Mr. Jackson then if he had, say, a lighter complexion?"

Jack could see that look in Archie's eyes and intervened as he had before. "Don't do this."

"Don't lecture me, Mr. Archibald." W.B. said defiantly, "I was an abolitionist long before your parents ever met."

Archie appeared calm, but it was that calm that your father always had that made you wish he was yelling at you.

"I see, so our consciences are satisfied that we abolished slavery, but we really don't need to believe that all men are created equal!"

Now W.B. was getting a bit miffed himself. "Mr. Archibald!" he fumed.

"What was it that my uncles gave their lives for in the war, to free Negroes from their shackles only to condemn them to second class status?"

Jack jumped in front of Archie. "We don't mean no disrespect!"

Archie referred to a sign on the wall that featured a Bible quotation. "You say you honor the Scriptures! How about the one that says, 'And he made from one blood all of the nations of the earth'?"

W.B. leaned into him. "Things are not as simple in life as they are in your imagination. There are forces at work here that you know nothing about!"

"The only force I see here is bigotry, sir. And I have seen it for far too long. Good day!" And with that Archie stormed out of the store with Jack in hot pursuit.

As they stepped out in to the street, Jack chased Archie down and stopped him with a hand on his shoulder in front of the bakery next door.

"I appreciate the sentiment, I do, but you can't just fly off the handle and insult people like that!" Jack recognized the volcano of bitter feelings burning in Archie, it had burnt inside him a time or two, but while it seemed out of place in Archie, Jack felt a sense of relief that someone else was carrying that burden for a change.

"The whole thing just makes my blood boil!" Archie was now pacing in the street to try to calm himself down. After a few moments he was calm enough to say half apologetically, "I didn't intend to make a scene. What'd he mean by 'Forces'? What Forces?"

Jack whispered in a conspiratorial fashion, "There's been a lot of talk about the Klan trying to reorganize out here."

Archie's hair was up on his neck again. "Is that possible? President Grant just outlawed them last year, didn't he?"

Jack looked both ways down the street. "I hear they're trying to lay low until all that blows over and they can get a Democrat in the White House."

Archie answered derisively, "Well, that isn't likely. Why would they come to this part of Indiana? You'd think all the Quakers here would make that pretty unattractive."

Jack shrugged. "Maybe this is the last place anyone would look. I don't know, anyway, it's all rumors at this point. So what do we do now?"

Archie was resolute. "We shake the dust off our shoes from The Cambridge City Marble Works..."

He gestured at the Marble Works' sign but then he was startled by a slap on the back. He wheeled around to see who it was and Amos Caldwell thrust his hand out in greeting. "Hey there, Mercer! How ya been?"

"Doin' well, Amos." Archie muttered. Caldwell was a schoolmate of Archie's but they had never been anything resembling friends.

Jack said, "Good day, Mr. Caldwell."

Caldwell pretended not to notice Jack standing there. "Are you looking into the Marble Works openings, Arch?"

Archie and Jack stood there for a moment and then Jack spoke up, "We was considerin' it, but after talkin' with the man we figgered it t'ain't right fer us."

Again Amos addressed Archie. "All the better for me then! Say, was old man Williams in a foul mood? I wanna hit him at just the right time."

Williams?

Archie and Jack panicked in unison. Archie bent over like he was looking for a coin in the dirt so Jack answered Caldwell. "We thinks you oughta give him a little time before you goes in there."

Caldwell tipped his hat. "Hey, thanks for the advice, Arch. See you soon." And with that he was off.

Jack leaned over to Archie, "Now don't jump to conclusions. It could just be a coincidence. Williams is a common name around here..." He thought for a second, "mostly because Emma's family nearly founded the county ...but that doesn't mean he's a direct relation... He could be another Williams... the less prominent kind."

Archie was turning green. "I think I'm going to be sick." And he leaned over a hitching post and lost it right there in the street.

10

Limping Home

From their vantage point beyond centerfield, Grandpa and Taylor were about to become part of the game. With two out and two men on base, one of which was a girl, a Cubs batter hit a long fly ball to center field. The first-string centerfielder went back on the ball but tripped over his feet as he tried to make the catch. He landed on his back just as the ball whizzed by him and hit the fence in front of Taylor.

Disoriented, the boy searched high and low for the ball as Grandpa stood and shouted instructions. "To your right! No, your right! Your other right!"

Taylor was back now after sprinting away from the oncoming projectile, and tried to help too. "It's to the east!"

Finally, with that piece of information, the boy grabbed the ball and hurled it toward the infield. Only then did he notice that no one was running around the bases any longer.

Grandpa's look of disgust at the boy turned to Taylor. "To the east? You actually thought that would help?"

Taylor held out her hands. "It worked, sorta."

"Purely coincidental. He just ran out of other places to look. Too bad Nicky wasn't playing. He would have saved a run." He started to enter the events into his scorebook and find his seat.

Now it was Taylor's turn to look at Grandpa with that cynical stare. "You think Nick would've caught that one?"

Grandpa chuckled. "Oh, no. Not a chance. But he would have known he couldn't catch it and turned to see where it landed. He does that very well."

"I suppose knowing your limitations is a skill." Then Taylor made

Grandpa's head spin again. "So, I'm confused about Emma's father."

Grandpa nodded, "And understandably so, since I haven't finished the story."

Then Taylor pivoted again, "Look Grandpa! Nick's getting a helmet on. Maybe he's going to hit next inning."

Grandpa's synapses were struggling to keep up. "Well, then I'd better hurry and squeeze in this next part. Okay, so on that same night, Emma had arranged for Archie to come over for dinner and meet her parents."

Taylor chuckled. "That can't be good."

The Williams house was all a twitter for most of the day. Emma and her mother had worked tirelessly to ensure that everything was just right for the big event and all of the children had done their part. George chopped enough wood to keep the fire burning for weeks, Mary Ina was on potato peeling duty, and little Lily set a beautiful table - almost on her own.

As the time drew near, Emma skipped down the street to Archie's house to retrieve him so he wouldn't be late; she was learning.

Just after she left, W.B. returned home after a tough day at work, threw his hat on the rack and collapsed into his favorite chair to read his paper.

Susannah greeted him. "How was the shop today, Father?"

W.B. took a while to respond but eventually offered, "This evening should be a great improvement."

The last thing Susannah needed was for Father to be of a foul disposition. "Oh, bother! Trouble with the Bakers again?"

There was a pause, then a sigh. "Indirectly. I had to turn down a young Negro man for the craftsman position today."

She put her hand on his shoulder. "You know it's for the best, dear."

He nodded. "Yes, but his friend let me know what he thought about it. Can't say as I blame him. 'Tis a shame, both young men showed promise. I'm afraid until I can find help down there my days will continue to be long ones. And today I got a wire from McMahon saying that he wouldn't be back until late summer."

"Well, thank you for coming home tonight."

He offered what for him was a laugh. "Did I have a choice?"

"Do you remember when you first met my parents?"

He lowered his paper momentarily. "That day is burned into my memory to such a degree that I still bear the scars." He raised it right back to where it belonged.

She scolded him, "It wasn't that bad. Was it?"

"I do have some fond memories of that evening."

"Which parts?"

"Limping home." He bent down his paper and gave her a wry little smile and his version of puppy dog eyes, intended to make her feel sorry for him.

"I agree. My father was a bit hard on you."

He tilted his head in empathy. "His daughter was very precious to him, as she should be. I understand now how he felt. Should I answer the door with some kind of weapon in my hands?"

Susannah turned on him, "William! The young man will be nervous enough."

He held his hands up in surrender. "I was joking. I will say that I'm glad to finally meet this mystery man. I half expect him to float in here borne on angel wings for all I've heard about him lately."

Susannah stopped what she was doing and put her hands on his shoulders, leaning in behind him. "Isn't love grand? Those days when your sweetheart could do no wrong?"

W.B. was a little taken aback by her romantic tone and felt he should reciprocate. "I had those days."

There was silence for a moment as W.B. awaited her response. Susannah sighed deeply and wistfully, grabbed a towel from the table and promptly returned to the kitchen. He didn't know quite what to make of that. Then in a fit of curiosity he yelled to the kitchen, "Did you have those days?"

With her hand to his forehead Emma snapped him out of his daze and asked, "Archie, are you not feeling well?"

He tried to laugh it off. "I suppose that depends on what you mean by feeling."

Archie and Emma started down Church St. on the journey to the Williams house. They both entered the evening with a fair amount of trepidation and for decidedly different reasons. Emma's fears were natural jitters that come with the territory, while Archie had real reason to worry.

The day's events, coupled with Emma's odd behavior when the marble shop had been mentioned the other night, convinced Archie that he was about to walk into the home of a man he had publicly berated just a few short hours before. There was no way to hide the fear in his eyes from Emma. He also began to wonder if he had been hasty in his assessment of the man's motives. If it was her father, a proposition he was resigned to by now, how could he raise a daughter with the sentiments on abolition Emma possessed if he did not possess them himself?

She wouldn't give up. "Are you concerned about tonight?"

"Shouldn't I be?" He jested. After all, even without the day's events this would be an anxiety ridden affair. He was justified in being a little concerned. "I will say that, if nothing else, preparations for this evening have had a positive effect on my prayer habits, if not on the knees of my pants."

Emma stopped him in his tracks and pulled him against a nearby tree. "There's nothing to worry about. They will love you. How could they not?"

"I can imagine a scenario."

Emma was starting to worry herself. "Come now. My parents are as excited to meet you as you are to meet them."

"Excited might not be the word."

That was one wisecrack too many. "What's wrong, Archie?"

Archie twisted a little and then, almost like a school boy, the giant whimpered, "Emma, if I told you about something I did that was wrong, would you still love me?"

Emma smiled mischievously. "You're thirty-four. I knew that."

She grabbed his arm and tried to drag him up the street but he wouldn't budge.

"Emma, I'm serious."

So was she. "What is it? You're scaring me."

He took her hand and with an odd solemnity said, "No matter what happens this evening you need to know that I will always love you, and that I will never give up."

Back inside the Williams house all the preparations had been finished and everyone eagerly awaited Emma's arrival with Archie in tow. By this time the whole household was aware of the identity of Emma's secret beau except for W.B. As usual he was the last to know, but this time it wasn't his fault. There had been a conspiracy to keep him in the dark; in fact, many of the neighbors had been enlisted in the plot.

Emma's reasons made sense, in a way. She expected that her father would be concerned about their relative ages and wanted to make certain of Archie's love before she put him through that ringer. Now that she was sure he was "God's man for her," they could approach her father with confidence knowing that they could survive anything he threw at them together. Ah, the naiveté of youth.

W.B. meanwhile was still on a fact finding mission and asked the whole room, "Do we know the young man's family name yet?"

Susannah sheepishly responded, "Yes." She hoped to avoid being the bearer of the bad news and that Emma would walk through the door any moment.

He pressed her, "And what would that name be?"

Now that was a direct question and Susannah could see that the two youngest were about to give away the surprise so she blurted out the first thing that came to mind. "I didn't want to upset you needlessly with all of your other worries."

W.B.'s innocent response has been repeated to succeeding generations with the same reverence afforded the Gettysburg Address. "As long as his name isn't Mercer, I can't think what could upset me."

The children sat stunned. Susannah squirmed like a child herself as she tried to think of a response that wouldn't light the fuse that would set off the bomb. The atmosphere became so thick that had there been a family dog it would have hid in another room - under the bed - in a box.

Then right on cue, Emma burst into the room and announced, "Here we are!"

11

How Unfortunate

In a voice that informed everyone that they were to now forget the last few moments, Susannah rushed to the door. "Oh, come in, come in!"

Emma ushered Archie in and time stood still for a moment. The children were staring at Archie as if they had never seen someone duck to get under the front door before. Susannah was looking at the gleam in Emma's eye, wondering if she had ever seen her so happy. W.B. and Archie reflexively turned away when they saw each other as if they were averting their gaze from an impending train derailment. Emma, being the only one in the room not somewhere else at the moment, broke the ice. "Father, Mother, this is Archie Mercer."

Now Archie and W.B. had to look at each other. Archie couldn't think of another time in the last few years when he had been afraid of another human being.

Maybe it was the fear in Archie's eyes but W.B. felt a little pity for him and decided to let him off the hook for the moment. "It is a pleasure to meet you, Mr. Mercer. Welcome to our home." He emphasized Archie's last name just enough to send a message to Archie that the day's events would stay between them for the moment.

All Archie could manage in reply was a meek, "Thank you very much, sir," but this time as it would sound if spoken by a native English speaker.

W.B. continued with the pleasantries. "This is Emma's mother, Susannah."

Susannah acted as if she had never met him either. "How do you do, sir?"

Archie greeted her. "A pleasure, ma'am."

She continued, "Do you know our other children, Mr. Mercer? This is George, Emma's brother."

George was a little annoyed that he even had to be there to meet Emma's new boyfriend when they'd known each other most of their lives. "Mother, Archie and I go way back. How are you, Arch?"

Archie smiled. "Good, George."

Susannah gestured for Lily to stand up straight. "Then I suppose you remember Mary and Lily?" Archie bent down to greet them and Lily let out a big giggle that put everyone at ease.

"Please have a seat, Mr. Mercer." W.B. pointed to a seat on the opposite side of the table. Emma went to sit down next to the spot and Archie pulled her chair out for her which forced W.B. to do the same for Susannah. George found his seat and Lily jumped into her seat with a thud. Mary remained standing. After watching what men were supposed to do for ladies, she stood there and stared at George, who was completely oblivious. After a couple of "ahems," much to the delight of the adults, George finally took the clue and pulled her seat out for her. All was now right with the world.

This was quite an event in the Williams household history as it turned out. None of the other children would court anyone seriously until the family moved to Richmond later in the decade, so this was the first and last of these awkward occasions on Church Street.

From his seat, Archie could see a stitched sign hanging over the hearth that read, "For I was an hungred, and ye gave me meat: I was thirsty, and ye gave me drink: I was a stranger, and ye took me in."

W.B. was equal parts bemused and sickened by the situation he found himself in. How could life be so cruel as to bring the son of his recently-deceased nemesis into the life of his daughter? On the other hand, their run in at the shop provided W.B. with endless entertainment for the evening.

"Mr. Mercer, it's a wonder we haven't met, Cambridge being

such a small town."

Not understanding what was really going on, Emma dove right in. "Father, Archie was around the house often when we were children, but you were away most of that time."

Archie tried to save her. "And I have been away at school for the last couple of years."

W.B. found a place for another subtle dig. "Ah, learning a new trade perhaps?"

Archie could see now that conducting two conversations at once was a family trait. "Something to that effect, sir."

"Father, Archie was studying at a military academy."

Archie had really hoped that his military ties could be avoided in the presence of her father. Mother rescued him with an attempt at humor. "Oh, you needn't worry Mr. Mercer, not all Quakers are strict pacifists."

Everyone laughed politely at what they perceived to be the awkwardness of that quip, but Archie's muffled response was more to the point. "How unfortunate."

Not hearing Archie's retort, W.B. was interested. "And where was that?"

Archie knew this was unavoidable so he just came right out with it. "West Point, New York."

"Oh, so THE Military Academy," W.B. said with a twinge of admiration.

"Yes, sir, I am afraid it was my father's idea."

W.B. suddenly changed the entire flavor of the conversation. "You have my sincerest condolences on his passing, son. It was a great loss for the town as well."

"Thank you, sir. Did you know my father?"

W.B. tried to be tactful for Emma's sake. "We had the occasion to supply him with materials on occasion."

The truth is W.B. had been nipping at Mr. Mercer's heels for years.

For a man like W.B., any relationship that could be forged with the most important man in town was a good one. Before he had gone to work for Carpenter's firm, W.B. had sold Mercer on the idea of using marble inlays in his passenger cars. Then he went to Carpenter and offered him the account with the stipulation that he could work for him in the shop in town and end his traveling days, a benefit for all parties concerned. Of course, when the Car Shops went under Carpenter was on the hook for a significant sum, and W.B. felt responsible.

Trying to avert his gaze from W.B., Archie spoke into his napkin. "I humbly apologize on behalf of my entire family if you were caught up in his most recent dealings, sir. It is a great source of embarrassment for all of us, but I promise that you will be made whole as soon the process runs its course and we sell the factory."

Williams nodded. "Thank you, sir."

Emma had never thought about that connection between their two fathers. Whatever their business dealings had been it looked as though there weren't any complications for her and Archie, so she moved the conversation on. "Father, Archie is planning on selling the house too and then moving his family back to Connecticut."

Archie was glad to not talk about either the military or the Car Shops. "It will be nice for my mother. Her family is there. I'll help them all get settled…"

Emma finished his sentence, "… but then he and Jack plan to come back to Cambridge."

"I see." W.B. didn't see, really. He was a bit confused as to why they had been at his shop looking for work if they were moving east. "When will that be?"

"That's still a bit up in the air," Archie volunteered, "certainly not until we have our finances settled. And as for Jack, I'm not sure he will be returning with me. If he finds work in Connecticut he may just stay."

Emma turned to Susannah to explain, "Momma, Jack is Archie's

Negro friend I was telling you about."

"He would be wise to do just that, sir, what with the way things are in these parts lately," Susannah said with a hint of disgust in her voice. "Why, it's a good thing Emma's great-grandfather is in his grave. He wouldn't have taken kindly to those folks trying to undo all the work he did."

Archie could see where Emma got some of her spunk. While it wasn't unique to the age, a woman speaking out on such things in mixed company wasn't common, though it appeared that it was common in this particular household. Archie could see that W.B. rather enjoyed listening to his wife rant about the topic. In truth, Mr. Williams had become accustomed to and tolerated the women in his household speaking their minds. In this particular case, however, it would prove quite advantageous.

Emma said, "My great-grandfather was William Williams the preacher. He was the first to invite Negroes to join the Society."

"And now those mongrels have set up shop right next to Father's store." Susannah had a bit of steam coming from her ears. "Excuse me." She took a dinner napkin and fanned herself a bit, looked at Father and gave him the universal "I'll be quiet now" expression.

Emma finished her thought for her. "The bakery next door to the Marble Works is where the Klan has decided to have their meetings in the middle of the night. Father's company had to stop hiring Negroes for their own safety a few months ago."

Susannah wasn't finished. "It absolutely broke our hearts. Of course, Mr. Carpenter has been able to find most of our men work in other parts of the county. Emma, could you help me put the supper on?"

As the ladies stood, the men pulled out their chairs and watched as they removed to the kitchen.

Archie felt like such a fool. He couldn't look W.B. in the eye. Surrounded by the children, Archie couldn't say what he needed to say to him. He tried the best he could to apologize silently and it appeared that when he did Mr. Williams both understood and accepted it.

W.B. admired the young man for his strength of character, if not his manners. He decided to put the whole episode behind them and never spoke of the incident at the shop again. He still had many concerns. This young man's age might not matter in a few years but right now it bothered him a bit. There was also the matter of his last name. The name Mercer was mud in Cambridge and that mud would soon be slung at his daughter. But his real reluctance, even if he would never admit it, was the idea that his daughter would be marrying "up." That implication would be obvious to everyone concerned when the daughter of a frontier salesman married the son of an important New England businessman, even if that name had been sullied. W.B. took solace in the thought that, at least, Archie was a Quaker.

12
Now Don't Cheat

As it turned out, it wasn't Nick's turn at bat after all. After the Cubs finally made their last out of the inning, Nick, helmet in place, ran out of the dugout and toward third base.

Grandpa exclaimed, "That's why he was getting a helmet on, Taylor, he's gonna be the third base coach." That solved the mystery. "The manager uses Nick as the base coach on the opposite side of the field a lot."

"Why, to get him as far away from him as possible?"

Grandpa gave her the requisite look of disgust. "No. Nick may not be the most physically gifted but he knows how to use his head. He says that base coach is actually his favorite position."

Taylor grimaced. "That's kinda sad, Grandpa. Well, at least he got on base, or close to it."

They sat for a moment and pondered the plight of the non-athlete on an athletic team, trying to look for a bright side. Not finding one, Grandpa lamented, "Third base has got to be a pretty lonely place to be on that team."

"Maybe he was sent over as a spy to hear the other coach's plans."

"What, his plans for the victory party? He's up by eight. What plans could he have?"

"Well, I was just trying to be optimistic, Grandpa,"

Just then Taylor's phone rang again and she jumped up and walked away to answer it, leaving Grandpa to mutter to himself, "So much for that."

"Hi Carter... Because you're about the only person that calls me." Taylor looked at her phone for a minute and then asked, "What's this number you're calling from? ... How'd you get to Conner's house? Okay, I'll check." She put her hand over her phone and pretended to check something with Grandpa and instead said to him, "Carter's phone is dead."

Grandpa muttered, "There is a God."

"I'll get rid of him, Grandpa." She went back to Carter with the voice of someone who was just following orders. "I don't think so. The game's only in the third inning and it's already eight to nothing so you'd be really bored... I can't... Nick hasn't batted yet, and my grandpa hasn't finished his story... No. It's only half way through." She looked at Grandpa who was shaking his head. "Or not even that far... The story? Nah, you wouldn't like it. It's a romance, and we all know how much you hate those."

Carter wasn't taking no for an answer so Taylor tried to make it sound like her phone wasn't working. "Car---? C--er? Are -- still --ere? I--you're break--ing --up. Call me-- when you--bet—re--cep--tion." Then she hung up.

Amused, Grandpa kidded her, "He's not going to buy that."

"Why not?"

Grandpa tilted his head at her. "Honey, he's on a land line isn't he?"

Taylor replied with a bit of a sigh, "He won't figure it out right away."

"And you say he's your boyfriend?"

"Yes."

"On purpose?"

"Could we get back to the story, Grandpa?"

"The story, right. Where were we? Ah, yes. Neither of the men mentioned the incident in the marble store ever again..."

Things went well for Archie that summer. He found a buyer for the house and his father's partner, Mr. Moore, struck a deal to sell the Car

Shops to a firm out of Indianapolis that intended to start production in the Car Shops facility under the name The Indiana Car Company.

It took a little longer to sell the rest of the family properties than Archie had hoped. Since much of the proceeds from those transactions would go to pay off his father's debts, including James Carpenter's Marble Works, the family was stuck in Indiana for the summer.

By the late fall, everything was finally set for the family's move back to New London. However, the prospect of traveling by train and coach during the cold of the fall and winter with their entire entourage of children, hired help, pets and belongings didn't sound very appealing to any of them. They decided to make the move as soon as the snow thawed the following spring of 1872.

Archie and Jack had found work during the fall and winter with the railroad, but the company was based in Dayton, Ohio. The trip back and forth was a little over sixty miles, so it was difficult to make it home. As anxious as Emma was to have Archie leave so he could get back, she was happy that he was still close, even if they didn't see each other much. He was home for Thanksgiving and Christmas and they spent that time dreaming about what their lives together would be like.

When Archie was home Emma was a regular fixture in the Mercer house. She loved getting to know the children and had fostered a special bond with little Frederick. That winter turned out to be particularly cold with temperatures getting down to below zero quite often from December through February, so going out to their hill was out of the question. Being home as little as he was, Archie figured he should spend as much time with his family as he could. Consequently, they rarely spent time with Emma's family.

At Christmas it was decided that Archie and Jack wouldn't be back again until mid-March when they would leave the railroad for good and prepare for the move. By February, Archie was getting tired of writing letters; and the painful thought of missing Emma's sixteenth birthday on the 22nd was impetus enough for him to schedule an unannounced visit.

He arrived in town secretly on Wednesday, the 21st, and swore everyone to secrecy. That the 22nd was also George Washington's birthday - so the school chose to shut down for the day - fit perfectly into his plan.

The next morning at ten sharp someone knocked on the Williams' door. When Susannah answered it, she saw a large, brightly colored gift box hanging in midair and below it a pair of very large feet.

"Emma!" She shouted, "Delivery!" Then she shut the front door so Emma could view the scene for herself as intended. While Susannah's intentions were good, it was a little odd for Archie having the door slammed on him like that.

In moments, Emma bounded for the door, threw it open, and stared at the legs. "Mr. Galt, is that you?"

From behind the box Archie answered, "Now what would Charles Galt be giving you a birthday present for? Is there something you've been keeping from me?" Archie lowered the box to his side and Emma dove at him and hugged him like he was a soldier coming back from war.

Archie visited briefly with Emma's mother and sisters and then it was time to open the gift box. Emma was a little disappointed that, 1) it was a large package - what she was hoping for would be much smaller - and 2) Archie was content with having her family present when she opened it. But, he was home for her birthday and that was enough.

As she started to unwrap it she couldn't help but notice the smirk of satisfaction on Archie's face. This told her that he was very proud of whatever it was and that she'd better love it. Then suddenly it hit her. She knew what was in the box and let out a squeal before she even saw it. Soon her eyes confirmed what her heart already knew; it was the winter coat she'd been coveting for months from the front window of Miller's on Main and Foote streets.

The coat was a beautiful deep brown with fabric covered buttons up the front, a notched collar and decorated in a floral brocade pattern. She quickly put it on and discovered that it was a little long on her, everything store bought was, but other than that it fit perfectly. Momma promised that she could do a little adjustment to the sleeves.

She ran to the full-length mirror in the hall and squealed again at how adult she looked. Mary Ina and Lily were envious, as all the ladies of the house admired her in the looking glass.

Archie stayed out in the front room and waited... and waited. Finally there came an "Oh, my!" from the hallway, then Emma came running in and bear-hugged him again. In all the excitement she had forgotten about Archie. No more of that.

It was a fairly moderate weather day, above freezing for once, and it was decided that they would test out her new coat up on the hill. Emma whisked Archie away as fast as she could.

It had become a custom that Archie would carry her up to the hill as she rode on his back and any other time it'd be nothing for Archie. Emma was a hundred pounds dripping wet, which was six pounds less than the railroad ties Archie had been carrying two at a time for the last few months. But the months of hard labor were catching up to him and, as they reached the summit, his back tightened up and a groan escaped before he could muffle it.

As Emma slipped off of him, he slumped to the ground and lay face down on the damp ground.

"Archie, what hurts you?"

"My pride, mostly," Archie groaned again, "which is located just below my shoulder blades."

"Can I rub it for you? Would that help?"

"It couldn't hurt any worse."

Emma tried to figure out just how she should approach this task. She found the spot he specified and gently rubbed her fingers in that area.

"Sweetheart, let me know when you've started," Archie quipped.

"But I've already started."

"Oh, well then you'll need to do whatever you're doing much harder."

Emma pressed down much harder using the base of her palms. "Is that any better?"

"I could use a bit more."

Now she put all of her weight into it. "That's all I've got, I'm afraid."

"Well," Archie said, "I suppose you'll have to resort to more desperate measures."

"And what would those be?"

"Stand on me."

"Stand on you? With my shoes? I'll break your ribs!"

"Oh, no, Jack does it all the time. He weighs twice what you do. Though, I'd prefer you not stand on me in those boots."

"If you're sure." Emma sat down on the stool and took off her boots. "This is a little strange, so don't get used to it."

Carefully, she put one foot in the middle of his back, shifted her weight on to it, and then stepped up with the other. Then Archie teased, "Tell me when you get up there."

"Oh, stop! Is that doing any good?"

"I think you'll need to jump about a bit."

Emma started bouncing on him and that started to do the trick. "Ah, there we are. That's good."

Then all of a sudden Archie winced and Emma jumped off of him as quick as she could. "Oh, did I hurt you? Are you all right?"

"That was wonderful. Try that again."

Emma dutifully climbed back up and bounced on him again. As she did she looked out onto the Lackey's horses and wondered what they might be thinking of this peculiar sight. Finally, Archie indicated that he'd had enough and she sat back down and put her boots back onto her frozen feet.

Archie crawled over to the stool, leaned up against her and put her hands on his shoulders, leaving the obvious hint that she should now rub his shoulders. She started in on her task and could see that she was making him feel a little better.

Archie sighed and took her hand and kissed it gently and said, "That's nice. Thank you, darling."

He had never kissed her before and, though this had been a little awkward, it felt so natural, like they were already married. That moment just froze in time for Emma. It crystalized the thought she'd had for the last year that she was only complete when she was with him. Even more, she was happiest when helping him. She whispered in his ear the God's-honest-truth. "There's nothing I love doing more."

Archie groaned a little and said softly, "It's never a good idea to be the largest man on a work crew. Even my hair hurts."

Archie, for his part, only felt like he was fully human when he was with her. He and Jack had talked about it at length while they were riding the train to their work site every day. Having Emma in his life made him a better person. She softened him, made him appreciate the beauty around him more, and even made him consider writing poetry. Fortunately, that urge wore off.

He had never really considered what he wanted to do when he grew up. Money had never been an issue before, and he'd always assumed that he would go into the family business. But with Emma in his life he was becoming ambitious. He wanted to set the world on fire and do something important like his father to provide for Emma - to make her proud of him.

Emma reminded him, "Only a few more weeks."

"That's right, I leave on Monday and then when we come back on March 15 we're done. Did I tell you we're taking William this time?"

"No. Is he excited?"

"He won't be once he gets a taste of the work. But between the three of us we should make enough to pay for the family's passage to New London."

Emma said, "I can't wait to watch you take care of our family the way you take care of your brothers and sisters." She started to tear up and paused for a moment. She was glad she was behind him so he couldn't see this display. Then the reality of the situation struck her. "What am I going to do without you for a year?"

They had always assumed that he would take the summer and fall to get his mother settled and then come back by train in the winter; but, if this winter was any indication, he'd probably have to wait until spring again. Archie had developed other plans. "I was thinking about that."

He paused and Emma didn't like it. "Out with it."

In his best casual tone he said, "What if you came with us?"

"I don't understand."

Archie slowly rose from his place on the ground and pivoted until he was facing her on one knee.

It took Emma a moment but finally she realized what was happening and jumped to her feet and screamed at the top of her lungs, "Yes!!!" Then she covered her mouth with both hands so she wouldn't blurt out anything else, though her giggles were nearly as loud.

"At least let me ask you first. I've got this speech prepared and all."

"I'm sorry." Then she waved her hand in his direction and said, "Go ahead."

Archie looked down to the ground to collect himself, raised his head to look her in the eye - as they were now about the same height - and softly said, "Emma..."

To which Emma replied just as she had before, "Yes!!!"

"Good grief, woman. Can't a man get a word in?" Covering her mouth again she gestured for him to continue.

"Emma, I've never been accused of being a sentimental man. I never even thought myself the marryin' kind. But you have made my life so sweet that I can't imagine living a life without you in it. Would you do me the honor of becoming my wife?"

Emma was afraid to say anything for fear she'd interrupt him again, so she just waited and stared at him.

After a few moments Archie nervously said, "It's traditional at this point for the woman to give the man an answer."

Emma was fully engulfed in tears by this point and could only say, "That was the prettiest thing I ever heard. Keep goin'."

"I'm afraid I'm all out of words. It's your turn."

She had rehearsed for this moment. "Then yes, a thousand times yes!"

She dropped down to her knees, making sure not to let her new coat hit the ground, and embraced him. As her face hit his chest she could feel his heart racing and then slowly calm down to a normal level. She pulled away a little so she could look up straight into his eyes and waited…and waited. Finally, she had to just say it, "We're engaged. You can kiss me now."

"There's nothing I want more, sweetheart, but let's save that for another moment."

Without missing a beat Emma replied, "I'm pretty partial to this moment."

"What if something happens and in the end you become another man's wife? I wouldn't want to harm that union."

Okay, noble is great, but this is ridiculous. "But I'm yours now, Archie. That's not going to happen. I could never love another man now."

"I understand, but unexpected things happen in life. I still think we should wait for 'you may now kiss the bride.'"

With just a little hint of sarcasm, Emma pulled away, started back for her stool and said, "Then you'll never kiss me."

"What?"

"They don't say that in Quaker weddings."

Archie pulled his stool up to hers. "They don't?"

"No, the couple just comes to a monthly meeting, stands up in front of everyone and says that with 'divine assistance they'll stay together forever'. They sign a paper and it's over. Not very romantic."

"Maybe you should pass around those Jane Houston novels you read."

"Jane Austen." She said with a bit of disgust.

Archie shrugged. "At least I knew she was from Texas."

Emma couldn't stay mad at him very long and let out a huge laugh. Then she realized that she had let her heart overtake her brain and that they had been too hasty. "The ceremony only lasts a minute but the preparations take months."

"How long?"

"There have to be at least two monthly meetings. One to announce it and get it approved, and then the ceremony is at the next one, but even that would be really fast."

The plan was falling apart. "I leave in a month and a half. Maybe we could get married at my church or by a justice of the peace."

Emma's eyes opened wide and she looked at him aghast. "Remember who my family is? My father would die a thousand deaths!"

"I suppose I can't very well take you with us if we're not married."

"Archie, it'll be all right. We'll just get married when you get back like we planned. It'll give my parents time to get accustomed to the idea. But, still, what will I do without you for a year?"

"I'll write every day."

"I will too."

Archie pointed up to its usual location. "And we'll have our moon. Eight o'clock every night just like we said."

"It will be later for you, now don't cheat!"

Archie looked her in the eye. "Every night, at about nine, I'll go outside, look at our moon, pray for you and your family, and thank God for giving me the most precious gift this life can offer."

She leaned her head on his giant shoulder. "God has been good to us, hasn't he?"

He put his cheek on the top of her head. "And I will be eternally grateful."

"Tell me you love me, Archie."

He turned to her and said, "I do, Emma Williams, with all my heart."There was silence between them as Emma looked preoccupied. Archie had to bring her back to the moment. "This is when you're supposed to say something. Do you love me?"

Emma broke out of her daze, giggled and said, "I do."

Archie was a little perplexed at what was so funny. "What is it?"

Emma put her head on his shoulder again and said wistfully, "We're not going to get to say 'I do' either."

13

What We'll Remember

Taylor pulled a tissue out of her clutch and tried to fix herself a bit, much to the delight of Grandpa. "If this is getting to be too much for you we can pick it up again later."

Taylor looked him in the eye and threatened, "Not if you value your life."

"Okay, just a little more then. I'll need to take a break soon. I hear a bad hot dog calling my name. So, the time came for Archie and his family to get started on their..."

Taylor's phone rang again and by this time Grandpa had taken about all he was going to take. He grabbed the phone from her, fumbled around a bit trying to figure out how to answer it and then in his best New Yorker accent said, "Morty's Mortuary! You kill 'em, we chill 'em. Can I help you?"

Taylor stared at Grandpa with her mouth wide open.

"Let's see, Taylor? Let me check." Grandpa half covered the phone and pretended to yell into the next room. "Hey, Murray! We got a corpse back there by the name of Taylor? No?" He went back to the phone and said, "Nope, 'fraid not kid," and hung up.

Grandpa gave Taylor a little Cheshire Cat smile, and the phone rang again. Taylor battled him for it, to no avail.

"Morty's Crematorium! You choke 'em, we smoke 'em. Can I help you? He hung up."

The phone rang a third time. "Well, he's persistent, I'll give him that." He answered the phone. "Morty's Burial at Sea! You slash 'em, we splash 'em. You clunk 'em, we dunk 'em. You crown 'em, we drown 'em. Oh, he hung up again." Grandpa put the phone back in the drink holder of Taylor's chair. "Good, I was running out. Next up, the cannibalism department. You beat 'em, we eat 'em. You crunch 'em, we munch 'em. You slay 'em, we filet 'em."

"Grandpa! Please just stop!"

The phone rang once more and this time Taylor snatched it before Grandpa could answer it.

"Hi Carter... Really? ... Three times? Hmm, that's strange... Nope, still third inning... eleven nothin'..." Something Carter said registered and her tone changed. "Oh, I'm sorry, did I not mention that I'm busy with my grandfather right now? I'll call you when I'm finished." She hung up the phone. "Maybe." Then she tossed it into the grass in front of her. After a few moments, she began to laugh a little, looked at Grandpa and then, almost apologetically, raised her hand for a high five.

Grandpa reciprocated her gesture but with real concern in his voice said, "You're gonna have to tell me someday what you see in him."

Taylor wasn't in the mood to talk about Carter any longer, so she urged Grandpa in no uncertain terms to move on with the story.

Imagine today trying to book airline tickets to get you from a small hamlet like Cambridge City, Indiana to New London, Connecticut. First you'd have to get to the closest airport. Cambridge City certainly doesn't have one, and Richmond only has one meant for private planes, so you'd have to travel the 60 miles to Indianapolis by bus or taxi with all of your belongings. Then you'd book a flight to the closest airport to New London, which is Hartford, Connecticut. Your flight to Hartford would have at least one stop in Washington D.C. or New York and then you'd have to make the fifty mile trip by taxi or bus to New London. Now imagine traveling this same route 140 years ago by coach and train!

Archie found the quickest and least expensive route, but it required getting to Richmond by carriage to catch the first of a series of trains to New London. The journey would take them through: Dayton and Columbus, Ohio; Pittsburgh, Harrisburg and Philadelphia, Pennsylvania; Trenton, New Jersey; New York, New York; and then up the Connecticut coastline through New Haven to New London.

The four coaches pulled up to the Mercer house the day before the move and the process of stuffing their belongings into every crack and crevasse began. Once they reached the train station at Richmond the family and their essential belongings would board the train; the rest of their things and their furniture would be consolidated into two of the four carriages to make the rest of the eight hundred and forty-four mile journey. Shipping their possessions by train proved to be too expensive.

Emma couldn't bring herself to help out. It all seemed so final, and she promised herself that she wouldn't cry so as not to be a burden to Archie. He was busy enough tending to the needs of his whole entourage of eleven.

The morning of the move, many of the townspeople came to pay their respects and say their goodbyes. Even Susan and Luna came into town to say goodbye - though really Susan had come to help Emma through the aftermath and Luna had come because Susan couldn't talk her out of it.

Emma decided that it was best that she not go down to the Mercer house to say goodbye, but rather wait up the street a distance so she didn't get lost in the crowd. She instructed Susan and Luna to stand in her spot and then signal to her when it was time.

Luna was in rare form that morning, as all of the commotion had clearly overstimulated her. She was badgering Susan about how they needed to prepare Emma better for the inevitable heartbreak. She had Susan to the point of considering sororicide.

"No, not a word. Do you hear me?" Susan yelled.

Luna pleaded her case. "What's the harm? After all, she should cherish every moment if it's going to be the last time she ever sees him. I just want to remind her is all."

"It was a dream. That's all it was, a silly dream!"

"A dream she's had every night for a week."

Susan tried to take a calmer tack. "A couple of nights ago I dreamt I was swallowed by a fish."

"Did you get out?"

Susan sighed, "What difference does it make?"

"It could be a sign."

"Yes, it could be a sign that I taught the children about Jonah that morning in Bible class. And the other night, after you put too many peppers in the stew, I dreamt that I could breathe fire."

Luna thought seriously for a moment and then asked, "Do you think Emma's had too much spicy food?"

"No! I think she's worried because the love of her life is moving a thousand miles away and her mind is playing tricks on her."

"Who's moving away?"

Susan couldn't help it and she yelled at the top of her lungs, "Archie!"

Calmly, Luna responded, "I already knew that."

Susan reacted with that famous Baldwin death stare. "How is it possible that we share the same parents?"

Luna put her right index finger to her lips and then alternately looked to the ground and then to the heavens for an answer. Finally it came to her. "Cuz we're sisters?"

There was silence for a few moments as Susan tried to regroup. Then she said as forcefully as possible without violence, "Today is hard enough for Emma. She doesn't need you reminding her about that ridiculous dream."

Luna only got out a meek, "Not even..." before she got a finger in her face.

"If you breathe a single word on that subject, I'll shove that bonnet so far down your throat you'll have a tail!"

From a block away, Emma mistook Susan and Luna's wild gesticulating for the signal to come down and she arrived just as Susan was about to make another untoward comment in Luna's direction. Susan felt Emma's presence behind her, spun around, changed her whole countenance, and with compassion asked, "How are you holding up today, pretty girl?"

Susan's theatrical talents had completely fooled Emma who responded in a daze, "Like this can't really be happening. It doesn't seem real."

Luna leaned in and whispered, "Like it's a dre…?" Before Luna could finish, Susan subtly backhanded her and pointed menacingly to the bonnet. Luna grabbed her head to protect herself and stayed that way for much of the rest of the conversation.

Susan turned her attention back to Emma and said, "He'll be back before you know it."

Emma recited to herself one of the many Bible verses she had memorized for the occasion. "Why art thou cast down, O my soul? And why art thou disquieted within me? Hope thou in God: for I shall yet praise Him, who is the health of my countenance, and my God."

"Is that a Psalm?" Susan asked.

"Forty-two. God has a plan, Susan. He just hasn't let me in on it yet."

Luna could see down the street that the Mercers were on their way to see Emma. "Here they come."

Emma started breathing uneasily and grabbed Susan's hand to keep her steady. "Help me, Susan. I have to be strong for Archie."

"We're right behind you."

As the Mercers approached, Susan and Luna stood behind Emma and she held on to them for dear life. Mrs. Mercer was leading the processional with the children behind her; Archie and Jack brought up the rear. She walked up to Emma and with a sweet and tender voice tried to delay the inevitable with disarming small talk. "Emma, you look lovely today, dear."

"Thank you, Mrs. Mercer."

"And Susan, is that a new dress? It's perfect on you."

"Thank you, Ma'am."

There was an awkward pause, and then Luna cleared her throat in an obvious attempt to receive a similar compliment.

Eleven-year-old Nellie said, "You look nice too, Luna," and everyone laughed nervously.

Susan got the ball rolling. "Are you all ready for your big trip?"

Thirteen-year-old John said excitedly, "Mother says we'll get to see the Ocean."

Mrs. Mercer offered, "You girls should come visit us some summer."

Susan politely replied, "We'd love that."

"If you're ever out in that part of the country then you'll always have a place to stay with us."

Susan wasn't sure that Eleanor's invitation was genuine, but appreciated the gesture. "Thank you, Ma'am."

The clock was ticking and this had to be done, so Eleanor uttered the dreaded words. "Come everyone, say goodbye to Emma so we don't keep these drivers waiting any longer."

The two littlest ones, Harriet and Frederick stared at the ground and held on to their mother's dress without saying a word. John stepped up and said, "Goodbye Emma. I'll pray for you."

"Thank you, John."

Then Nellie stepped up to Emma, took a long look into her face and finally said, "Goodbye Emma. Aren't you going to miss Archie?"

The whole lot of them cringed silently and Emma grabbed Susan tighter and said meekly, "Very much, Nellie."

Nellie turned slowly and then said to her mother in hushed tones that everyone could hear, "I thought she'd be cryin' or somethin'."

Eleanor grabbed her by the sleeve and shoved her into William's grasp and stepped forward herself. "I do so wish you were coming with us, child."

"So do I, Mrs. Mercer."

"Courage, dear, the Lord has a plan."

"That's what I hear."

Eleanor gave Emma a big hug and while they embraced she said softly enough so only Emma could hear, "I love you like you were my own flesh and blood. You just put your mind to other things and he'll be back before you know it."

Emma was trying so hard to not cry she was hyperventilating. All she could muster was a faint, "I hear that too."

"Goodbye, honey. Come along children." And with that Eleanor gathered her brood and whisked them away.

Now it was William's turn. He approached her with his hat in his hands in front of him and his chin in his chest. Emma said to him, "Take care, William."

He lifted his head a bit and offered, "You too, sister. I'll come back with Archie next spring. Gonna be his best man." Archie was a bit surprised by that since he hadn't asked him and had no intention to do so. Then William turned his attention to Susan and said, "Susan, I hope when I get back I'll see you again."

Susan was in no mood for him. She wanted to be nice, but what she was thinking slipped out anyway. "Well, I imagine that will be hard to avoid."

William was unaware that he had just been verbally slapped across the face and cheerfully said goodbye to all three ladies. He turned to go but Archie grabbed him and said matter-of-factly, "William, why don't you and Susan take a little walk? Don't you think that would be a good idea, Susan?"

Emma nodded her direction and Susan took William's outstretched arm and followed him back to the carriages.

Jack didn't need to be told that it was his turn. "Don't you worry none now. I'll take good care of him."

"I know you will Jack. Thank you for being such a good friend." And with that Emma gave him a big hug that caught him a bit off guard.

Jack would have fallen in love with Emma too, if only for the way she always made him feel fully human. Still, a white girl hugging a black man in public could cause an unwanted reaction. Emma was oblivious to the ramifications of such an action - Jack was not.

"Thank *you,*" he said as he backed away from her without making his intentions obvious. "You made him a very happy man. He's better company now. He actually talks every once in a while."

"Bring him back to me in one piece?"

"I will."

As Jack turned to go Archie stopped him. "Jack?"

He knew immediately what that meant. "That thing again? Okay, this-a-way, Miss Luna. Hurry up, time's a wastin'."

"Which thing is it this time?" Luna said sarcastically.

"A different thing."

She took his arm and started to walk away with him but continued to object. "You can't fool me. There's no thing. You're just trying to get rid of me. I'm too sharp for that."

Jack sighed. "Yes, Miss Luna, you sure are sharp. As sharp as a bowl of pudding."

Luna looked up at him with the wonder of a small child and said, "You always say the nicest things."

Now they were alone. They looked at each other for a moment - neither one knowing what to do. Emma started to cry and they ran together and embraced.

Emma buried her head in Archie's chest and was trying to

surreptitiously wipe her tears on her sleeve when a giant hand placed a handkerchief near her face. She grabbed it and dabbed her eyes as she backed up a bit and said unconvincingly, "My eyes perspire in the sun."

With a chuckle Archie said, "Of course they do."

With a little determination in her voice Emma told herself out loud, "There is no need for tears. He's just taking another trip like he did when he worked for the railroad."

"It'll be over before we know it," Archie said.

Again they looked at each other not knowing what to say until Emma blurted out, "What we say right now will be what we'll remember."

"Then let's make it count. Emma Williams, I love you more than anyone or anything in this world."

"You are a part of my soul, Archie. Without you I'm incomplete."

"I will always love you and I will always come for you."

"And I will always wait for you." They embraced again and then Emma looked up at him and whispered, "Kiss me, Archie."

He leaned in as she wished and then suddenly John appeared out of nowhere. "Come on, Archie. Momma says the drivers are getting impatient."

Archie didn't know whether he was more mad or embarrassed. "I'm coming!"

He tried again and this time Nellie was poking at him. She whispered so only he and Emma could hear, "Come on! They're gonna leave without us."

"We're the only passengers!" He said in exasperation.

As Nellie ran back to the carriages, he would have tried a third time but he could see his mother approaching with everyone else, so he just drew Emma in and they embraced while they waited for her.

"I'm sorry, Archie," Eleanor said gently, "They say if we don't leave now we won't make Richmond by sundown."

Without a word, Archie started to pull away. Jack put his arm around him and led him out. The look of panic on Emma's face started Susan and Luna weeping as they rushed to her and held her up.

Archie didn't look back, for a few yards. When he finally did, seeing her in such pain caused all of his protective muscles to twitch uncontrollably; he broke through Jack's hold of him and ran back to her.

He grabbed her face in his giant hands and pressed his lips to her forehead. What ensued was the most passionate forehead kiss in the history of forehead kisses. It may have only lasted a moment or two but both of them seemed to be trapped in a timeless state. Though they were standing on a crowded street corner the only thing that mattered, the only thing that existed, were the two of them and this new creation that had just been brought into being, "Them."

The whole world had gone silent. Neither could hear anything, not even their hearts beating out of their chests. Then all of a sudden, like a spell had been broken, Archie could hear the commotion of his family calling him and he let go of Emma and ran away. He ran right past his family and didn't stop until he got to his place in the third carriage. He buried his head in his coat and hoped the world would just go away.

Emma was so lost in that moment that she almost fell over when he let go of her. Susan caught her and held her as they watched Archie run. Emma clutched his handkerchief to her face to breathe him in as he left. She was fairly calm, until the coaches began to move.

They began down the block toward her and as they passed, all of the Mercers in the window seats waved goodbye to them. As the third carriage approached, Emma strained to see if she could get a glimpse of Archie. She thought that seeing him as miserable as she was might make her feel better. Instead, what she saw was little Frederick sitting on his momma's lap sobbing and pointing at the only home he had ever known as it disappeared in the distance. For a moment he looked right at Emma and then wailed again and buried his head in his mother's coat.

Emma bit her cheek, bounced on the balls of her feet and waved at the coach trying desperately to keep it together for just a few more moments. As soon as the last coach turned the corner and was out of sight, she groaned in agony. She fell to her knees and sobbed so hard and convulsed so violently that Susan was convinced that this healthy young woman was going to have a fatal heart attack right there on the street. Susan and Luna held her and stroked her hair and encouraged her to breath for the next few minutes.

Emma slowly started to breathe again, but she would never be the same. You see, she had given her heart away, and it was currently traveling by coach toward Richmond, Indiana on its way to a land she had only read about. Though her lips were quick to say that it would be back before she knew it, and her mind could calculate that the distance of eight hundred miles soon separating them wasn't insurmountable, something deep inside her whispered that she wouldn't see her heart again for a very long time.

Part Two

14

A Lost Art

When Taylor went to the concession stand behind home plate to fetch Grandpa his bad hot dog, she also picked up a package of candy insects. She was making a snide remark about her bugs being more appealing than his dog when a player on Nick's team hit a scorching liner down the left field line.

"Atta boy!" Grandpa bellowed, "That's the way, Justin! Good hit!"

Taylor was duly impressed. "He really hit that one hard, didn't he?"

"Yep, the coach teaches 'em to swing as hard they can in case they accidentally hit it."

Without a hint of sarcasm Taylor observed, "Now all they have to work on is hitting it fair." She offered some Creepy Crawlies to Grandpa. "You want some?"

"No, no. Thank you, though."

"You want to get started again, Grandpa?"

Grandpa groaned a little as they both sat back down. "You've gotten quite involved in this story, haven't you?"

Taylor took his inference as almost accusatory. "Is that okay?"

"Well, of course." Grandpa was happy she was enjoying it, but he sensed that this story was going to provide an opportunity for a significant teachable moment so he started set the stage. "Why do you like it so much, do you think?"

Taylor wasn't just going along to make an old man feel better about himself; she really connected with the story, but even she didn't know why yet. "I don't know. I guess... maybe that love back then was the same as it is now, but more..."

She couldn't come up with the word she wanted so Grandpa filled in the blank. "Noble?"

She tilted her head a couple of times. "I was trying to say deep, but I guess noble works. It's just fun to think of your great-great-grandma as a teenager in love."

Grandpa leaned in and delivered the bad news. "Your parents were once teenagers in love."

Taylor shivered a little. "Okay, that's just gross." Taylor meant the information he had just imparted and not the half chewed garden pest in her mouth. Then she asked, "Why was Emma so broken up? I mean it was only a year."

Clearly, Taylor had never been in love. "Well, to a teenage girl back then who had never been more than twenty miles from her home, Connecticut was so far away it might as well have been on the dark side of the moon. They both had a feeling that they'd never see each other again. Emma had that dream and Archie – well, he just had a sense. They never breathed a word of it to each other. The letters began arriving just as they promised."

Richmond, Indiana
30th of April, 1872

My Dearest, Darling Emma:

As the wheels of the coach clicked along the many miles of our very familiar journey to Richmond today, my courage waned with each revolution as I realized that each one took me further from the one I love. My only solace is the assurance that they can just as easily turn in the opposite direction, as they surely will one short year from now.

Cambridge City, Indiana
May 15th, 1872

My Dear, Sweet Archie:

They arrived today! Your first letters arrived just as I thought they might! I sank gloriously into my bed and snuggled with my pillow to read them. I read them so many times and with such great affection that I'm afraid they are quite the worse for wear. Your letters are like a healing balm for my soul. The time between them dare not be long lest I be overtaken by a great sickness.

Mystic Harbor, Connecticut
4th of June, 1872

To My Love:

We took the trip out to the harbor today to see the ships come in. As we sat this afternoon and looked out over the river I recalled the many beautiful sights we had taken in during our travels. God's creation is a wonder to behold. I thought of you today as I sat there, which is my custom when I see something beautiful, and I realized that of all of God's masterpieces it is only when I gaze at you that my heart stops, my throat parches, and I cannot avert my eyes to another subject. You are the greatest of God's works of art, and the fact that he finds me worthy to call you mine own baffles me beyond words.

Cambridge City, Indiana
June 30th, 1872

To my only love:

Since receiving your letter extolling my beauty I have had the occasion to be complimented on my appearance by a great many acquaintances and even some complete strangers. Mr. Galt at the postal office is quite persistent, truth be told. This had never happened before you sent your greatly exaggerated lines. I can only surmise that you have created beauty in me by praising it when it did not yet exist. Your love for me has made me worthy of being loved. That may be your greatest gift.

New London, Connecticut
1st of August, 1872

Emma Darling:

I am afraid that I am not a very accomplished writer. I cannot seem to translate the depths of my heart onto lines of paper. You will have to fill in the blanks with the thoughts you know my heart wishes to express. I have so little imagination, something you have in such abundance, that I am beginning to lose you. I can no longer easily see your face when I close my eyes, nor smell your hair in the garden, nor hear your voice in the wind. But I can imagine that day when we are reunited in body as we are now united in heart and in soul. Will not our suffering these many months make that moment all the sweeter? That is the moment I am partial to.

Cambridge City, Indiana
September 5th, 1872

Dear Archie:

Your letter dated August 1 pained me so deeply that I can scarce cease my eyes from releasing streams of compassion for you in your distress. I long to come to you that I may participate in your sufferings, or else, as I suspect I might, relieve them altogether.

Perhaps I am cleverer than you as I can recreate every detail of you in my heart without aid of the senses. But I do have an advantage as I can revisit our former haunts and breathe you in more fully. Kiss me in your dreams, my love.

New London, Connecticut
15th of September, 1872

My Dearest Friend:

I apologize for my penmanship. My fingers are so excited to send my love to you that I can scarce make out what they have been saying. As I gaze at our moon tonight my mind has replayed the short years of my life and has come to the conclusion that my greatest success in life was winning your love, and even that was given to me freely and without merit. My greatest hope is to one day become a man worthy of your love.

Cambridge City, Indiana
October 8th, 1872

To the friend given to me by God, the soul He has married to mine own;

Your love has built for my soul a great castle, impenetrable to the enemies that seek to destroy it. Am I not the most to be envied? For I have what every little girl dreams of and every woman covets, a prince. Yes, a prince in disguise so that his royalty is unknown to all save the damsel who has won his heart. This prince cannot navigate the day without telling his lady that she is loved.

Archie, it has been nearly six months and yet your absence is still unreal to me. I feel as though I have been sent off to the land of dreams by the prick of the spinning wheel, waiting for my prince to return and revive me.

Taylor was envious and a little repulsed at the same time. “Wow, they had it bad!”

Grandpa chuckled. "Yes, they did, but it was a different day, and folks who might not dare let any of their innermost thoughts out of their mouths, wrote them instead."

"I wish we still did that."

"Did what?" Grandpa asked.

"Well, had a different way of communicating with each other."

Grandpa corrected her, "You do. Your generation writes very differently than it speaks."

"No we don't."

"Really? When was the last time you said LOL to someone? Or ROFL, BRB, G2G, IDK?"

Taylor was strangely amused by Grandpa's grasp of internet shorthand, even if was a little behind the times, as usual. "Ok, I get it."

"But, you're right, Taylor. It is a lost art."

"Grandpa, do you think it has anything to do with all the technology we have now?"

"How do you mean, sweetheart?"

"Well, it's so easy to communicate now that we don't have to think about it. I mean, I can just send Carter a text or call him no matter where I am or what time it is. I can't possibly make every one of those messages deep and meaningful so I've gotten used to having meaningless conversations with him. You think that could carry over to other parts of our relationship?"

Grandpa tried to be careful. "Are you asking me if I think your relationship with Carter is meaningless?"

"No, Grandpa," Taylor said, "I know how you feel about that, thank you very much. I mean, do you think that it being so easy makes us not care about it?"

"I suppose that's possible. Grandma and I just got one of those DVR thingies and now I find that I've stopped listening to her - thinking that I can rewind her if I missed something important."

Taylor thought for a moment. "If you have a long distance relationship now you can still see and talk to them every day. It must've been really hard back then."

Grandpa sighed. "I imagine so."

15
Getting Settled

By the time the Mercer clan arrived in New London, all of the financial transactions had been finalized. Mr. Moore had done very well in settling all of the accounts and paying off the Car Shops' creditors. The Mercers were no longer in debt, but things would certainly not be as easy as they had been back in the salad days in Cambridge. Housing prices in New England were a bit higher than either Archie or his mother had expected, so buying a home proved unrealistic. Since they didn't spend their money on buying property, Eleanor had a little bit of a cushion to get them settled, but they needed to get some kind of business up and running, and quick.

New London was still home to many of Eleanor's siblings so they were able to stay with relatives until she found the perfect house to rent. After a few months of living out of suitcases they finally settled at 111 Huntington Avenue in what is still called Whale Oil Row. Four large houses were built on spec by Ezra Chappel between 1835 and 1845 in the Greek revival style, Ionic columns and all. The four buyers were two men who had made their fortunes in the whaling industry - thus the name - plus a merchant and a physician, one Dr. Enoch Vine Stoddard.

Dr. Stoddard married Eleanor's oldest sister, Mary Allen, in 1832 when Eleanor was only four years old. Mary was twenty years older than Eleanor and had always been more of a second mother to her than a sister. Mary died suddenly after coming down with the flu in January of 1848 at the age of forty, about four months after Eleanor had married William with Mary at her side as her matron of honor. The whole family was devastated. Dr. Stoddard was left with four small children (Mary, Enoch, George and Harriet) ranging in age from ten years to eleven months.

Dr. Stoddard was an important man in town so the memorial service at the Allen home and then the graveside service at Cedar Grove Cemetery were very well attended. With all the arrangements that needed to be seen to, Eleanor's sister Sarah, the only unspoken for sister of the five living Allen girls, took the children in and cared for them for weeks.

Eleanor and William moved to Buffalo that spring against Eleanor's better judgment, as she felt the family still needed her. William had already made business commitments so they moved in May, right after her youngest sister Jane's wedding.

It wasn't more than a few months after they left for Buffalo that a letter arrived from Sarah announcing that she was marrying Dr. Stoddard and raising Mary's children, a prospect Eleanor found both comforting and disconcerting at the same time. You could imagine that had Dr. Stoddard married a woman from another family the children might not have remained connected to the Allens, so this was a relief; and yet still... They were to be wed January 15th of 1849, so Eleanor made the trip back home to New London for Christmas alone as William's business interests didn't allow him be gone for that long.

As she stood as a witness for Sarah and Enoch, all she could think of was her dear sister Mary and standing at the alter as a little girl at her wedding. She committed right then to naming her first baby girl after her sister. Little did Eleanor know that Mary Stoddard Mercer was already in attendance that day and would make her official entry into the world just eight months later.

We moderns can't always appreciate the love and reverence for family that would cause someone to name their child after a sister, grandparent or family friend who has passed on. We want our children to be individuals with their own identity, so we even resort to making up names. That's all well and good, but in order to understand our forebears we need to know that a child named for a departed loved one kept that person alive in a sense. Nearly everyone was named for someone else.

Unfortunately, little Mary Mercer was never well, in fact, when Archie was born two years later, in May of '51, the Mercer home looked like a M.A.S.H. unit. A midwife cared for Eleanor and baby Archie upstairs while another live-in nurse cared for Mary as she battled one of her fevers downstairs.

In October of 1854, Eleanor's mother, another Mary, passed away at the age of sixty-five, but Eleanor couldn't leave to attend her funeral because her daughter Mary (5) was sick again. She never recovered, passing away three weeks later. That made three deaths of three Marys in five years – Eleanor's sister, her mother, and her daughter. It was as if her grief was tripled at each passing.

Fast forward to February of 1871, just after Archie and Emma found each other, and two months before Charles Galt delivered the terrible news about William's passing. Word reached Cambridge about a horrific railroad disaster in New Hamburg, New York, a little hamlet about eighty miles up the Hudson River from New York City and about 130 miles from New London.

An oil tanker derailed on the frigid cold night of Monday, February 6th and lay helpless on the tracks as the Second Pacific Express hurtled toward it. Helpless to stop his engine with the weight of eight passenger cars behind him, Simmons the engineer refused to jump off to escape the inevitable calamity. He and his engine, the Constitution, slammed into the tanker and immediately burst into flames. The intensity of the heat incinerated the engine, tender, baggage and the first of the five sleeper cars as they hurtled into the icy river. Fortunately, perhaps due to Simmons' heroism, the other passenger cars decoupled and the surviving passengers and crew were able to push the remaining charred carriages back off of the bridge before it collapsed.

The total death toll was eventually rendered at twenty-three, but the bodies of the passengers in the unfortunate sleeper were not identified for several days as the remains in many cases were burnt beyond recognition. By Wednesday, the local papers were reporting that three of the first bodies recovered were that of a mother and her two small children, one of whom, about four years old, was found still cradled in his mother's arms.

William had remarked about the accident to Eleanor but neither thought anything more about it until they received a telegram from her sister Sarah informing them that Enoch and Mary's grown daughter, also named Mary, her husband, the Reverend Morelle W. Fowler, and their three children, Robert (7), Agnes (5) and Morelle (4) had been recovered from the rubble of the passenger car. They had just left Enoch and Sarah in New London and were headed to their greatly anticipated missionary post in Salt Lake City, Utah.

Where was God? How could He allow such horrible suffering year after year after year? When Eleanor arrived in New London, the first person she sought out was Sarah. They wept in each other's arms for days.

Enoch and Sarah had four children of their own, the youngest of which was fourteen when the Mercer clan arrived in 1872. With all but two of their brood out of the large house, the Stoddards invited Eleanor to join them and turn their house into an inn.

Huntington Street made for a breathtaking sight, as if one had just stepped into the pre-Civil War South with a row of magnificent sycamore maple trees framing each grand house. On the corner, northeast of the houses, was the new location of St. James Episcopal Church, the congregation Eleanor had grown up in with her family. She and William had been married at her father's home, as had Enoch and

Sarah and their sister Jane, because the new church building was still under construction, but the parish rector, Rev. Hallam, performed the ceremonies nonetheless. The sanctuary would be dedicated in 1850 and still houses an active congregation to this day.

The first floor of the house was really a basement, but you could enter it from the rear at ground level. Though it featured the kitchen, furnace and new plumbing fixtures, its five rooms still made for a nice home for the family.

Nellie and Harriet shared a room next to Eleanor, as did John and Frederick. Toward the front of the house there was a nice place for Harold and Alice that gave them a smidgeon of privacy. Since Archie was only staying another six months or so, he let William have the last room for himself.

The formal entry way was on the second level and opened onto Huntington Street. The entry hall had exquisitely crafted parqueted floors leading to the focal point of the room: the staircase. The bannisters were designed to match the crown moldings throughout the house, which meant they were beautiful to the eye but not to the touch. Frederick and Harriet found out the hard way that this was not a staircase meant for sliding down like the one back home.

To the right as one entered was the parlour, which was connected to the formal dining room. Eleanor and Sarah could seat up to sixteen for dinner, a number that was stretched to the extreme from time to time. A serving room at the top of the basement stairs was connected to the dining room and featured a dumbwaiter, which Alice and Harold were very thankful for. Their room downstairs was just off the kitchen, so this made things very convenient. The second floor also had two guest rooms in addition to the two rooms occupied by the Stoddards.

The third floor featured another four guest rooms and the latest in indoor plumbing facilities.

The fourth floor had been used just as storage to that point but was a good candidate to be turned into more guest rooms. There was a room on the south end of that floor that Archie took a liking to and made his own. Though there were only a select few places in the room that he could stretch out his six foot four frame without hitting his head on the ceiling, he felt very comfortable there. The room's grandest feature was its window overlooking the city. From that vantage point Archie could see the Thames River and the town of Groton on the other side. The Congregational Church spire was the only obstruction to the entire New London harbor and on a clear day he could see Fisher Island in the distance where his grandfather, Lewis Allen, had grown up.

The prestigious nature of the house's location made keeping the rooms occupied rather easy in the warmer months. Winters would prove to be more of a struggle. Eleanor now had a business she could run that would keep her independent, but still she needed Archie's help in many areas, so rather than seeking an outside job for the year, he worked for her, and that allowed him to save up for his married life.

Eleanor had insisted that Archie, William and Jack be paid back with the proceeds from the sale of the properties for their arduous labor on the railroad, so with those savings and what he made working for his mother, Archie was convinced that he could not only find a suitable home for him and Emma but also start a business. This next year would be dedicated to researching what kind of business would be both suited for them and needed in Cambridge City.

By October of 1872, with his family settled and all of the monetary issues resolved, Archie was finally getting over the shock of being so far away from his best friend. Once the halfway point of their separation had been crossed it felt as though it was all downhill from there. He had finished job number one of settling his family and was now free to prepare for his future with Emma.

He eventually settled on the idea of going into the dry goods business. "Dry goods" was the term in those days for a business that sold fabrics, ready to wear clothing and miscellanies. It was the business his father had been in back in the Buffalo days, so he had grown up in it and that gave him some confidence. Plus, a few of his father's old contacts were still around, and he was able to make some important connections. Even the name Mercer derived from the term for a merchant who worked in textiles. It was truly the family business.

In a day when women still made much of their family's clothing, selling the needed fabric, patterns and supplies was an important enterprise. He would also sell the latest styles of ready to wear fashions, toiletries and other trinkets and knickknacks. And with the contacts he was making in New England, he would have access to suppliers that would give him a leg up on his competitors in Cambridge City.

Since his customer base would largely be women, he took care to consult Emma and his mother for their opinions and was careful to follow their instructions. In fact, it was both ladies' constant complaining about how difficult it was to find good materials in Cambridge that convinced him to go into the business.

In their letters, Archie and Emma strategized on location, inventory and many other issues. Not only did it help pass the time, but they felt that they were being productive in their letters.

For Emma, it gave her a purpose as she waited for his return. The town's existing dry goods shop owners couldn't help but notice how often she visited them as she tried to take mental notes of what was missing.

There was much to do and being eight hundred miles away from most of the people Archie needed to contact was very time consuming, plus there were his duties at home getting the boarding house in proper condition. He was so involved in the work on his various projects that the time began to fly by.

16
You'd Better Write Her about That

A house this big with a large family, staff and house guests running about tended to be a chaotic place. Some days Eleanor wasn't sure that she was cut out for the day to day bedlam that came with this venture. One Monday she was dusting off a set of her china as she unpacked it from the move. She had a question for Archie and thought she heard footsteps behind her. "Archie, is that you?"

It wasn't. It was William and he answered, "No," as he made his way from the serving room, through the dining room and parlour, and up the front staircase.

Eleanor never actually laid eyes on him from her vantage point in the parlour but could tell he wasn't Archie. "William, do you know where the china got to?"

"You're dusting it!" William said as he bounded up the stairs. He actually thought he was being helpful. Then he disappeared into the third floor of the house.

Eleanor didn't realize he was gone and kept talking to him. "No, the other set. This is my mother's!"

Nellie had nearly been run over by William as he sprang up the stairs, and she came down. "What about your mother?" Nellie asked.

Eleanor was a bit startled by the small female voice coming from William but pursued her line of questioning anyway. "Her china?"

Now it was Nellie's turn to be confused. "Your mother's in China? Didn't we just visit the gravesite the other day? Did it sink?" Nellie disappeared into the kitchen.

Out came John at whom Eleanor yelled, "Where is the china?"

John thought that was an odd question but answered it. "Near India

I think. Least that's what I hear."

Eleanor was about to have a seizure. "John, I need to find the other china!"

As John bounded up the stairs he said in all earnestness, "I don't know where the other one is, maybe Europe?" And he was gone.

Muttering to herself now, Eleanor was done with this cruel game. "I don't need a geography lesson; I just need to find the other china!"

On cue, Archie came up from the basement with a wooden crate filled with dishes wrapped in blankets. "Will these do?"

"What would I do without you?"

"You'll manage, Mother."

"I guess we'll have to soon, won't we," she groused.

Archie sat down on the sofa and began to unwrap the plates.

After a few moments Eleanor asked, "Any news from Emma?"

"In her last letter she said she'd talk to her father about starting the process with the Society soon. Hopefully, we can be married about a month after I get there."

"We can have a lovely celebration at the church for you when you return."

Archie caught her inference. "Thank you. We aren't sure when we'll be able to come back. I suppose it depends on what develops with the storefronts we're looking into."

"I see. Well, whenever it is that you can make it back we will be sure to throw you the biggest celebration New London has ever seen." Then Eleanor remembered which son she was speaking to and added, "Or, if you prefer, an intimate get together with just your closest friends and relations."

Archie snickered, "You thought I was William there for a moment didn't you, Mother?"

They had a good laugh together and went back to their dishes. Archie could tell that Eleanor wasn't finished, but let her bring up whatever was of concern. With a couple of sighs and then a burst of energy, Eleanor blurted out, "Is Emma going to be happy, Archie, giving up Quakerism and becoming a Presbyterian, or whatever it is you call yourself these days?"

Archie was caught a bit off guard and tried to joke his way through. "I prefer Presbypalian, if you don't mind."

Archie had never had a serious talk with his mother about religion, at least not a talk surrounding the unspoken but obvious religious division in the family.

It's hard for us in our rapidly changing, post-post-modern culture to grasp just how different we are from our ancestors, even just a few generations back. Twenty-first century Americans tend to think of our differences in terms of color: black, brown, white etc... In fact, it is common now to err in believing that people who look similar must also think similarly. But in the nineteenth century differences were viewed through the lens of national origin and religious affiliation, which in many cases were the same thing.

Back then "white" was not an ethnicity. You were Scottish, English, Welsh, Irish, French, Dutch, Danish, Swedish, etc... And the cultural barriers between the Scottish and the English, who had been at war with each other for centuries, or the French and the English, or the Danes and the Swedes were just as or more difficult to bridge when they all arrived in America as ours today.

Their languages were different, even if many of them were speaking a form of English, making it difficult to communicate, and their religious beliefs were different, even if they were all Christians of one stripe or another. In the end though, when these disparate groups became Americans, they intentionally tried to lay down their affiliations in the old country and melt together, largely through intermarriage. What has resulted, after generations of laborious change, is a country of descendants of northern and western Europeans who no longer think of themselves as French or English or Scotch-Irish or any other hyphenated group but just American. Maybe we can get there too, eventually.

The Mercers came from a long line of Scots that can be traced all the way back to the Norman invasion at the beginning of the second millennia A.D. When John Knox led the separation of the Scottish Church from the papacy in the sixteenth century, one of his lieutenants was John Row, whose great-granddaughter, Lily Row, married a Mercer. From that time the Mercer line features one Scottish Presbyterian Minister after another, including Rev. William Mercer who first came to America with his brother Hugh in 1747.

Like the story of so many other immigrants to the new world, those affiliations quickly began to fade for the Mercers. Archie's great-grandfather Archibald married a Swedish immigrant, his grandfather Archibald married a French immigrant and then his father married (gasp!) an English woman.

The Allens, Eleanor's family, were of pure English blood and can be traced back to at least five different Mayflower passengers including William Brewster, the elder of the Plymouth Colony, and John Howland, the young man who had to be fished out of the sea after he fell overboard during a storm. Consequently, with those English roots, the Allens were members of the Anglican Church and then the American Episcopalian Church when they arrived in the new world.

When Archie's parents married, they left New London right away and tried to establish a new life together away from their family traditions, but it wasn't easy. In Buffalo they had attended the Episcopal Church, but when they moved to Cambridge City there wasn't an Episcopal church in Eleanor's tradition, so the family attended the Presbyterian Church instead.

Archie preferred the reformed theological bent of the Presbyterians but enjoyed the familiar liturgical aspect of the Episcopalians, so when they moved to Connecticut he was content with following his mother's wishes and dutifully attended church with her. It hadn't occurred to him that this new family he would soon create might suffer from the same malady.

Archie said, "Actually, Mother, we haven't really talked about that yet. I suppose we should."

Trying not to sound alarmist but having experienced this pressure herself, Eleanor calmly responded, "Yes, I suppose you should." Then causally she offered, "It is a wonderful thing you're doing; waiting and getting married at her church to honor her parents."

Archie acted oblivious to her palpable casting of motherly guilt in his direction and replied, "It's not a church. They call it a 'meeting.'"

"A meeting, of course."

"It's the least we can do." Archie's brow furrowed and his leg began to bounce uncontrollably. "But, you know, the more I think of it, I'd better go write her about that."

"You never talked about this at all?"

"It was never a concern."

"Do her parents know that you aren't a Quaker?" Eleanor could see from Archie's silence that this was going to be a problem and insisted, "Son, you'd better write her about that."

Arms flailing in the air, Taylor huffed, "After all that they get separated by their denominations?"

"Now, don't go ruining it for yourself," Grandpa said... well... grandfatherly.

"Aren't they both Christians? I mean, isn't that all that matters?"

"Do you want to tell the rest of it?"

"I'm sorry. It's just so stupid! Who cares how many angels can dance on the head of a pin?"

Grandpa tried to slow the conversation down and take the emotional charge out of it. "Well, I'm not sure that's fair, honey. Theology isn't trivial. I can't think of anything in life more important than how we understand God. Now, we may have gotten past some of the things that divided us years ago, but that doesn't mean that to these folks the differences between them weren't real."

17
God is Still on His Throne

Archie wasted no time in penning his next missive to Cambridge City.

New London Connecticut
October 19th, 1872

Sweetheart:

In conversation with my mother this morning it occurred to me that we have never spoken about what arrangements we would make after we marry in regards to church membership. I am embarrassed to say that this vital part of our union never entered my thinking in any significant way.

I had always assumed that you would join me in the Presbyterian persuasion but after more reflection I recognize that your Quaker heritage is such a deep anchor in your life, and that of your family, that perhaps such an arrangement would be difficult.

While I will take my role as the head of our household very seriously, I am resolved to consult you on all decisions as the equal partner God intended you to be, however odd that might sound to you. What are your opinions on the issue?

Emma's Quaker heritage was not as straightforward as it might have seemed to an outsider. In those days the meeting habits of the Society were still very different from those of other Christian groups. The central place of worship for many Quaker families was still the home and the clan might not meet with other Quaker families for official meetings more than once a month. This was largely due to the fact that they were so spread out around Wayne County. The closest Quaker meeting house to Cambridge City was in Dublin, a little more than two miles away. The next closest was all the way to Richmond.

What this meant was that the Williams only ventured to "Meeting" once a month and, depending on Father's traveling schedule, sometimes not even that often. Most Sunday mornings were spent in the front room together, and in the Quaker tradition, mostly in silence. Emma had learned to use the time to read her Bible, but she very much felt the absence of other believers in her life. She had never told anyone this, even Archie, but she looked forward to joining the Presbyterian Church with Archie when they married while still being involved with the Society as much as possible.

Back in Cambridge City life was as it always was. Well, that's not entirely true. The Car Shops' debts had been paid off, so W.B. breathed a little easier. George went off to college in the fall, but unemployment in town was still very high. The Indiana Car Company didn't open its doors until early 1873, so all of 1872 was difficult in town, to say the least.

In other news, Susan and Luna had decided to stay in Cambridge City for the foreseeable future and were staying with cousins half way between Cambridge and Dublin. There were Baldwins just about everywhere in those days, so when Susan decided to stay, it wasn't difficult to find family. Emma had tried to convince her father to let them stay in George's old room, but no luck.

Emma was trying to keep herself busy. The impulse to stay in her room with the covers over her head or to sit and read Archie's letters all day was overpowering at times. Some days it was the best she could do to just get out of bed. Susan being close was a big help. She didn't feel quite so alone.

By fall she got absorbed in school as she tried to cram the last three years of high school into one. She really wanted to finish before they got married, if it was possible. It wasn't, but she made an admirable attempt.

She got Archie's letter in early November, and it frightened her some. It had occurred to her that the church they attended might pose a problem, but as she thought about it more it became clearer to her that this was going to be an obstacle. But any obstacle can be overcome, right?

She determined that she would begin the process of talking with her parents about the wedding arrangements with the hope that the subject could be broached naturally, or maybe avoided altogether.

Early one evening she was pacing in the front room with Archie's letter in hand when her mother caught her. "Did you get a letter from Archie, today?"

"Oh, no, Mother. The last ones came Wednesday."

"Well, your eyes shine like you did."

"Joy and fear can look much the same. Is Father coming home soon?"

"Any time now, I hope," Susannah answered. Then she sidled up to Emma and asked conspiratorially, "Is this the talk?"

"Which talk is that?"

"Oh, I don't know. Perhaps the one you've been rehearsing in your room."

Emma feigned indignation, but her heart wasn't in it. "You eavesdrop on me, Mother?"

"Of course not, dear. The hallway has just been very dusty." Everyone in the room knew that was a lie but it didn't matter.

Emma looked at her mother and her eyes started to well up with tears. "Momma, I'm scared. I'm afraid I'm going to lose him."

Susannah held her close and whispered in her ear, "God is still on

His throne, child. Nothing will keep you two apart."

"How can you know that? For months I've been having these dreams, Momma, like God's preparing me."

"This is God's man for you," was Mother's answer. "I am as sure of that as you are."

Just then Father came through the front door and tossed his hat on the rack and his paper on the table. Emma quickly pulled away from her mother and turned away to wipe her face on her sleeve.

Susannah greeted him warmly and helped him off with his coat. "Welcome home, Father."

"Greetings, Father," Emma half whispered.

"Good evening, ladies."

Susannah asked, "A good day at the shop?"

"In a manner of speaking," he responded with a sigh, "I finally hired someone today to take care of some of the paperwork."

Susannah put her hands on his shoulders as he sat in his chair. "Well, that's wonderful!"

W.B. countered abruptly, "No, it isn't."

She was a little perplexed and looked to him to get more information, but he wasn't interested in speaking anymore about it. It was as if he were keeping horrible news from her. Finally after a bit of head bobbing and beard scratching, out came the truth. "I hired Emma's cousin."

Susannah didn't know what the trouble could be and admired him for being forward thinking enough to consider hiring a woman. "Susan is a very bright girl..."

Then he said with all of the sullenness of someone making a notification to the next of kin, "Not Susan."

Incredulous, Susannah gasped, "William, you didn't!"

With shame he hung his head and admitted, "When a man is desperate he sometimes clings to things that will only cause him to sink faster."

After a moment of silence Susannah tried to cheer him up. "It appears she's already been a help. You're home early."

He replied grimly, "A man can only take so much for one day."

With that, Emma tried to slip out of the front room and into the kitchen. "If you'll excuse me I have to... take care of a thing."

"Oh, that's right. Father, Emma has something she wants to talk to you about."

Emma's eyes widened and she stared at her mother aghast. "It can wait, Mother. Father has had a difficult day."

"They aren't likely to get easier any time soon," Father added, "What's on your mind, child?"

"Really, it's nothing that can't wait."

Susannah knew that this bridge needed to be crossed and there was no time like the present. "Emma wanted to ask you how we should go about getting the meeting scheduled for a declaration of marriage."

W.B. smiled and said, "I see. Well, that would be up to the young man and his meeting on how to proceed." Then he gave Susannah a knowing glance and said, "Unions between meetings can be complicated, but not insurmountable."

Here we go. Emma still hoped she could avoid the inevitable. "Archie's... meeting... is a little different from ours. For them it's traditional to have the ceremony in the bride's... meeting house."

W.B. was oblivious to Emma's deft verbal swordplay. "I assure you his meeting knows what to do. The Society has been celebrating marriage the same way since George Fox."

There was just no way of avoiding it now. Emma winced and said, "So have the Presbyterians."

The impact of that blow and all of its ramifications dropped on the house like a cannon blast.

After a few moments of excruciating silence, W.B. responded as calmly as he possibly could. "Do I understand you to say that this man of yours isn't a member of the Society?"

His calm was, as usual, concealing his wrath at having been misled. Emma panicked. "I thought you knew that Father. Mr. Mercer built the Presbyterian Church."

The calm was gone now. "I was under the impression that he had converted, and that you would not dishonor your family by pursuing this courtship if that were not the case!"

Nearing tears again Emma pleaded with him, "I don't understand what the trouble is. Archie is a follower of Christ."

W.B. pivoted and fired straight at Susannah. "Madam, were you aware of this?"

She had never seen him this angry and his use of that formality scared her. "I suspected, but I..."

"How could you let her go on like this, knowing what was to come?"

"We survived, William."

"You were from a neighboring meeting of the same Society and we were disowned! Imagine what would have happened if she had married someone outside the faith!"

Those words would burn in Emma's ears for the rest of her life. How could he be so cruel and small-minded? She lost control of herself and forgot who she was talking to for a moment and yelled at him, "Archie isn't outside the faith! He's just as much a friend of Jesus as you or I!"

Susannah had wanted to remind William that much had changed in the last twenty years, but Emma's reaction derailed any chance of ratcheting down the volume.

How curious it is that a relationship that has taken a lifetime to build can be broken permanently by a few simple words - and true ones at that. Having been disparaged by his daughter for the last time, W.B. reigned in his emotions for fear that he would lose control. He said in eerie coolness, "There will be no more discussion. You will write him one last time and do him the courtesy of informing him that you will not be writing in the future."

And with that it was over. Not just the conversation but their entire association.

Emma yelped, "Momma!" just as Susannah implored him to reconsider.

All he would say as he grabbed his coat and hat and slammed the front door behind him was, "That is the end of the matter."

As distraught as Emma was as she sobbed on her mother's breast, the only thought that went through her mind was defiant. *Oh, no. This is just the beginning.*

Grandpa leaned into Taylor and confided, "Emma and her father didn't speak to each other for weeks."

"Ya think?" Taylor had been clenching her fists and grinding her teeth for the better part of the last five minutes.

"Emma wrote Archie to tell him what happened and say that she was ready to catch the next train to New London. But it was November so she told him they'd be better off waiting until the spring as they planned." Grandpa cleared his throat. "Unfortunately, Archie never got that letter."

18

A Problem with the Mail

As busy as Archie was, his week was still organized around the arrival of Emma's letters. For the sake of their finances, they had decided to send a week's worth of letters at a time rather than sending one each day, but still, he could count on them arriving on Wednesdays pretty much like clockwork. Railroad mail service had become a reality in just the last couple of years and that made delivery far more efficient and timely. Every once in a while he'd miss a week, and then get two bundles the next, but they were generally on schedule.

The letters served a multitude of purposes. Most obviously, they kept them connected to each other and informed on what was going on in their respective lives. News went back and forth ranging from the vital, as it pertained to their business and wedding arrangements, to the trivial small-town gossip and hubbub.

The letters also served as a confirmation or assurance of their love for each other. Both of them considered failure to write each day an act of betrayal against their beloved, and by extension, would take the same failure in the other somewhat personally, even if they would never admit it.

But, let's be honest, it was also intoxicating. In the beginning when God declared that it was "not good for man to be alone," He wasn't just referring to physical, existential or even emotional "aloneness."

We were all designed with a built-in need to be complemented, not just complimented. We're just not good alone. All of the weak and unflattering sides of us are apparent when we look in the mirror, so we need someone to remind us that we are okay; that we are loved for who we are rather than in spite of it. That's not a twenty-first century, pop-psychology concoction, it's human nature. It is also the reason we were designed to be completed by a different but complementary partner who can admire our abilities without envy and root for us to win without fear of being diminished.

That "oneness" is what Archie and Emma had begun to develop and what was so painfully missing now. The letters could only do so much, but that didn't minimize their importance.

As Christmas of 1872 approached it had been three weeks since Archie had received anything and he had become concerned. He was never one to bring others into his personal sphere, but Jack noticed one day that Archie seemed a little… off.

"What's eating at you, Arch?"

After the requisite hemming and hawing Archie said, "I don't understand it. It's been weeks since I received anything from Emma. She's beginning to worry me."

"It's been a hard winter."

"I've received other mail from Cambridge. Her last letter is dated 20 November!"

"Maybe she's busy with the wedding plans."

"No, she finds time to write every day no matter what, even if only a few lines."

Jack had seen Archie panic for no reason before and wasn't going to let him go to that place. "Archie, you're gonna worry yourself right to death. There's probably just some kind of problem with the mail."

And Emma had an idea of what that problem might be. Letters from Archie had stopped coming as well, but unlike Archie, who was in the dark, Emma smelled a rat and knew the rat's name. In mid-January she got a tip from a friend who thought that a conversation she'd overheard Charles Galt have with a postal customer might interest

Emma. It did and she went directly to the Postal Office to see if she could get some answers.

When she arrived, the only person in the office was Galt. As motivated as Emma was to get to the bottom of "this treachery," as she referred to it, being alone in a room with Charles Galt was not at the top of her to-do list. He wasn't a bad guy, maybe a little socially awkward, but still a decent man. The problem was that as soon as Archie left town, Charles had not so subtly appeared in Emma's life in the oddest places. It seemed that everywhere she went she would just "bump" into him and each time he would go out of his way to praise her for her appearance. He seemed to have developed a particular fascination with her wardrobe as well, complimenting it every chance he had, sometimes at multiple points in a single encounter.

As soon as Emma entered the room, Galt saw her and practically leapt toward the door. "Why, Miss Williams! 'Tis such a pleasure to see you!"

Emma did her best to be polite and not make eye contact at the same time. "Good morning, Mr. Galt."

The term "Personal Space" wasn't used back then but the concept is universal. Nowadays we understand there to be a region called Public Space. This is "greeting someone across the room distance." Once they acknowledge your greeting and come over to talk to you they will enter into "comfortable conversation distance," or Social Space. The most notable characteristic of this region is that another person could walk between you and not necessarily realize that they were interrupting. This is typically anywhere from four feet to about twelve feet from the tip of your nose.

If that person then feels the need to tell you something in confidence they might slip for a moment into "I can smell your breath distance" or Personal Space. It is a natural, reflexive response for all of us to react with our flight instinct if someone we are not comfortable with enters this protected, forbidden area from a foot and a half to four feet away from us. However, when someone passes that zone and enters "you really should have asked me to dance first, distance," otherwise known as Intimate Space, a more violent reaction is likely to ensue.

Charles Galt didn't know from space. In the time that it took him to say, "How long have we known each other? Please, call me, Charles," he traversed Emma's Public, Social and Personal Space and would have entered her Intimate Space had Emma not escaped. She left him in the dust and pretended to look at the pictures of the fugitives on the wall.

Businesslike, Emma refused his familiarity and proclaimed, "Mr. Galt, I came this morning to see about my mail."

Not to be thwarted, Galt crossed to her and again violated the space/distance continuum as he said, "That is a lovely dress you're wearing today, Emma. Can I call you Emma?"

The faster Emma moved away the faster Galt pursued her. What ensued was the ridiculous sight of two people having a conversation whilst almost running around the room.

"My coat is covering my dress, Mr. Galt, so you are in no position to comment on its loveliness."

"Well, that is, Emma, I meant to say that, just from the hem of your dress sticking out from below your coat, I can imagine that it is very lovely."

"I would appreciate it, Mr. Galt, if you would not be so imaginative when it comes to me or my apparel!"

"You're here. There is no need for imagination," Galt said with a big grin.

Emma searched for a rejoinder but came up nearly empty. "I should point out to you that I haven't had a good night's sleep since November and haven't eaten in almost a week!"

Realizing that made no sense whatsoever, she tried to come up with a follow-up comment but Galt's improvisational skills were maddening.

"You are a remarkable woman, Emma, looking as good as you do with the cards stacked against you like that."

She put an abrupt halt to the chase, stretched out her hand, thrust it right into his chest and barked, "We are going to talk about my mail now."

Like a lapdog just smacked with a rolled up newspaper, Galt stopped and said meekly, "Of course."

There was a moment of silence as Emma waited for him to volunteer the information she wanted. Failing that she asked directly. "Where is it?"

"Where is it?"

"As you well know, I have been receiving letters from my *future husband* in Connecticut since the middle of last May. Then suddenly in November they stopped."

As if he just saw another opening, he came a little too close to her again and said, "Well, perhaps your friend stopped writing?"

Emma was desperate to get the information out of him and resorted to veiled threats, thinly veiled threats, but threats nonetheless. "Now, Mr. Galt, you know Archie," she raised her hand over her head as if to remind Galt how big Archie was, "and how much he enjoys writing. It gives him great comfort after coming home from a long day of snapping useless things in half."

Galt gulped just a little and took a healthy step back, into Social Space, and said, "Emma... that is... Miss Williams, it isn't appropriate for me to talk to you about that."

Now it was Emma's turn to invade his space. She thrust her finger in his face and roared, "You're a postman! How is it inappropriate for you to talk about the mail?"

Galt was wilting like a fragile flower. "You see..."

"Out with it!"

"Well..." Emma took one more menacing step his way and he broke. "It's all being sent to the shop now. Your father told me that I was to deliver all of the mail for his household to the Marble shop. He can be very persuasive."

Emma collected herself, casually straightened her coat, adjusted her hair and as she exited, calmly said, "Thank you, Charles."

19

How Many Letters?

Emma raced over to the marble shop as fast as she could, even if she wasn't exactly sure what she would do when she got there. To her surprise when she arrived, Luna was standing behind the counter looking as though she knew what she was doing.

As Emma entered, Luna looked up at her and in the most disinterested tone she could manage said, "Can I help you, Miss?"

Still fuming but slightly amused, Emma responded with a feigned smile, "Hello Luna. Where's my father?"

"Welcome to the Marble Works, Baldwin and Williams proprietors. I'm Baldwin. How can I help you?"

"Come now, Luna, where's my father?"

"Mr. Williams isn't present at the moment. He's left the business in my capable hands."

Taking a page out of Susan's playbook Emma just yelled at her, "For crying out loud! Would you stop that?"

Luna broke out of her false formality and like a scolded child whimpered, "You don't need to yell."

Emma caught herself. "Luna, you're right. I'm sorry. I'm just having a difficult... life. How are you? Do you like your new job?

"Oh, yes! I feel so important!"

"That's nice. So, do you know where my father might be?"

Luna gestured outdoors. "Oh, he's out on one of his walks."

"He takes walks?"

"When I first got here he'd take a walk every day to stretch his legs. Now he's just walking all the time - sometimes for hours. I think he feels more comfortable leaving with me here."

Emma tried to be kind. "That's a creative way of looking at it. Now, what is it you do for him exactly?"

With a giggle of pride Luna said, "Oh, I handle all of his correspondence!"

"Really? Does he get a lot of letters?"

"Quite a few, yes. Some are even addressed to you. I think they're from Archie."

Emma tried to stay calm. "How do you know that, Luna?"

"Well, it's just a hunch really. The returns are all from somebody named Mercer in New London, Connecticut but I suppose it could be someone else."

Emma was starting to lose her manufactured tranquility. "Luna, where are Archie's letters?"

"Oh, you're father takes them and puts them somewhere, but he doesn't tell me where. I think he's afraid I might tell you about them. He should know me better than that by now. We've become very close."

Emma was too desperate to be patient. "How many have there been, Luna? How many letters?"

"Oh, I don't know."

"Think Luna. Exactly how many? It's very important."

"Well, let's see, they started around Thanksgiving and this is January..." It sure sounded like Luna was going to continue her thought but then it just stopped and she went back to her paperwork.

Getting information from Luna was like climbing a wall that's leaning toward you. "The letters, Luna! How many?"

"Oh, I don't know for sure but I can guess.

"That's fine, Luna, just guess. Give me an estimate."

"Okay... there's been one every week... so nine or ten maybe, oh, and a little package at Christmas."

The blood drained back into Emma's face as she now knew for certain that Archie had written her faithfully. The relief she felt quickly turned to anger at the prospect that her father had confiscated her property. Had he read them as well? Had he kept her letters from Archie? Without a word to Luna, she stormed out of the store to find her father.

"Grandpa?" Taylor asked, "What's the technical term for killing your father?"

"Hey, would you look at that. We got a base runner!"

Nick's team was now facing a new pitcher and he had walked the first batter on four pitches.

Taylor looked at him like he was living in the wrong universe. How could he think about baseball at a time like this? "What?"

"Remember the game? The reason we're here?"

"Oh, yeah. How'd that happen?"

"The Cubs took out their star pitcher. I guess they didn't want to waste him with a fourteen run lead. This new kid isn't very good. He hasn't thrown a strike yet... oh, there, look, another walk. Just think, he only has to walk fifteen more and we're tied."

"You're the ultimate optimist aren't you?"

Grandpa leaned into her, "My father-in-law applied for a thirty year mortgage when he was ninety-two, that's optimism. I just like to be hopeful."

"So, did Emma ever find her letters?"

"No. Her father destroyed them all. It's patricide, by the way."

Taylor was becoming distraught. She had started to live vicariously through Emma, and the lines between the story and reality were blurring faster by the minute. "Did she ever talk to him again?"

"Uh, yes, but only because she wasn't fully aware of what he was up to."

20

If You Truly Love Her...

About that same time, Archie had undertaken another project. He had become so concerned about Emma's failure to write to him that he began some detective work. Since he had received several letters from business contacts in Cambridge recently he knew the problem was not with the mail service. He fired off letters to several school chums from Cambridge and asked them if they had seen Emma, and if she were okay.

New London, Connecticut
January 13, 1873

Dear James:

I hope this letter finds you in good health and spirits. I remember last winter you remarking that we might be wise to go into the ice making business if we could only master the obvious storage issues involved in such a venture. If only we could keep the ice from melting so we could sell it in the summer.

Well, my dear friend, I believe Connecticut has solved that problem for us. It was a very simple solution after all. The temperature simply never rises above thirty-two degrees Fahrenheit.

I wonder how the weather is treating you out in Indiana these days. I worry about my friends in Cambridge from time to time as mail seems to be spotty in its arrival this winter.

As example, I have received much correspondence from business associates but none from my dear Emma, of all people. The time has drawn on so long since her last letter arrived that I have begun to worry about her safety. Have you seen her recently?

Best Regards,

A. Mercer

Four such missives found their way to Indiana and returned with assurances that Emma had been seen walking about town as always and seemed in fine health, and yet still nothing from Emma herself.

One terribly cold day in early February, Archie was in the basement patching an iron pipe that had begun to leak. Indoor running water was a fairly new convenience and their new home had been retrofitted just before their arrival. Plumbers were nearly non-existent but Archie was beginning to get a handle on the basics. Soaking wet and freezing cold, Archie was relieved when Nellie came running down to the basement.

"A letter came for you Archie! It's from Cambridge! The return says Williams!"

They both ran upstairs. Archie had to do some serious washing up and thawing out before he went into the public hallway, a rule his mother steadfastly impressed upon everyone. After he dried himself off he grabbed the letter and climbed the three flights of stairs for his room. He flopped onto his bed, and at first glance, he could tell it was not from Emma. He paused for a second, said a quick prayer, and then began to read. It was from her father.

Cambridge City, Indiana.
January the 22nd, 1873

Mr. Mercer:

Let me first say that I find you to be a fine young man and to possess a strong moral compass. I am sure that you will succeed in your chosen field and would otherwise prove to be an adequate match for my daughter.

However, it has come to my attention that you are not, nor have ever been, a member of the Society of Friends. For this reason, and this alone, I cannot give your union with Emma my blessing. I can only presume that you are not acquainted with the Society and its practices or else you would not have pursued this courtship. The Society strictly forbids marriage by Friends to those outside the membership. Violation of this rule would result in the member being publicly disowned by both the Society and her family. Our family is not unimportant in Quaker circles and Emma's banishment from this community would lead to not only her own but also her family's ruination. Marrying you, sir, would cause Emma to give up her heritage, her family, her home and her faith; the very things that make her who she is and which, presumably, caught your eye.

In a year and a month from today Emma will come of age, and therefore, I will no longer be able to choose for her. As a man of honor and as a man who loves my daughter as I do, I appeal to you that you no longer follow this course. If you truly love Emma, you will disappear from her life and allow her to live her days in peace.

Cordially,
William Baldwin Williams

Archie was stunned. When the shock finally started to wear off the first thing that crossed his mind was… *Maybe he's right.*

When that went through his head he shivered, almost convulsed, like someone or something had jabbed him between the shoulder blades. *How could he be right?*

The thought was ridiculous. "Live her days in peace?" How could either one of them ever live in peace apart? He was as positive that they had been brought together by Providence as he had ever been about anything in his life. What God has brought together let no man put asunder, right? *Don't we deserve to be happy?*

Then his back stiffened a little and he started to seethe. He figured Williams was still mad about that day in the marble shop or maybe about his business dealings with Archie's father. *He got paid back in full with interest. What more could he want?*

He imagined himself face to face with "that man" and the only question was how badly he would beat the living daylights out of the scoundrel. *How dare he?*

Then he thought, *We'll just wait until she's eighteen and then he won't have anything to say about it.*

But then it struck him how important a person's history could be. He thought about how much he cherished his own family's heritage. Would he leave his family forever for her? Of course he would, but what about Emma? He was confused a little by organized religion, to the extent that he considered himself a Presbypalian, but Emma had Quaker blood running all through her. Come to think of it, the letters had stopped coming right after he wrote her about the issue. Then he remembered how close she was to her beloved sisters. But wait a minute, weren't they supposed to "leave and cleave?" Doesn't that have to mean ignoring your parent's wishes at times? Or is it just for after they choose someone for you? *I'm a grown man. Am I supposed to ask my mother what she wants for my life?*

A seed of doubt began to creep in and he wished he had as much scripture memorized as Emma. Does God bring people together, or is that just a modern idea made to sound churchy? What does "Honor your father and mother" mean in this situation? Are we supposed to go back to arranged marriages? *Would I cause Emma to sin if we ran away together?*

This had to be the explanation for the weeks of missing letters from Emma. There were only two possibilities: either her father forbade her to write and she complied, or she agreed with him and chose not to write, but neither option sounded plausible. *Then what happened?*

Since that dreadful day last April when his carriage pulled out of

Cambridge City for good, he had heard whispers from the mocking voices in his head. Now the murmurs were turned to shouts. So many times back in Indiana he would glance at her or hear her voice and scoff at the very idea that such a creature could be his. How could it be possible that God, in His great wisdom, would entrust such a treasure to him? Archie thought of himself as "weighed in the balance and found wanting." He was so easily consumed by rage that he was more animal than man. Maybe in His omniscience God knew that one day Archie would unintentionally turn that rage on Emma or their children. This was God's way of sparing them pain. Surely he didn't deserve her. Maybe he didn't deserve to be happy. This letter was the confirmation. *I'm not good enough for her. Maybe he's right.*

21

I'll Spare You the Trouble

Taylor was beside herself but too embarrassed to let Grandpa see that she had to fight away tears. She didn't know how to feel. Was she supposed to feel sorry for Archie or be angry at him? And what about W.B.? She was just a little conflicted about the heart-felt loathing she was developing for her own great-great-great-grandfather.

Grandpa had told this story a time or two and suspected what Taylor might be feeling. "I think sometimes the hardest part of obedience isn't doing what God wants but rather knowing what He wants."

"How do you figure that out, Grandpa?"

"Well, most of the time it's clear, but when it isn't, you have to go back to what you do know for sure. Archie knew that he had to put what was best for Emma before anything else. He just wasn't sure he knew what that was yet."

It was February now and Emma had failed in her attempts to find Archie's letters. She figured they must be hidden in the house somewhere, but weeks of tearing it apart in the hours after her father left for work had yielded no results. So with Susan in tow she went to the marble shop to confront him, hoping that they might be hidden there or that at least he would be forced to be reasonable if they spoke in public.

When they arrived, Luna was at the front desk and W.B. was working on some papers in the back. When he heard the front bell he made his way to the doorway and stuck his head through the curtain.

Luna was very excited to see the girls but tried to maintain her professionalism. "Good afternoon ladies. Welcome to the Marble Works, Baldwin and Williams proprietors. I'm Baldwin, he's Williams. How can we help you?"

Susan swallowed hard to keep from laughing. "Good afternoon, Luna. Uncle William."

"To what do we owe this pleasure?" W.B. asked as he stepped out from behind the curtain.

It was Susan's task to get rid of Luna. "Lunch. We thought we would drop by and take Luna out for lunch."

Luna wasn't accustomed to Susan going out of her way to be nice to her, so we can pardon her suspicious tone. "Really?"

Susan didn't want to get ahead of herself. "Yes, if that's all right with Uncle William."

With concern in her voice, Luna asked W.B., "Can you get along without me, Uncle?"

"Hmm, I will try to muddle through. What's the occasion?"

Susan and Emma hadn't talked about that one and at once they gave him two different answers. Just as Susan answered, "Her birthday," Emma said, "No occasion."

Susan kept her cool and tried to fix it. "Occasionally we like to celebrate her birthday."

Luna was confused as usual. "It's my birthday?"

Susan went behind the counter, grabbed Luna's coat, and began to lead her out by the arm. "There you go again, always so selfless."

Luna objected, "But my birthday isn't until September."

Susan walked her to the door and said, "Is that so? Then let's go celebrate that."

Emma started out with them but stopped at the door as they left and called out, "You ladies go ahead. I'll catch up."

The charade didn't fool W.B. in the slightest. "What really brings you here, Emma?"

Emma took a deep breath and said matter-of-factly, "I'm told that my mail is being routed through the shop now and I've come to collect it."

Knowing they were about to have an argument but determined to stand his ground, W.B. answered, "We have no mail for you here."

"And the package and ten sets of letters that have come?"

"Emma, I told you that there would be no more correspondence between you."

"That is not your choice to make, sir."

It was the "sir" that got him. It wasn't uncommon for a daughter to refer to her father in that way as a show of respect, but this was anything but. Her voice dripped with disrespect.

His back stiffened accordingly as well. "In case you have forgotten, you are still my daughter and reside under my roof."

"Situations that can be remedied quite easily."

That one stung and his tone softened. "You would leave your family for this man?"

Emma recited from Genesis in the desperate hope of bringing God in on her side. "Therefore shall a man leave his father and his mother, and shall cleave unto his wife: and they shall be one flesh."

He didn't appreciate being Bibled at. "Child, do you not know what this means for you?"

"Yes I do, it means a lifetime with the man I love."

"No, it means you will be disowned by your family and the society."

"*When* I become Archie's wife I will attend whichever gathering he chooses for our family. Being disowned by a society one has left voluntarily is hardly a consequence. As for my family, I'm afraid that is your choice Father, not mine."

W.B. couldn't believe that his daughter didn't share his values. "You would throw your life away for this man?"

"*Give* it away, Father!"

Neither of them spoke for a moment as each was afraid of losing their composure, especially in a public place, though no one else was in the shop at the moment. W.B. ratcheted down his tone. "I do agree with you on one point. He is a good man. And as such I don't expect he will allow you to make this mistake now that he is aware of the cost?"

Emma's shoulders slumped. "Aware? What did you do, Father?"

"I wrote to the young man and explained the situation to him. He will not be coming for you nor will he be writing again."

Emma started to get light headed. If she didn't yell at him she would pass out. "How dare you?"

You could practically see the steam coming from W.B.'s ears as well. "Because it was my duty as your father!"

Emma shot back, "I do agree with you on one point. Archie is a *very* good man and as such he won't break a promise he has made repeatedly!"

W.B. said coolly, "Believe what you want, but that's the truth. You should be thankful that he loves you enough not to ruin your life."

Emma casually picked at her gloves to mask her trembling hands as she said, "Clearly, you don't share that sentiment, sir."

The sadness in both of their voices was unmistakable by this time as they knew where this was heading. Almost pleadingly W.B. said, "Emma, you know that isn't the case."

"Do I?"

Then she straightened up, gathered herself and in an eerily business-like tone said, "You needn't go to the effort of disowning me, I will spare you the trouble. I will have my things out of your house within the week. Good day."

And with that the conversation and their relationship ended.

22

How Do We Get You to Connecticut?

Emma walked out of the store in total control but as soon as she turned the corner and started down the street the floodgates opened. She ran as fast as she could down the street toward home, sobbing all the way.

When she arrived no one was home, so she went to her room and found her suitcase. She threw in everything she could find that really belonged to her, closed it up and walked outside.

She paused on the porch as she realized that she didn't have the vaguest notion of where to go next. She knew she couldn't stay but she had nowhere to go. She ran through all of the possible scenarios in her head in a matter of moments. She couldn't stay with Susan, she was a houseguest herself. The Huddlestons would probably take her in but they just had a new baby. If she could get to Richmond somehow, her uncle would surely help her, but how to do that? She decided to run up to her hill so she could think.

It hadn't snowed in a couple of weeks so the climb was manageable, but it was still a little slippery. She pulled her stool out of the brush, grabbed pencil and paper from her suitcase and began to write Archie. He wouldn't get it for quite a while and she didn't know what to put down as a return address but those details could wait until she was finished.

Cambridge City, Indiana
February 18th, 1873

My Dearest Archie:

I have just been made aware of my father's treachery in confiscating both your letters to me and mine to you since late November, so this may indeed be the first time you have heard from me in many months.

I assure you, dear friend, that, as I promised, I have written every day without fail, as I am sure you have as well. I have also heard of his wicked letter to you and need you to know that he no longer speaks for me...

Just then she heard a familiar groaning coming from the bottom of the hill. She peered over the side only to see her mother struggling up the incline. When Susannah came within reach Emma grabbed her hand and pulled her up the rest of the way. Out of breath, Susannah straightened herself as she quipped, "I thought I might find you up here."

After she lent her mother her hand, Emma took a few steps back. She had no sense of whose side her mother would be on. When Susannah had gotten her bearings she looked at Emma and, as only a mother can, held out her arms and without words told Emma everything she needed to know.

Emma ran to her and threw herself into her arms, sobbing again like a little girl. Her mother kept whispering to her, "I'm so sorry, child," as she stroked her hair.

Suddenly, Emma's cries became fits of rage. "I'm so mad I could...!"

Susannah held her tighter to let her get it all out. "I know sweetheart, I know."

Still crying, and nearly hyperventilating, Emma sobbed. "God brought me the perfect man, Momma, the perfect man! And now he's gone! I don't exist without him!"

Susannah continued to calm her, whispering, "I know, I know." When Emma finally began to catch her breath, Susannah pushed her away a little, held her at arm's length and looked right into her eyes and said, "So, how do we get you to Connecticut?"

Emma was stunned. "You'll help me, Mother?"

Susannah was almost hurt that Emma thought she would do anything else. "Any way I can."

Emma pulled Archie's stool out of the brush and offered it to her mother and they sat as they tried to catch their collective breath. Emma, always the planner, had looked into transportation costs. "Passage on a coach to Richmond and then the train to New London is fifty dollars; at least it was last spring, plus accommodations on the trip. I need about seventy all figured, but I only have six dollars that I've saved."

Susannah reached into her bag and grabbed a little coin purse. "I've been putting a little away for an emergency. This certainly qualifies. It isn't much but you're welcome to it."

"Thank you, Momma! How much is it?"

"Only twelve dollars and seventy-five cents I'm afraid," Susannah said sheepishly.

Emma crashed as quickly as she had soared. "Leaving over fifty to raise. How am I going to find that kind of money?"

"I'm sure Archie will send help if you ask him."

"Yes, I'm writing him about that right now. Susan and Luna will help too, I think."

Susannah pulled a scrap of newsprint from her bag.

"I confiscated your father's newspaper and found this notice for a live-in nursemaid for an elderly lady. It would solve both of your problems at once, and it's in Richmond."

Emma took the paper from her mother and read, "Five dollars a week. Free room and board! That's about ten weeks if I can save every penny… that is except for stamps and paper."

Momma reached into her bag again and pulled out a pile of stationery. "Here's paper to last a few weeks."

Emma was amused and touched at the same time. "Anything else in your magic bag?"

Susannah changed the subject. "I know the lady from years ago, a Mrs. Harrison. The poor woman is suffering from consumption and doesn't think she has but a few weeks. She wants someone to keep her company and make her comfortable in her remaining days."

"I suppose you've already written her then?" Emma asked, knowing the answer.

Susannah feigned insult. "I would never presume to involve myself in your affairs…" Then she came clean. "She's expecting you."

"Thank you, Mother."

"We'll need to rely on the Lord to provide the rest. Hopefully, Mrs. Harrison can hold on until spring. It won't be safe to travel for a while yet."

Emma thought for a moment and looked quizzically at her mother and asked, "How did you know, Momma?"

Susannah didn't know quite how to respond. She hemmed and hawed for a bit then finally said, "The only person I know more stubborn than you is your father. It was bound to come to this so I took some precautions for you."

They both smiled a little, then Emma asked with tears in her eyes, "Why aren't you mad at me, Momma?"

"Oh, darling, I could never be mad at you. And I had to make the same decision when I was your age."

That brought a little of Emma's resentment back to the surface. "Why doesn't Father remember those days?"

"Oh, he's just trying to protect you like my father tried to protect me."

Then Emma asked the question every child asks about their parents eventually. "Why can't he trust that I know what's best for me?"

Susannah could have answered from her own experience as a parent but at the moment she thought of herself more as one woman talking with another. "I am afraid it may take many years before we can enjoy the faith of a man in our ability to think for ourselves."

Emma's eyes lit up and her desperation showed. "But that's one of the things I love about Archie. He listens to me. He treats me as his equal partner."

Susannah couldn't even imagine what that might be like. She rose and said, "Well then, we do need to get you to New London, don't we?"

Emma was surprised at the boldness she was hearing from her mother. "I didn't know you felt this way, Momma."

Susannah donned a defiant visage, checked to be certain no one was listening, and then recited, "It is a downright mockery to talk to women of their enjoyment of the blessings of liberty while they are denied the use of the only means of securing them."

Emma was dumbfounded. "That's Susan B. Anthony!"

With her nose just a bit in the air, Susannah boasted, "I read... secretly when your father is at the shop... but I read."

They both laughed a little and then Momma looked at Emma lovingly and said, "You'll visit Mrs. Harrison then?"

"Yes, Momma."

Then Susannah had her moment of maternal panic; that inevitable and understandable moment when a mother realizes that can no longer keep her child from harm. She sat in silence for a moment, took a deep breath and then did the only thing she could do to avoid becoming a weepy mess and making Emma's life even more difficult. She changed the subject. "I do have something else in my magic bag." She handed Emma a small package.

Emma started to shake. "From Archie?"

"It came around Christmas. Your father thought he hid it."

Emma carefully unwrapped the brown paper to reveal a white lacy handkerchief. "Oh, Archie." She put it to her face to breathe him in and whispered, "You're here again."

Momma pointed to the corner. "I think it has a monogram on it." She was right. In the corner were embroidered the initials E.W.M.

Emma clutched it to her face and started to cry but quickly pulled it away as to not get any tears on the handkerchief. She wiped her eyes with her dress so as to not cover up his scent with hers and then neatly folded it back up and put it back in the paper.

Then Momma produced something else from her bag: a letter. Emma lunged for it but Susannah pulled it back and warned, "I think this letter is in response to your father's and it may not bring news you wish to hear."

Emma opened the letter carefully and said a quick prayer as she turned to the first page. Then holding his handkerchief to her nose so she could breathe him in, she read the last letter Archie would ever send to her.

New London, Connecticut
4th of February, 1873

My most trusted friend:

I received a letter from your father this week detailing the ramifications for your family and your reputation should we marry. I must say that my heart sank in disbelief as I read his lines. My mind wanted so violently to respond in defiance that it concocted a scheme to come and spirit you away under cloak of darkness. My body yearned to deal him and all else who might stand in our way a mortal blow to avenge the pain caused to my broken heart. Thanks be to God that my eternal soul soon won the day and dissuaded its compatriots from their intended mischief.

I love you, my darling, more now than ever have I expressed before, and only one thought pains me more deeply than the thought of losing you; that by loving you, and keeping you selfishly to myself, I might cause you to be thought of as less than you are. You are the fairest and purest creature God has created and the idea that I might somehow be responsible for corrupting that purity, even if only in the minds of a few, grieves me to no end. I cannot, I will not, be responsible for such a crime.

You must know, my love, that though I take these steps in faith and assurance that I do what our most gracious God wishes, my heart, body and mind want none of it. They want to run to you as if we had not a care in the world. Alas, my eternal soul must win out so this is the last letter you will receive from me. I will not be coming for you as I had promised.

Though it kills me to break that promise to you, I also promised that I would love you forever. I find that I cannot do both so I must choose which promise to keep and I have chosen the latter. Please, I beg of you, do not come to New London. Seeing you only to lose you again would strike the final blow to me.

I will pray earnestly for your happiness and that you will soon forget me. But I do look forward to that day when with all the saints we will be reunited in eternity. I will always remember you.

I love you, my darling,
Archie

23
The Only Ones Here

There were moments in early February when Archie wanted to chase down that letter and keep it from reaching Emma, but then he'd eventually come to his senses. He was convinced that this was the right thing to do, and he kept reminding himself of that, though he and God had a number of angry exchanges as the days passed. Still, he felt like a traitor, and not just to Emma, though that was the worst of it. He felt as though somehow he was betraying love itself; that by doing the right thing he was doing the wrong thing. How could his heart ever trust his head again?

As her seventeenth birthday approached on the 22nd, he slipped deeper and deeper into a depression. Everything hurt. Getting out of bed in the morning, or the afternoon some days, was becoming more difficult all the time. All of his plans, everything he had been working toward, had gone up in smoke and there was nothing left for him. What would he do now?

As happy as his mother was that he wouldn't be moving to Indiana, she could see dangerous signs in him that reminded her of her husband. William had become depressed when the train car deal fell through and she had come to believe that the shame of it all had been what killed him. Now she could see Archie heading down that same dark path and it frightened her.

She tried to fill his days with work to keep his mind occupied, but nothing helped. She sent him to market one afternoon to pick up some supplies when he saw a woman wearing the same style coat he'd bought Emma and it ended his day. This giant man could be brought to his knees by a fleeting glimpse of a woman with red hair. Everyone could see it, but they were powerless to help. It was just painful to watch.

We humans want so desperately to believe that we are a proficient, capable and strong race; that we have this life figured out and conquered. We celebrate independence and value our freedom. We champion concepts like choice, liberty, autonomy and self-determination. No one gets to tell us what to do.

Perhaps that's why the sight of a grown man crying is so difficult for us to watch. A powerful man is the epitome of strength, so when he is broken and weeping, we have to look away. It crushes all of our illusions of self-sufficiency. More important, the man himself feels that he must run and hide so as to not let anyone down. He cuts himself off from the comforts he needs and, if he isn't careful, puts himself in danger of losing his soul. Because the paradox of life is that even the greatest among us are all just orphaned children anxiously waiting for someone to claim us.

Archie had always preferred to go it alone. Whatever the crowd was doing he did the opposite. Being the biggest and the strongest tends to lead to a relaxed attitude when bucking societal expectations. This tendency explained a lot about his friendship with Jack. But he also preferred to *be* alone. His time with Emma was the only time in his life when he got energy from being with someone else; any other time he'd prefer to spend his days in peace and quiet.

When the Mercers had arrived in New London the previous summer, Archie quickly realized that there would be no quiet time in the house, so he looked for a spot on the river where he could look out over the harbor.

On the other side of town, the oldest cemetery in New London, "The Antientist (or Ancient) Burial Ground," was situated on a hill overlooking the Thames River with the town of Groton visible on the other bank. On a clear day, if he sat clear of the trees, he could even get a glimpse of Fisher Island. This also happened to be the spot where traitor Benedict Arnold presided over the burning of New London on Sept. 6th, 1781.

Archie discovered that many of his ancestors were buried on those grounds, including Lucretia Bradley Christophers - his fifth great-grandmother who was herself the great-granddaughter of Mayflower passenger William Brewster - her husband Richard Christophers, and his parents Christopher and Mary Christophers, who emigrated from Devonshire, England about 1665. Up in the northeast corner he found Governor Gurdon Saltonstall, also his fifth great-grandfather, who was the Governor of the Connecticut Colony from 1708 to 1724.

In the southwest corner was the section reserved for Negro gravesites. Mostly unmarked, there were some notable people laid to rest there, including Flora the wife of Hercules the reported Governor of the Negroes, a reference to the custom in some parts of New England beginning in the late 1700's of African Americans electing their own leaders. As the Revolution began, New London County had the "distinction" of having the greatest number of slaves in all of New England.

As the months passed, Archie began to feel more and more at home on that lonely hill watching the ships come in. On his worst days he struck up conversations with the family members interred there; they were excellent listeners. It became a metaphor for his life, sitting among the dead, watching the living go about their business from a safe distance.

The cemetery was a twenty minute walk from his house but he spent time there nearly every day that summer and wrote his letters. It became his hill. Coincidently, a few years later a young Eugene O'Neill would grow up in a house just a few blocks away and watch those same ships come in and out. O'Neill turned his maritime hobby into a successful career as a playwright, often including nautical themes in his work. Archie just wrote letters he never sent.

When winter came he couldn't spend much time there but after he sent that horrible last letter to Emma he went anyway. Having his hands and feet go numb only made them match his heart.

Every once in a while Jack would meet him there to keep him company and try to bring him back to life. On Emma's birthday, no one could find Archie, and the family was worried so they sent for Jack. He knew where he could find him so he headed for the cemetery with a couple of blankets.

Jack found Archie shivering under a tree. He was sitting atop a stone table monument trying to escape the scattered flakes of falling snow. After he warmed him up a bit, Jack told Archie a story he'd been saving for a special occasion. "So, once there was this man who died and stood before the pearly gates, and the angel standing guard asked him why he thought he deserved to get into heaven. The man said, 'I ain't got no merit of my own, but Christ died for sinners.' Sure enough the gates opened and the angel invited him in."

"Is there a point to this story, Jack?"

"I'm getting there. I can only tell it from the beginning. So another angel started giving the man a tour of the place. He saw millions of folks from every nation and from all ages rejoicing and praising God. But then the man noticed that there was a big wall on one side of heaven that stretched as far as he could see in both directions. When they got close to it he could hear music and the sound of folks praising God on the other side just like everywhere else he'd seen. The man asked the angel who those people were and why they were behind that wall and the angel said, 'Oh, those are the Quakers. They still want to think they're the only ones here.'"

Jack let out a big belly laugh but Archie didn't respond at all. Then without batting an eye Archie quipped, "When I heard it they were Presbyterians."

Jack laughed again. "That's okay, when I heard it the first time they were Lutherans, but the point's the same. Look, everybody thinks they're the ones who got it right and some folks take the next step and think everybody else must be wrong. But it don't change the simple fact that Christ died for sinners and we all fit that description. We Quakers can't go thinkin' people ain't Christians cuz their theology sounds a little catawampus to us."

There was a long silence. At times like this it's important to have a friend so close that you can sit in silence without worry. Finally, while trying to secretly wipe away a tear, Archie said softly, "I have to do this, Jack. They're her people, no matter what they may think of me."

Jack didn't know what to say but under his breath he prayed, "Lord, have mercy."

They stared off into the river in front of them and kept silent again for quite some time. Jack was hoping that either the conversation would continue or they'd call it a day because he was so cold he was afraid his beard would shatter.

Then Archie tried a little gallows humor. "Maybe Emma should have fallen for you. At least you're a Quaker."

They both laughed for a moment and Jack said, "I think that woulda made for a whole mess of new troubles. Besides, she's too smart for me. I couldn't keep up with her."

Archie replied, "I never could." He thought for a second and then asked, "Jack, why did you join the Friends? Cuz they were abolitionists?"

Jack recited, "'Henceforth I call you not servants; for the servant knoweth not what his lord doeth: but I have called you friends.'"

Archie wasn't sure. "Gospel of John?"

"Yes sir, I liked the idea of being God's friend, not his slave."

As his voice cracked with emotion, Archie said, "I need you to help me get through this, Jack."

Archie stopped trying to wipe his own tears away and then Jack said, "Lots of times, great blessings are disguised as great suffering."

24

God Seems to Like Surprise

February 19, 1873

"So, he just gave up." Taylor wasn't trying to hide her tears anymore. "What happened to all of those promises?"

Grandpa had always defended his grandfather at this point in the story, but he could see that Taylor was more involved in it than he had remembered anyone else being. He was still trying to get the hang of "Millennials" who saw the world so differently than he. What was it that Taylor was really upset about? He decided to not go there quite yet. "Well, except for coming back for her, he kept 'em."

"He didn't write anymore," Taylor said with a bit of indignation in her voice.

Grandpa corrected her, "No, no, he wrote every day. He just didn't send them to her."

Taylor seemed to be satisfied to some extent by that. "Did Emma give up?"

Grandpa chuckled. "Oh, no. She was relentless. She followed through on her plan to raise the money to get to New London."

The only thing keeping Emma from traversing the same dark path as Archie was hope; Archie had none, but Emma had plenty because she was still in control, or at least so she thought. Nothing could convince her that their life as a couple was over, because in her mind, God had brought them together. She was certain that as soon as Archie read her letter he would change his mind, so she went about the task of raising the money she needed to get herself to Connecticut.

She stayed with the Mendenhalls that first night and then hitched a ride to Richmond first thing the next morning on a logger's cart taking a load of red oak to market. The ride was on the bumpy side but the aroma of the fresh cut trees she sat on more than made up for it. She had been to Richmond on many occasions, but this time as she watched Cambridge City disappear in the distance, it felt so final, like she was moving that day from one chapter of her life to the next. Indeed, this was the last time she would ever see her childhood home or her beloved hill. Years later in Richmond, as camera technology developed, she gave serious consideration to hiring a photographer to take pictures of and from her hill so she could relive better times, but she never followed through.

Emma sat on the logger's cart with shoulders squared and aimed at her future. There were no tears in her eyes, either for what she was leaving behind or in fear for what lay ahead. All she had coursing through her was determination. She would not let the dreams they dreamed together die.

By the time Emma arrived at Mrs. Harrison's door it was dark out and Emma was trembling from the cold. It had been a fairly warm day for mid-February but the temperature had still been in the 40's and was now descending rapidly. Emma's legendary confidence notwithstanding, she had no idea what she would do if Mrs. Harrison didn't answer the door.

She knocked quietly but didn't hear any movement. She could see a candle flickering inside through the window so she knocked a bit louder. Finally she heard a faint, "I'm coming" and in a few moments the door opened. She was invited in as if she were a long lost granddaughter.

Mrs. Harrison was in her early sixties, but the years had not been kind to her. She appeared on the outside to be a much older woman as deep lines cut into a face that once lit up a room. Her blond locks had turned prematurely white after the death of her beloved husband, who had moved them from Tennessee to Indiana in search of greener, and less hostile, pastures. They had not been blessed with children, so she was now completely alone in the world - though he had left her a good deal of money, which at least kept her from that worry.

Her doctors had recently diagnosed her with consumption, a now archaic term referring to tuberculosis, but she didn't have the tuberculosis bacteria. She had simply never recovered from her husband's death, and it was killing her.

As Emma stepped into the front entrance she noticed solid oak arches that looked all too familiar. She later learned they had come from the same logger's cart as her seating arrangements on the trip from Cambridge. The hexagonal entryway led on the left to the front sitting room, directly ahead to a stairway and to the right to another sitting room. Except for the Mercer house, Emma had never been in a home with more than one living space but soon learned that the one on the left was called a receiving room and the one to the right was the parlour.

Mrs. Harrison hurried Emma to a chair by the fire in the parlour, and they introduced themselves as she thawed out.

Mrs. Harrison's home was not a palace, but it certainly belonged to a different station than anything Emma had ever encountered. Looking around the front room, it was clear to Emma that just about any painting on the wall was probably worth more than her father's entire house, plus the oriental rugs, crystal vases on nearly every surface and the chandelier. *The chandelier! Oh my, how does one clean that?*

The time flew by as Mrs. Harrison, in her southern drawl, regaled Emma with stories of her youth growing up in the same mountains Emma had heard about so many times from her grandmother. She told of her trip with her husband to Indiana and any number of other tales she had saved up for a time when she would again have a willing ear. Two hours had passed when Mrs. Harrison noticed that Emma was fading from her long day.

"Now Emma, let's get something straight right now."

"What's that Mrs. Harrison?"

"I've got a bushel basket of stories, and when this one's empty there's plenty more down in the basement."

"Do you need me to fetch one for you?"

"Silly girl!" She said with a laugh. "What I mean to say is we have plenty of time. You don't need to hear 'em all tonight. Why, you've been getting better sleep the last few minutes than I have in years."

"I'm sorry, Mrs. Harrison. It's been a long day. And I'm afraid I didn't sleep at all last night."

"You've come to the right place then. I've been told that I am a fine cure for insomnia."

Mrs. Harrison showed her back to the stairs leading to the second floor.

"You can have your choice of any of the three rooms upstairs. I never make it up there anymore, so I can't vouch for their tidiness."

In all of the excitement they hadn't spoken about the terms of Emma's employment, but that could be taken care of in the morning. Mrs. Harrison was right. They had nothing but time.

"Thank you again, Mrs. Harrison. I'm sure I will be very happy here."

Emma chose the room with the unobstructed view of the street and found some linen in the closet that really should have been washed first, or at least shaken out, but as tired as she was that could wait until morning as well.

Writing Archie a few lines about her day couldn't wait, so she set up the desk in the room to become her writing spot, told him about her trip, and went to bed. As soon as her head hit the dusty pillow she fell asleep.

The next morning they talked about Mrs. Harrison's plans for Emma and what her days would look like. All she really wanted was someone to keep the house, run errands and listen to her, though the last requirement was less stated than understood. For that, Emma would receive free room and board and ten dollars a week, double what she expected! This was truly a Godsend. Emma went right to work.

Job number one was to write to Archie and give him her new address. *Check*. Her second task was to get the lay of the land. She found the post office, the druggist, the local market and the bank, among others. Every morning she ran over to the market to get fresh eggs or whatever else they were out of and then ran back home and made breakfast. After that she'd do the daily rounds; picking up the mail, Mrs. Harrison's medicine if any, and then at least once a week she'd go to the bank to tend to her benefactor's financial transactions. After a while she felt like she was becoming quite the mogul, dealing every day with more money than she had seen in her entire life to that point.

At first, dealing with the men in the various offices was a bit intimidating, but she had one tremendous advantage: she was young and pretty. She learned that if she played a little dumb, they were all very interested in helping her navigate her tasks, especially the banker and the postman. *What is it with postmen?*

After her rounds were done, she'd start on the house. She was determined that the house would look, and most importantly smell, like a happy home before she left; she had a lot of work to do. She started with the downstairs but she made sure to leave a couple of hours in the day to work on the upstairs and eventually turned it into her own little home. She felt as though she were a princess. Instead of sharing a small room with her two sisters, she had three rooms all to herself, each of which was nearly the size of her living room in Cambridge.

One of the highlights of her day was to buy the daily paper, the Richmond Gazette. It was a highlight because she was buying it for herself, not for Mrs. Harrison. Now that she was on her own, she had no expectation that she could ever finish school, so she set out on the task of educating herself.

Every evening after her work was done, and she'd put Mrs. Harrison to bed, she would write Archie and read her Bible and the paper. She read every word on every page, though she liked the advertisements the best. Through the stories of world events she was transported to exotic places and met interesting people and, of course, paid careful attention to any news coming from New England.

After a couple of weeks had passed, she started to become concerned that Archie hadn't written yet. Surely he would. What could be happening? Had her letters not reached him? She decided to send her letters daily and included her new address in each one just in case he wasn't receiving them all.

On Sundays she alternated attending St. Paul's Episcopal Church on A and Eighth and the Presbyterian Church on A and Eleventh. Both were just down the street so she spent several months trying to decide which one to attend regularly. She understood why Archie had trouble deciding but was just excited to be part of a larger group than six.

By summer she had settled on the Presbyterians but mostly due to the brand new church building. The Gothic architecture made her feel like she was entering another land, Scotland to be exact, and that made her feel closer to Archie and his family. And, on a more practical note, if she was going to become a Presbyterian when they married, she might as well get used to it.

As spring began to thaw the ground in the large front yard, Emma began to miss her hill. Caring for Mrs. Harrison didn't allow for much solitude and even when she did get a moment to herself there were no suitable places anywhere near the house. Even if there were, it could never be the same. She decided to, in effect, make her own hill in the front yard. Her hill, after all, was just a quiet spot overlooking beautiful scenery. She had the porch, now she needed to create the beautiful scenery. Maybe she could make some new memories.

She asked Mrs. Harrison if she could make the yard a project. Lillian gladly offered her whatever resources she needed to make her vision come to life and she went to work.

Emma hired some men to dig out a couple of old tree stumps that were in the way and then hired some young men from church to dig out a suitable gardening spot.

She didn't have to start from scratch. There was a nice elm tree near the front fence and some bright pink and lavender azalea bushes on the side of the house, but everything else had been let go.

She planted every flower she could get her hands on, but the peonies became her favorite; the peony plants would eventually vie with her rose bushes for garden supremacy and win. By the following spring of 1874 the garden was a sea of pink, red, orange and purple flowers, and Emma had the tranquil spot she missed so much.

One late summer's day, about six months after she arrived in Richmond, Emma bounced back into the house as usual after her morning trip to the market and found Mrs. Harrison standing in front of the linen closet. "Why, you're up early, Mrs. Harrison!"

"Hello, dear, yes, I wanted to get an early start on the day."

Mrs. Harrison never got up before breakfast was ready any day but Sundays, so seeing her up and about on a Tuesday was an odd sight. "You must have a little bit of your spunk back then. Good for you!"

Mrs. Harrison's head was still in the closet but Emma could hear the warmth in her voice. "That's all your doing, Emma. I was thinking I'd clean out this closet today."

"I'm planning to get to that soon, Mrs. Harrison."

"Oh, I'm sure you will, but when I wake up with some vim and vigor I figure I'd better use it before it escapes me."

Emma helped her drag all of the linens from the closet and stack them on the sofa and then started breakfast.

After the dishes were done, Mrs. Harrison asked Emma if she would set up her chair on the porch so she could sit outside. "It's such a beautiful day."

Emma dragged her rocker out onto the porch and brought a side table out for her things. After she was all situated Emma asked, "Is there anything else I can do for you, Mrs. Harrison?"

"I wish you would call me Lillian now, dear." Emma had become so much more than a hired servant.

"If you'd like."

Emma started back into the house but Lillian grabbed her hand and said, "It's such a joy for me to have you here, Emma. I just wish it were under better circumstances."

"No, I enjoy being here with you."

Lillian brought Emma down to her level so she could look her in the eye as she said, "I want you to reconsider and let me pay for your passage to Connecticut."

Emma had already saved all the money she needed and didn't really want to have this conversation again. "Then who would take care of you?"

Lillian waved her off. "Oh, I'll manage. I hate to see you waste your life with an old woman when you could be with the man you love."

Emma shook her head and rubbed her eyes. "Do you mean the man who hasn't written in six months?"

Lillian squeezed her hand tighter. "Now don't you go and lose hope, dear. Archie is a man of his word."

Emma broke free of her grip and under her breath said, "That's what I'm afraid of."

They'd had this conversation before, several times, and it always resulted in Lillian getting a little frustrated with Emma. This time she practically yelled at her, "Oh, just go to him!"

That stopped Emma in her tracks as intended. She came back and squatted next to the rocking chair and said, "I can't. Mrs. Harrison... Lillian. You've been very generous and I appreciate all you've done for me, but to just show up on his doorstep without invitation... Call me old fashioned but I need him to make that decision. I've explained the situation to him. He knows where to find me."

Lillian answered sarcastically, "You two are quite the pair. Ignoring what's best for each other by doing what's best for each other."

Emma got up and took a little walk on the porch and stared off down the street. "Is it possible for a man to be too honorable?"

Lillian thought for a moment. "That's a very good question." Then she thought some more. "Too good a question. Do you have another?"

Emma turned to her. "I have many. Why did God let this happen? Why Archie and I? What did we do wrong?"

Lillian continued, "How can a woman get three proposals and no husband?"

That embarrassed Emma a bit, but she giggled and said, "That would be four."

Mrs. Harrison was aghast. "The postman again?"

"I'm afraid to go get the mail."

They laughed together a little and then Lillian said in her motherly tone, "Always be cautious of asking questions that start with why."

Emma asked, "Why?"

If you asked Emma about her answer she would tell you that she was being intentionally ironic, but that was not so evident at the moment, and they both laughed at her.

Mrs. Harrison began to cough violently and Emma put her arm around her as the fit subsided. Then with her handkerchief still to her mouth Lillian said, "Because there aren't answers to those questions. The reasons why don't present themselves until so far down the road we aren't interested in hearing them anymore."

"Don't you ever ask why, Lillian?"

"Like, why am I so sick? Why did I lose my husband so young?" Then she took Emma's hand. "Why has God sent an angel to take care of me? No, asking why is just an excuse to blame God for our dissatisfaction. This sickness is here whether I like it or not and asking why isn't going to change it."

They continued to hold hands as they looked off into the garden in front of them until Emma whispered softly, "We have our plans all worked out, but God seems to like surprise."

"That he does, child. That he does."

The U.S. economy, really the world economy, took a serious nosedive in 1873 due to what was then called the Great Depression. It wasn't until the 1930's that the next Great Depression took over that name. The Panic of 1873 resulted in banks being overrun, railroad strikes, massive factory layoffs and unemployment going all the way to 8.25%.

Small town economies were less affected than the big cities like Boston and Chicago - who also suffered from devastating and expensive citywide fires - unless they were heavily involved in the railroad business. Unfortunately, Cambridge was so involved and the new Indiana Car Company struggled from the start.

W.B. saw the handwriting on the wall and moved the family back to Richmond when another sales opportunity opened up. The family was reunited in a way. George came back from college and got a job with the city which would eventually lead him to running for public office and serving for many years as the Wayne County Clerk. And of course Emma was there, though the family settled on the opposite side of town, which in Richmond actually meant something. It afforded Emma the opportunity to see her mother and sisters when she wanted and avoid other family members as desired.

25

Please, Stop Flirting for Me

No... It's the sixth... fourteen to three... Yeah, the new pitcher walked in three runs..." Taylor stepped away to talk on her phone but was still close enough for Grandpa to hear.

Grandpa interjected, "There was a hit in there."

Taylor was getting progressively louder. "There's no need for you to come down here... No, I don't need you to come... Why can't you just trust me to know what's best for me?"

With that, she glanced sheepishly at Grandpa who pretended not to have heard. "Look, no, you know... don't call me again. I'll call you when I get home." Taylor hung up and added, "Not likely." Mere seconds later it rang again and she promptly declined the call and turned off her phone. "I'm really sorry, Grandpa."

"So am I, Taylor." Taylor was referring to the constant interruptions but, of course, Grandpa was not.

Taylor sat back down and after a moment to gather her thoughts she asked, "How did we get so far away from that time? How did we get to this place where love is so about us and not the other person? Notice I didn't ask why."

Grandpa was getting a little distracted as he kept his mind on Taylor but one eye on the game. "It sure seems like another world doesn't it?"

Taylor said, "Two people denying their own happiness to do what's best for the other? That just doesn't happen."

Grandpa was trying to come up with a response when the game sidetracked him again. "Neither does that. Look, he walked in another run!"

"Don't they have another pitcher, Grandpa?"

"I just overheard someone say they used their other two good ones yesterday, so they can't pitch today." He marked his scorecard appropriately and then shifted in his chair so he could look at Taylor and said, "Don't despair, sweetheart. There are still men in the world who believe in antiquated ideas like devotion and commitment."

Taylor knew Grandpa had to be right, but other than men in her own family she was having a hard time coming up with many examples. "So, when do they see each other again? I really need a happy ending."

"Well, not for quite a while I'm afraid. Archie tried to figure out a way to live without Emma, but he never really succeeded."

The New London job market was hit pretty hard by the combination of the depression and the droves of Bostonians trying to get fresh starts after the fire. As much as he wanted to find work that would take him out of the house and distract him, Archie couldn't find much. He did attach himself to a carriage repair outfit as a machinist, but the work was intermittent at best. The only real boom in town was in the shipping industry, as the seemingly regular railroad strikes made moving cargo down the eastern seaboard by ship attractive again.

When Archie got the chance in the spring and summer months, he'd catch a ride out to Fisher's Island. His great-grandfather, Thomas Allen, had leased a portion of the east end of the island, and his grandfather Lewis Allen had grown up and started his family there. Eleanor was born after the family had moved back to New London, but it had remained a favorite holiday destination. It was one of the first places she had taken the family when they moved home, and Archie had grown to like it.

There was a small strip of land between Barlow Pond and Island Pond on the south side of the island that was, and still is, one of the most beautiful places on earth. A few minutes of listening to the crickets chirp and the birds trying to outdo each other, feeling the cool summer wind on your face, and watching the gentle ripples wash up on the rocky beaches and the occasional squirrel or cotton tailed rabbit scamper by was the cure for just about any malady.

It could make you forget that there was anything wrong in the world; in fact, there might not be anything wrong in the world if more people would sit there and listen, feel and watch. The problem with places like this, though the problem isn't with the place itself but the condition we all find ourselves in, is that you can't stay there forever. Eventually you have to go home.

When Archie was on Fisher's Island the only thought on his mind, other than the majesty of his Creator, was wishing Emma could experience it too. As soon as he got home all he could think of was her absence. He could take her with him in a way to the island, but she could never come home with him.

In 1874, the Mercers took in a tenant by the name of Miller, who was first mate on a cargo ship that called New London Harbor home. He and Archie began to develop a friendship. Miller had broken his ankle on his last voyage and was spending the winter in town to recuperate. With nothing to occupy his time, he regaled Archie and the children with stories of his days on the great whaling vessels of the past - at length.

As the weeks passed, Archie transitioned from humoring the man by listening to his tales to developing an actual interest in the maritime trade. The idea of being out at sea and away from everything he knew was alluring. Eventually, Miller arranged a job for Archie on a replacement crew making the round trip down to Long Island and back once a week. It was part-time work, but it got Archie out of the house. Having a bit of a life and making new friends was just what Archie needed to take his mind off his troubles. When he was at sea the urgent tasks that required his attention gave him brief respites from the torments of his own mind.

It had been a couple of years now but Emma never left his thoughts;

in fact many was the night that he woke up in a cold sweat dreaming about her in some kind of peril from which he was helpless to rescue her. The guilt that he carried weighed on him like he had gained a hundred pounds.

As the years went by the dreams grew darker and eventually merged into one particular nightmare that he would have virtually every night. In it Emma would die in some fashion: sometimes of natural causes and sometimes in horrific accidents on boats, trains, carriages, in thunder storms... Anything Archie had seen recently could appear and cause her demise. But no matter how she met her end it was always somehow his fault. The dream would always end with him sitting in front of her tombstone. No matter what year it was in real life, it always read:

Here lies
Mrs. Archibald Mercer
1856-1872
"What God has brought together-
Let no man put asunder."

The dreams were driving him crazy and many nights he would stay up until near morning just so he wouldn't have time to dream the whole dream. He really needed a change in his life.

He had instructed Harold to hide all of Emma's letters from him but to keep them in a safe place. Without reading them he knew exactly what they said. No matter how adamant Emma was that she would choose him over her family, he knew that she would regret it in the end and he couldn't allow her to do that to herself. He saved the letters because he expected that someday he would be able to move past his current misery and that they might become a source of comfort for him. He also recognized that he was far too weak presently to resist their temptation so he made Harold promise to indulge him in his silly bout with his own psyche. Harold's instructions were to tell no one where the letters were kept and only reveal them to Archie if he came to him in person every day for a month. He figured that at least one day out of thirty he would have enough strength to resist. Given that he was away for two days at a time each week on the ship this would be easy.

"I hope you find everything to your satisfaction."

"You have a lovely home, Mrs. Mercer. I'm sure I will be very happy here."

Eleanor had just met a young woman named Charlotte Parker who had enquired about renting a room. Charlotte was twenty-two years old, impeccably well-groomed and had one hazel and one blue eye. They were quite striking.

Eleanor asked, "We do have a room open on the third floor with a lovely view of the church. When do you plan to join us?"

"Next week, if that's acceptable."

Nellie, now fourteen years old, entered the parlour on her way to the kitchen with her nose stuck in a book, but Eleanor grabbed her on her way by. "Let me introduce you to my daughter, Nellie. Nellie, this is our new tenant, Miss? Parker."

The ladies laughed a bit and Charlotte admitted, "Yes, it's still Miss. Please call me Charlotte. It's a pleasure to meet you."

Nellie responded, "You as well. Where are you from?"

"Ohio, originally."

"Which parts?" Eleanor asked.

"Just west of Dayton."

Eleanor laughed. "Well, then we were practically neighbors. We came here from Cambridge City."

"Oh, yes. I've been there many times."

Nellie ran to the base of the stairs and yelled at the top of her lungs, "Archie!"

Eleanor scolded her, "Nellie, please!"Then she turned to Charlotte apologetically, "Please pardon her manners... or lack of manners."

Nellie, ignoring her mother, ran back to Charlotte and asked frantically, "When was the last time you visited?"

Charlotte was caught a little off guard. "In the spring. I have cousins in Dublin."

Nellie practically shouted at her, "What are their names?"

Archie came bounding down the stairs expecting to find someone dead on the floor, or at least a rat or a spider that needed disposing of. "You shrieked?"

Eleanor tried to minimize the damage done by Nellie and switched gears nonchalantly. "Oh, Archie. There you are. Let me introduce you to Miss Charlotte Parker. Miss Parker, this is my bachelor son, Archie." She emphasized the words "Miss" and "bachelor" in what she thought was a cleverly subtle fashion, but her intentions were so obvious that these two complete strangers were compelled to give each other a knowing glance.

Their shared moment of embarrassment ended abruptly with Nellie dragging them back to her narrow conversational interest. "Archie, she has cousins in Dublin."

Eleanor would not be outmaneuvered. "And the loveliest eyes I have ever seen. Don't you think her eyes are lovely, Archie?"

Archie looked at Charlotte again and apologized with a gesture. "Of course, it is a pleasure, Miss Parker."

Eleanor just smiled at the them and let the silence linger, hoping one of them would be forced to speak. Finally, Charlotte gave in. "Have you been back to Cambridge recently, Mr. Mercer? Your face is very familiar."

Nellie interrupted, "He just has that kind of face. Now, who do you know in Dublin?"

A silent skirmish broke out as Nellie and Eleanor tussled for position. Eleanor covertly grabbed Nellie's dress and pulled her back as she stepped in front of her and addressed Charlotte. "Archie worked in Dayton for the railroad a few years back, didn't you Archie?"

Charlotte dutifully said, "Perhaps that was where we met then."

Entranced by the wrestling match going on behind him, Archie answered, "Yes, perhaps."

Eleanor was able to keep Nellie distracted long enough to try again. "So, what brings you to New London, Miss Parker?"

She answered, "Oh, restlessness I suppose. I was planning on heading up to Boston, I have some family there, but the coach stopped in New London and I just fell in love..."

Eleanor interrupted, "Oh...?"

Charlotte countered Eleanor's obvious insinuation, "...with the town; the ocean to be more specific."

Eleanor found that very interesting. "Oh, yes, Archie is quite smitten as well, aren't you Archie?"

He didn't take the bait and answered in the affirmative with a grunt.

Eleanor continued, "Many is the day he just sits out on the shore and stares at the harbor..."

Nellie finished her sentence for her, "...writing letters to Emma."

Eleanor had had enough. "Yes, of course. Nellie, darling, don't you have places to be?"

Nellie looked at Archie and said with more than enough disdain in her voice, "It appears that I'm needed here."

Archie was beginning to enjoy the floor show. "Yes, please stay, Nellie."

Harold overheard the last few minutes of the conversation from the kitchen and came to Archie's rescue. "Mr. Mercer, another stack of letters from your fiancée arrived. Shall I place them with the others?"

"Yes, *thank you*, Harold."

Charlotte, becoming more and more uncomfortable, sensed the need to escape. "I should be going. I'll send word on my arrival date."

She began to make her way toward the entrance hall and Eleanor followed after her asking, "Would you like to stay for lunch with Archie... and the family?"

Miss Parker didn't even slow down. "No, thank you. I'm afraid I must continue preparations for my move. Good day." And she was gone.

From the front porch Eleanor waved good bye. "Good day, Miss Parker."

Archie repeated her greeting with a little sarcasm, "Good day."

Then Nellie followed in the same tone. "Good riddance." Nellie grabbed Archie's hand as they went back into the house and pulled him toward the parlour again. His little sister was persistent. "Why won't you read the letters, Archie?"

Archie wanted to explain to her why he had avoided reading any of the hundreds of letters that had arrived since he had sent his last letter to Emma, but anything he'd say would only point out his failings as a man, so he only answered, "I can't."

She insisted, "You never know, there might be an important one."

Tired of Nellie's interrupting, Eleanor grabbed Nellie's book and stuck her nose back in it.

Archie lit into her, "Why must you do that, Mother? I can't have you flirting for me with every woman that crosses our path."

Eleanor brushed off his complaint and pronounced, "It's been three years, Son. You need to move on."

From behind her book Nellie chimed in, "Archie loves Emma, Mother."

In unison both her mother and brother snapped at her, "Please, stay out of this."

"I can't love another woman, Mother. It would be cruel for her to be compared in every measure and come up short."

Eleanor wasn't really listening. "She does have lovely eyes."

"Yes, Mother, and I'm sure she is a lovely person. I'm also fairly certain that we will never see her again." He was right.

Eleanor was not going to give up. "But you could learn to love someone."

Archie turned to his mother and said the last thing he would ever say to her on the subject. "I already have, and I already do. I'm afraid I don't know how to turn that off. Now, if you'll excuse me." And with that he headed for the stairs and went up to his room.

Nellie waited for Archie to leave and then gave Mother a look that said "I was right."

To which Eleanor responded, "She did have lovely eyes."

That was the last straw. Archie had finally had enough and decided he needed a permanent change in his surroundings. Miller was now the captain and part owner of his own vessel, the Magellan, and agreed to bring Archie on full-time; he could use a man Archie's size. The only catch was that this would not be a two-day excursion. Miller had inherited an Asian supply route from the ship's previous owner and explained that Archie might be gone as much as a year at a time. The longer the better as far as Archie was concerned.

There was no time for long, tearful goodbyes; the ship set off for Britain two days after Archie signed on. The night before he shipped out, Eleanor had a goodbye dinner for him with as many family members as she could find. The children, especially Frederick, were horribly sad to see him go.

Archie was saddened most that he wouldn't get to say goodbye to William. William was in his final year down at Yale, so word couldn't get to him fast enough. After he graduated he joined the army and moved west. As it turned out, their paths wouldn't cross again for more than twenty years.

As Miller's ship left the harbor that next morning and New London disappeared in the distance, Archie looked forward to starting the next chapter of his life. He had no sorrow for what he was leaving behind because New London held nothing but painful memories for him. What lay ahead on the open sea was a fearful mystery, but what could the future hold that could possibly be any worse than the present?

26

Life had changed

As Emma was preparing to celebrate her twenty-first birthday in February of 1877 the United States was entering another tumultuous period. The election of 1876 had been a contentious one and there were even rumblings of possible renewed hostilities in the Civil War. Republican Rutherford B. Hayes from neighboring Ohio and Democrat Samuel J. Tilden of New York squared off in the most disputed White House contest to that time or since. At the end of a long battle in Congress and the courts, Hayes was declared the winner despite having lost the popular vote. His victory did not come without cost.

The Compromise of 1877 allowed for Hayes to become president in exchange for all Union Army units being pulled from southern states, among other concessions. This effectively resulted in the end of Reconstruction and any progress in civil rights for Negroes. In fact, some African-American scholars still refer to the compromise as "the Great Betrayal."

That year also saw the "Great Railroad Strike of 1877." Labor strikes in Martinsville, West Virginia and then Baltimore, Maryland by disgruntled railroad workers over reduced wages touched off similar protests from Pittsburgh to San Francisco. Most of the strikes turned into riots. Nearly two–thirds of the nation's rail mileage was within the strike areas and it might have become a national strike if President Hayes hadn't reluctantly called in the army. The resulting violence and disruption of a service that had now become a central cog in the new economy nearly brought the country to its knees…again.

It might seem odd to someone looking back more than a century later that an industry which had scarcely existed forty years prior could become so necessary. After all the Golden Spike had only been driven in eight years earlier.

But imagine what would happen in the second decade of the twenty-first century if an entirely new industry that was scarcely forty years old, say cell phones for example, got together and decided to reduce wages for their employees by twenty percent and every worker walked out: sales people, technicians, account reps – all of them. It's not that we moderns could not survive without a phone in our hand – after all most of us still remember what life was like before they were invented - the problem is that universal cell phone usage has effectively eliminated the communication mediums that preceded them. Good luck finding a pay phone in an emergency. In fact, many of us don't even have home land lines any longer. We don't carry watches, own alarm clocks or know how to read a map, but at the same time our expectations for speed and convenience have increased.

It was no different in 1877. The train had become such an established form of transportation and communication, even in just those few years, that there was just no going back. Life had changed.

Emma found herself in the same situation. It had now been five years since Archie left Indiana and four years since she'd moved into Mrs. Harrison's home. She still wrote to Archie every day and she was never very far away from losing her composure if reminded of his absence. Yet as much as her heart still ached for him, life had changed and she had to move on - or at least that's what she kept telling herself.

As the years rolled by, Mrs. Harrison's health improved. There was never anything physically wrong with her that wasn't brought on by her broken heart. Before Emma arrived, she was all alone in the world and had given up hope, but when Emma entered her life, it was as if someone had opened the shades and let the sunshine in again. Of course it didn't hurt that Emma did open the windows and let the sunshine in again.

Mrs. Harrison became more and more independent and even started to venture out to do some of her own errands from time to time. Even though Emma wasn't truly needed any longer, she couldn't leave her. Mrs. Harrison had not become a surrogate mother - her real one lived across town - nor grandmother - no one could or needed to replace Grandma Becky – she just became a friend. There were nearly fifty years separating them but their relationship more resembled sisters than anything else. Emma had all the money she needed to travel to New London twenty times but she didn't leave simply because she didn't want to be alone. Now that it was clear that Archie was not coming for her and was not reading her letters, Emma started to itch to do something with her life.

One day while running her usual errands, she passed D.B. Crawford's general store on Fifth and Main like she had nearly every other day. She'd purchased many things there over the years and had struck up an acquaintance with Mr. Crawford and his son John. John's fourteen-year-old son, Wilbur, had quite the crush on Emma, and as she passed he mumbled something inaudible her way as he swept the walkway in front of the store. As she turned to address the grunts aimed her direction, she beheld a gangly young man with wiry brown hair, ears that would have been more appropriate for a head the size of a basketball, and a toothy grin that blurred the lines between heart-warming and pathetic.

As she turned she giggled a little and said, "What was that, Wilbur?"

Caught, Wilbur panicked. "Uh... mmm...er...what was what, Miss Williams?"

"Did you ask me something, Wilbur?"

"Oh...no...I...er...uh..."

Emma could see that this was going to be a long conversation so she moved it a long a little faster. "It's a beautiful day out, isn't it Wilbur?"

"Yes, it is, Ma'am."

"There we go. I knew you could do it. Now what is it you said to me as I passed? I couldn't make it out."

"Oh, Ma'am, I's jist sayin' that we got a paper in the winda' 'bout a sower; thought you'd like it."

What Wilbur was trying to say was that there was a notice in the window about an opening for a seamstress. He had never intended to say that out loud, but as soon as his father put up the notice Wilbur's adolescent imagination started running wild with the possibility of having Emma working there with him every day. His infatuation wasn't lost on Emma, but nevertheless, this was an interesting opportunity.

"Thank you, Wilbur." And she started inside to see about the details.

The Crawford's were planning to branch out into dry goods and needed someone to help their customers pick out the right patterns and materials, as well as decide which products to stock.

It was a little eerie that she'd be taking on the role she would have played in her own business with Archie, but the more she thought about it the idea grew on her. She had spent a year scouting all of the dry goods stores in Cambridge and dreaming about what they would sell so this would allow all that effort to not have been a complete waste. The bigger question was whether working in dry goods without him would make her life better or worse.

In those days many of Emma's decisions centered on whether she would be reminded of Archie or not. The thought of him made her insides churn and could reduce her to a useless wreck at a moment's notice. But she had also come to understand that the thought of him was what kept her going. It gave her hope.

What would Archie want me to do? It was a thought that was seemingly always on her mind. She could still hear his voice ring in her ear, and she intentionally tortured herself with his memory. This misery had become her friend; she enjoyed its company. She talked to him when she was alone and chose to be alone much of the time so she could be with him. Just the thought of him caused her deep pain, but the only way to stop the pain was to think of him.

Emma needed a life and she knew it. She took the job.

27
Adrift at Sea

Life at sea was growing on Archie. It took him a few weeks to get his sea legs under him, meaning he learned to walk in a straight line while being bounced around randomly like a beach ball at a sporting event. He was proud of the fact that he was the only crew member not to vomit during a storm in the North Atlantic, at least not on deck.

The Magellan was a mix of steam and sail power, but with Archie's size there was no use wasting his strength down below decks in engineering. His job was to do whatever needed doing above decks that required an abnormal degree of muscle. He spent some most of his time as a rigger, but he really enjoyed the infrequent watches when he was assigned as navigator. Although the job came with a lot of responsibility, he liked that it forced him to concentrate all through the four hour watch. His mind tended to wander less.

He liked the night watches the best. The sea breeze in his face and the stars too numerous to count made him feel small, yet inspired him to want to do great things; to be somebody again. Most nights it was so quiet he felt all alone in the world, and then a glimpse of their moon would remind him that he truly *was* all alone in the world. Emma still followed him wherever he went, even to the ends of the earth, from her perch in the night sky; if only they hadn't made so many memories together.

When the ship hit port he was a major cog in the loading and unloading of cargo. Crew members tended to come and go, and when the ship hit port in Hong Kong in July of 1876, Archie was a head taller and about fifty pounds heavier than any man on board. The dock workers were agog as he carried two and three times the weight they could handle. Archie began to tire of being a spectacle.

The Magellan stayed in port for the American centennial, but aside from blowing some improvised fireworks there wasn't much of a celebration on the ship. Nearly two years at sea was now starting to take its toll, and he was ready to come home.

His first and, as far as he was concerned, last sea voyage had taken him around the world twice. He had seen four continents, sailed on three oceans, met interesting people and made a lot of money, but he was very glad to be home as the ship pulled into New London Harbor in January of 1877.

When he arrived, he dragged himself and his belongings the half mile up Huntington Street and arrived at 111 to find that his family was no longer there. The death of Dr. Stoddard a few months before Archie left in '74 had caused a ripple effect that forced his mother and family to find another living situation. The new residents at 111 directed him to 3 Amity St. He thanked them and trudged another quarter mile toward his new destination.

He wasn't quite prepared for what he found; his mother had not done well without him. With William gone the oldest sibling with Eleanor was John (17), and then Nellie (16), Harriet (14) and Frederick (11). They had struggled to find a place large enough for them to live and rent out rooms. They finally found a four bedroom house, so John bunked with Freddie, and Eleanor roomed with Nellie and Harriet so they could rent out the other two. They were forced to let Harold and Alice go in '75 so the family that numbered twelve back in Cambridge was now down to five. Archie made six, but they had nowhere to put him, so he quickly found them a better situation at 12 Prospect Street about a quarter mile east. The money he'd saved put them in good stead for the present, and he was able to get his machinist job back. Their financial world had stabilized for the moment.

The children had grown so fast in his absence. John was pretty much full grown and a fairly impressive specimen himself, though nothing like Archie. John was dabbling in various business enterprises, and it wasn't long before it became obvious that he had inherited his father's penchant for dreaming up schemes to make a quick buck. You can understand how a child who grew up knowing nothing but ease would not take kindly to being in dire financial straits so regularly. John was never going to let that happen again. He may have overcompensated a little - more on him later.

Nellie had decided she wanted to become a schoolteacher so she could support herself and had become very studious. She ended up teaching lower elementary school ages, traveled west in the early 90's and became the head of the Spring St. Kindergarten in Los Angeles. She married Judge Henry Brubaker in 1893 who took her back home with him to Lancaster, Pennsylvania, where they had two children. He was seventeen years her senior and died in 1898. She returned to California soon and lived there until her death in 1935; she was seventy-five.

Harriet, or Hattie as she now wanted to be addressed, was travelling a different path. She was hell-bent on learning everything there was to know about being a lady in hopes that she could snag a doctor or someone of importance. She became the wife of Dr. Edward Prentis and stayed in New London until her death in 1939 at age seventy-seven.

Frederick was just tired of moving around. He had no ambition to sail around the world, meet heads of state or conquer the world of business like his brothers. He married a local girl, Lavinia Parker, had one daughter, Eleanor, and lived the rest of his eighty-four years in New London. Uncle Fred, as Grandpa knew him, remained an active member of St. James Church all of that time.

The property at 12 Prospect was sold out from under them, so the family was forced to move again in 1878, this time back to Huntington Street at number 36, just a couple of doors down from the Catholic Church. That move made five homes in six years. This house did not allow for renting rooms, so the family depended on Archie to be the breadwinner. He was doing well now as a machinist, and John was contributing a little, but things were tight. Eleanor was doing the household chores for the first time in her life and, though she thought she'd despise the menial work, she actually grew to like it. It took her mind off of being so lonely.

During the latest move, Archie was both relieved and saddened to learn that somehow between the loss of Harold and the relocation of the household, all of Emma's letters had disappeared. No one was quite sure where they had gotten to, at least no one had confessed, but there was a common suspicion that Eleanor had tossed them in a moment of foul temper.

Late in '78 Captain Miller's ship limped back into New London Harbor. The year had been a difficult one, and most of the crew had called it quits. To get back into business Miller needed to find an experienced crew, which was proving to be a difficult task. Most of the available men were from ethnic minorities and Miller needed to find some officers to lead them, and most importantly, men who spoke English.

He ran into Archie while looking for some parts at the carriage repair shop and offered Archie a position on the voyage. Archie refused him even after Miller offered to double his current pay. He almost said yes but figured he could hold out for more and eventually got Miller to agree to pay him four times his current wage and promise a voyage of no more than a year.

As reluctant as Eleanor was to let him go again, she had to admit that this brief voyage would go a long way toward making them financially solvent. It was agreed that Archie's salary would be paid out of the New London office directly to Eleanor, with Archie getting just a small bit of it for necessities on shore leaves.

As the day approached for the Magellan to depart, he spent more and more time on his hill. He'd developed the same loathing for the idea of leaving New London again as he had for leaving Cambridge City nearly seven years earlier, and had an eerie foreboding that something else was going to go wrong. He also couldn't help but notice the parallels between the two trips. In both cases he was dragged away from everything he loved for the sake of his family, who didn't seem to understand, or even appreciate, the sacrifice he was making. He no more wanted to leave New London now than he had wanted to arrive at New London then, but his father had left the family as his responsibility, so he didn't have much of a choice.

As the crew began to arrive and prepare the ship for the expedition, Archie was eager to see if there might be someone on this voyage he could befriend. The two years of the last journey were the loneliest of his life, mostly due to his own decision to wallow in his own misery. He wasn't much use as a companion in any case, staring wistfully at the moon every night as he was wont to do, spending any shore leave he had gathering supplies, and volunteering to stand guard on the ship at every port. But now he felt as though he might just be slowly crawling out of the rabbit hole he had descended down.

He kept telling himself that the years of mourning were enough; that he needed to move on. He was nearly twenty-eight years old, and if he had any hope of making something of himself, he needed to get started. The sea was not his final destination, nor was operating machinery, but he hoped that the solitude would allow him the time to decide on a new path for his life. A friend to bounce his ideas off would be so helpful. He remembered that he was at his most creative when he could share his dreams with... well... a friend could prove very helpful.

The Magellan's crew of nearly fifty was an unfortunate collection of the dregs of society. Captain Miller must have been desperate. Many had prison records, including one man who had been accused of killing his wife but was acquitted because the body was never recovered. As Archie got to know him a bit it was clear that either he had indeed killed her or she had run away in fear that he would. Not that Archie felt threatened, he was not exactly the easiest target for someone with nefarious inclinations, but he slept with his side arm for the first few months nonetheless.

At first glance Archie despaired of finding a companion. Only half the crew spoke English and only half of those spoke it well. He was one of only seven or eight Americans - he wasn't sure about one of them - including the captain, the first mate and boatswain. As it turned out, while he became friendly with a couple of the men, one a former slave from Louisiana, he never did find a real companion. He later recognized that as a gift from God.

The scheduled route of the journey would take them to Boston, then England, France, Portugal, Italy, Greece, Egypt, Bombay, Ceylon, Singapore, the Philippines, Hong Kong, San Francisco and many points in between, then home. The Suez Canal had been built ten years earlier and connected the Mediterranean Sea to the Red Sea, which saved weeks of travel around the continent of Africa. Now if someone would just cut another canal to connect the Atlantic and the Pacific, it would do everyone good. Archie said good-bye to his family, Jack and his new wife, and his friends at work and set off on a journey that would change his life forever.

The expedition began just as planned. The Magellan picked up its cargo in Boston and then dropped it at Liverpool, picked up more goods in Liverpool and delivered them to Le Havre and so on, right on schedule… until it arrived in the Philippines.

When Archie had passed through the Philippines three years earlier, his ship had the good fortune to find a time of calm in what had been a tumultuous period of nearly three hundred and fifty years of conflict between the Spanish and the indigenous Muslim Moro people. Ferdinand Magellan had claimed the islands for Spain in 1521, and from that time the Moro sultans and the Spanish had fought battle after battle that would erupt and subside for a while and then flare up again.

The years of 1874-75 were a time of relative peace, but just after the Magellan had headed for the Chinese mainland in January of 1876, the Spanish launched another offensive to colonize one of the Moro held islands. Reminiscent of the American Revolution, the Moros were vastly outnumbered and outgunned, so they were forced to resort to what we now refer to as guerilla warfare. For the next few years, really until the Spanish were finally forced to abandon the Philippines at the end of the Spanish-American War near the turn of the century, Moro pirates looted and pillaged any merchant ship they could get their hands on. The tradition of Moro piracy was nothing new, but now the official Moro navy and the Moro pirates were virtually indistinguishable. Captain Miller had no idea what he was getting himself and his crew into.

"Whoa! Back up the train!" Taylor threw up her hands. "Pirates? I was totally tracking with you but you've lost me now! You really expect me to believe that?"

"It happened." Grandpa put his right hand up as if to say "Scout's honor," but inadvertently gestured "Live Long and Prosper" in Vulcan instead. Taylor corrected his fingers for him and he continued. "He didn't like talking about it, but Uncle John was able to pry the details out of him over the years."

28
Shanghaied

With the Philippine Islands in its sights, the Magellan made its way to Alexandria, Egypt and then into the Suez Canal for the grueling 3,400 mile trip to Muscat, Oman, once a British colony and still an important trading outpost. The next stop was Bombay, India and then Colombo, Ceylon (now Sri Lanka) and then Singapore. Both Ceylon and Singapore were major rubber exporters, and the Magellan picked up as much as it could carry. Some of it would be traded in Hong Kong and the Philippines but most of it would be sold in San Francisco. These were the most lucrative transactions on the trip.

After setting off from Singapore, the ship headed east into the South China Sea toward the Philippines and its next stop in Iloilo City. Iloilo was an exporter of sugar and Miller planned to trade some of the rubber there. It was then that Captain Miller made his fatal mistake.

After you pass the northern portion of the island of Borneo, now the country of Malaysia, you have a choice to make. You can either take the more direct route through the Sulu Sea or you can go north around the island of Palawan and then turn south. The problem with the direct route was that the Sulu Sea was the hunting grounds of the Moro pirates. Captain Miller had gotten behind schedule by a couple of days negotiating the Arabian Peninsula and, though he had planned to take the safer route, he decided to pick up the lost time traversing the Sulu.

Archie was below decks asleep when the lookout alerted the boatswain that a pirate "proa" was approaching from the starboard side. These smallish ships were extremely fast but no military match for an armed merchant ship. They carried swivel guns that had very little range, so as long as they kept their distance they posed no significant threat. The Captain ordered the lookout to keep an eye on it but did not order the crew to general stations. The sea had been choppy the night before and the crew needed rest.

Suddenly, an artillery blast burst from the proa, and then another and another. The first two whizzed by without damage but the third caught a piece of the yardarm on the mainsail and it exploded into a thousand pieces. Those weren't scatter guns! That was significant cannon fire and apparently they had three of them. How did blasts that large not sink the proa? The captain ordered the crew to battle stations but before they could get off a shot the proa let fly three more volleys. Everyone braced for impact but there was none; all three missed their targets. Captain Miller shouted, "Fire!" and the six starboard cannon of the Magellan returned fire.

The two ships traded broadsides for the next ten minutes but with the noise, smoke and confusion no one noticed that three more ships had snuck up on them to the rear on the port side. There were already six boarding vessels at their heels before the first mate could alert the captain of their existence. Riflemen started to pick off pirates one by one, but there were too many of them, and they began pouring on to the ship. The furious battle began with men falling by the dozen on both sides.

Below deck, Archie was jolted awake by the splintering yardarm and the siren calling for general stations. He bolted out of his bed and grabbed his shoes. He had one foot in the air when the Magellan's first cannon blast rocked the ship and sent him sprawling. He landed face first on a nearby bunk striking his forehead on the edge of the wooden bed frame. He rolled onto the floor and remained conscious for the moment but blood was gushing from a gash just above his right eye. He reached for the first cloth he could find and pressed it to his head, but in a matter of seconds he was out - face first on the ground with the blood soaked shirt still on the wound.

The next thing he knew he was on his feet being held by three men who were yelling at him in a language he didn't recognize. They were small men that he could have easily taken, but he was in no condition to put up a fight and passed out again, chained to an iron pole.

Above decks the battle was over. All but twelve of the Magellan's crew were dead, including every officer save the captain, who had been severely beaten and taken a gunshot wound to his shoulder. The pirates threw the bodies of the dead on both sides overboard and assembled the remaining crew on the deck. Archie was hauled on board and lined up with the rest of his mates for what all presumed was an execution.

The adrenaline surging through Archie broke him out of his haze as he began to understand what had happened. The leader of the pirates began to yell at the crew. Diego, one of the South American crew members that had survived, recognized some of the words as they were a blend of Spanish and something else. The pirate leader paused as if he had asked a question and was awaiting the answer. Diego answered slowly in Spanish that they were going to Iloilo to trade. Then the pirate spoke to Diego and pointed Archie's way. Diego turned to Archie and, in broken English, asked if he wanted to be the engineer.

This made sense. They wanted to use the steam engine and couldn't manage it on their own. That explained why they left the rest of them alive, though it was foolish to think that twelve men could operate such a large vessel. Archie realized that the real head of engineering was not among them so he said, "Yes, I'm the engineer."

Diego "translated" and the pirate, seeming to like the answer, walked up to Archie, looked him up and down and motioned for one of his men to release Archie from his chains. But before he did the pirate wheeled and shot Captain Miller through the head at point blank range. He was the captain now and there would be no confusion about who was in charge.

The whole crew reacted as you would expect and Archie reflexively lunged forward at the rogue but the new "captain" stuck his sword in Archie's chest as if to say, "That's what will happen to you if you try anything."

Archie's blood began to run hot in him again and he struggled to keep from doing something stupid. He stuffed down his anger and relaxed his posture in submission which satisfied the "captain", but there was nothing but defiance in his glare. This would be revisited, perhaps not right away, but eventually this scum would pay.

The months of Archie's captivity passed painfully slowly. He was expected to run the ship's engines and make repairs. He had picked up enough to be at least semi-competent as long as nothing out of the ordinary happened. Diego had been assigned as his assistant and his English was improving daily. It didn't escape Archie that necessity had finally found him a friend. Diego was a relatively large man as well so they were both confined below decks for security purposes. Any time the pirates brought them food or came down to check on them they came in threes and were heavily armed.

Once a week or so they were allowed on board to stretch their legs and they used that time to survey the situation. They had no idea how many of the crew remained, where on earth the ship was, or how much time had passed. Archie did know that they had made two stops in port but had no idea where those ports were or what business had been transacted, though after the second one the ship felt a little lighter so he assumed they had off-loaded the rubber. That was a good thing for two reasons, 1) it meant that the lighter ship would use less fuel and, 2) he didn't have to unload it.

He knew that it wouldn't be long before he ran out of coal to power the engines. To save fuel the captain had used wind power whenever possible, so the reserve was intended to last the year. They were at the nine month point of the journey on the day of the attack so they had already stretched it beyond expectations. Once the fuel ran out, Archie and Diego wouldn't be needed anymore.

On one trip topside, they noticed that the yardarm had been repaired and that all of the sails were operational. Did the pirates know they would run out of fuel soon? Had they already made provision for life after the engines died? This news jumpstarted Archie and Diego's urgency to finalize their escape plan. It appeared that the pirate crew had been thinned a bit as Archie only counted six armed men on board instead of the usual ten. He also counted eight of the nine crewmen who had survived, in addition to Diego and himself; God help the other man.

The best they could do to communicate with their friends was to drop body language hints as to what they were up to, but finally Diego was able to speak secretly to one their mates for just a few moments. They hoped that had been enough to set the plan in motion.

They waited for some kind of audible cue to tell them that they were headed into another port, and finally one afternoon they got it. One of their friends started singing a tune in Spanish and Diego told Archie that was the signal. The man had also worked the number eight into the song several times which they took to mean that there were eight armed guards on board; hopefully that's what it meant. They had stoked the coal level as low as they could get away with for the last few weeks in preparation for their escape. Diego started to shovel whatever coal he could safely reach out of the burner and into a metal bucket and then they waited.

The engines shut down for lack of fuel faster than imagined and they hurried to lie in wait for the expected reaction from the pirates; they just hoped it hadn't been too soon and that the ship wasn't too far from shore. Diego hid under the stairs and Archie laid in wait behind the engine with the bucket of coal. His brief military training hadn't exactly prepared him for this.

Soon they heard the lock on the door rattle and the sound of men descending the stairs. The difference between life and death for both of them would be how many men came into the engine room. They figured they could only handle two or three since their weapons were just the coal bucket and the shovel. They would be up against pirates armed with a four-chambered pistol, a sword known as a kris, and a dagger called a barong, each designed to inflict optimum damage.

The first man reached the bottom of the stairs with gun drawn and the second man right behind him. Archie lunged out from behind the engine and threw the burning coals right into the first man's face. Both men screamed in agony as the second man had also been hit in the neck. Then Diego dashed out from under the stairs and struck the second man so hard with the shovel that he nearly decapitated him. Archie grabbed the first man's pistol as Diego stabbed him with the second man's dagger to silence his cries.

They looked up the stairs expecting more to follow but they were in luck; only two had been sent. They took the weapons from each of the bodies and dragged them both back behind the stairs and waited. They checked their pistols - Archie's was empty and Diego's had only one round; this was good news and bad. They heard the next set of footsteps approaching and made ready. As the descending man reached the mid-point of the staircase, Diego plunged his dagger into the man's calf that sent him hurtling down the stairs. Archie was there to greet him and with one punch knocked him cold. This one's pistol was empty as well which was a very pleasant trend indeed. Perhaps all of their captors were running low on ammo.

Archie liked their chances in close combat given the small stature of the pirates in general and because Diego had already proven quite adept. They had only five more armed guards to go, assuming their intelligence was correct. They hid the third body with the others and waited. The footsteps they were expecting didn't come but they could hear commotion on the deck so they slowly made their way up the stairs.

Suddenly, gunfire broke out, and Diego ran for the door with Archie right behind him. Diego found himself face to face with one of their captors, fired his pistol and the man fell. Archie grabbed the pirate's sidearm and they reached the deck. It was chaos on board. The other crewmen had attacked the pirates with anything they could get their hands on. Apparently ammunition was indeed in very short supply as the gunfire had stopped, and the struggle was now hand to hand as Archie hoped. The crew was out-numbered two to one by Archie's reckoning and the count of eight armed guards was clearly not the case. He and Diego split up and engaged the battle.

Archie snuck up behind a pirate who was wielding his sword against one of the crew, who was armed with only a piece of wood, and decked him with one blow of his fist. The crew member grabbed the sword and plunged it into the pirate's chest. Archie now had a pistol, two swords and a dagger so he tossed one of the swords to his friend and each engaged another opponent. Archie checked the chamber of the pirate's pistol and found there were two rounds in it.

A few yards to his rear he heard a call for help in English, and Archie found one of his crew, Abner, the Negro man from Louisiana, pinned down by three pirates. Archie fired his gun and kneecapped one of the pirates and then shot another in the shoulder just as the third slashed his friend through the heart.

Archie had been so panicked and filled with adrenaline up to now that he hadn't had time to get angry, but this did it. He disarmed the pirate quickly and, in a furious rage, beat him so ferociously with his bare hands that what was left of him was unrecognizable. All he could think of were those mongrels who had attacked him and Jack so many years ago. He kept beating him and beating him, well beyond the point of death, until he heard another gunshot behind him. It was the pirate captain.

He ran toward the sound and found Diego lying in a pool of blood. Blinded by his fury, he ran toward the rogue who aimed his gun at

Archie and fired, but the weapon was empty. Before the pirate knew it Archie was on him with his giant hands around his throat. Archie lifted him off the ground by his neck and then hurled him to the ground, smashing his head into the deck. Archie kept smashing his face onto the deck until the man stopped moving, all the while screaming, "Diego!"

He ran to his friend, but he was gone. The shot had hit him right in the heart and he had died instantly. Archie was seething and looked around for another poor soul on whom he could exact his revenge when he heard, "Aqui! Aqui!" He looked up and realized that the battle was over. The three remaining crew members were loading into a landing craft and one was motioning for him to come. He grabbed his weapons, ran to the boat and he and his three best friends in the world made their escape.

29

We're Silly Girls Aren't We?

When the Williams family moved to Richmond in the mid-seventies they had inexplicably begun attending services at St. Paul's Episcopal Church. Emma stayed at the Presbyterian Church. She had made a home there and Mrs. Harrison had begun attending with her, but, more importantly, the thought of seeing her father engaged in a congregation that didn't bear the name Society of Friends, therefore making all she and Archie had gone through utterly meaningless, was more than she could bear. Clearly, if Quakerism was something he could so easily give up then it couldn't have been the real reason he had driven them apart. While she was curious as to what his real motivations might have been, finding out would require speaking with him; she wasn't that curious.

The year of 1878 turned out to be the year of awkward weddings. Emma's sister, twenty-year-old Mary Ina, and Benjamin Chandlee were married by the Reverend Isaac M. Hughes on April 25 at the First Presbyterian Church and then twenty-five year old George and Sarah Elizabeth Campbell were married by Pastor W.G. Virgus on December 19th at the Pearl Street Methodist Church. Not a Quaker ceremony, regulation or tradition to be found among them.

As Emma stood at the front of the church as Ina's maid of honor with Sarah, the soon to be Mrs. George Williams, at her side, she couldn't help but wonder how it came to pass that she could very well end up as the last of the Williams children to marry rather than the first. No one was sure, let alone Emma, whether those were tears of joy streaming down her face as her sister came down the aisle.

As it turned out, Ina and Ben only had twenty years together as he passed away in 1898. Ina was remarried in 1903 to George McAlone and they moved soon after that to Los Angeles where Ina lived until her death in 1933 at the age of seventy-five. Neither of Ina's marriages resulted in any children.

George and Sarah's wedding was a little more lavish as she came from the powerful Gaar family, one of Richmond's richest clans. They had two children, Gaar Campbell in 1880 and Inez Rich in 1883. Gaar ended up having a very successful career as a cartoonist for the Indianapolis News and the Chicago Tribune. George and Sarah lived in Richmond, many of those years with George serving as County Clerk, until his death in 1910 at age fifty-nine.

The 1880's did not begin well for Emma or the United States. The winter of 1880-81 went down in history as one of the worst ever. Known as the "Hard Winter" or, as Laura Ingalls Wilder's novel called it, "The Long Winter," the blizzards and accompanying spring flooding in the Midwestern states set the country back for years.

In July of 1881, newly inaugurated President James Garfield was shot by a deranged individual who was upset that a speech he had written, and never delivered, was not getting the credit it deserved for winning the White House for Garfield. Garfield was shot in broad daylight right on a Washington D.C. street as presidents had no security details in those days. This was almost exactly one hundred years before and just three miles away from the spot President Reagan would be shot. Garfield died from infection as a result of his wounds in September. This was the second of three presidential assassinations in Emma's lifetime. After President McKinley was killed in 1901 the Secret Service was finally tasked with protecting the president.

In 1882 another economic recession began that lasted for thirty-nine months. On the bright side, Thomas Edison's electric light was being mass produced and resulted in whole cities being illuminated, and out west, Billy the Kid, Jesse James, Billy Clanton and Frank and Tom McLaury were eliminated.

Emma continued to work at D.B. Crawford's store. It was still a novelty for a woman to work outside the home back then and Emma's situation; specifically that she was in her mid-twenties and still single with no prospects, or desire to develop any prospects, was a regular topic of conversation for many of the women who now frequented the establishment. She tried to not let it bother her, but their constant insinuations into her affairs began to wear on her. She tried to focus on her work.

Victorian era fashion sensibilities kept women covered head to toe in heavy fabrics, so the summer heat didn't do them any favors. The result was the loss of many a fine garment to underarm sweat stains. In the early 80's dress shields became all the rage to solve this problem and Emma sold hundreds of the oval shaped fabrics to her clients. She began to recognize though that, depending on the dress and the wearer's choice of undergarments, fastening the shields in place was a significant problem.

She tried various ways to solve the problem for "her ladies" but it wasn't until the late 80's that a real solution presented itself. It was so simple she didn't know why it took her so long to figure it out. She simply took two shields, placed one of them under the arm and one on the shoulder, and fastened them together with a couple of little clamps. It took her a while to find the right materials and to come up with a design, but once she had one Mr. Crawford enlisted a machine shop down the street to start mass producing them. Women loved them because they were easy to attach one handed and were so thin they were completely unnoticeable. The shop sold them by the box full. Soon Crawford's was shipping the fasteners to stores in other towns and Emma was becoming known for something other than what she didn't have. In '92 it became necessary to apply for the contraptions to be patented, so Emma enlisted patent lawyers Denis and Stockman and finally on April 4th, 1893, Emma officially became a U.S. patent holder. Take that.

Emma's days were full now. Her work at Crawford's had made her an independent woman, even without her income from taking care of Mrs. Harrison, and she was filling the other hours of her day pursuing a variety of interests. She was teaching Sunday School now for grades one through three at the church, and she had developed a love for poetry. And, of course, there was her garden. Frankly, Emma had developed so many pastimes she scarcely had room for them all.

By the mid-eighties little, freckled-faced Wilbur Crawford had finally grown into his ears and his affections had shifted from Emma to her youngest sister Lily. Wilbur was beginning the long process of taking the store over from his father, who had long ago lost interest, and his grandfather, who had just turned eighty-six. Emma noticed that Lily's visits to Crawford's had grown increasingly frequent and that less and less of her time there was spent looking at patterns. In fact, it was becoming rarer every week when Lily's calls on the store actually resulted in a purchase. Wilbur Oran Crawford and Lillian (Lily) Rich Williams were married November 13th, 1888. Emma was yet again a bridesmaid and not a bride.

On an unseasonably warm afternoon near Christmas that year, Emma returned from work and her errands and found Mrs. Harrison out on the porch again.

"Oh, hello, Lillian! How'd you get out here?" Lillian was in her seventies now and actually needed Emma to take care of her again, so it was surprising to see the rocking chair out on the porch.

"Hello, dear. I thought I'd get some fresh air."

"You must be feeling better to drag the chair out here on your own. Can I get you anything?"

Lillian thought for a moment and then said, "Tell me about your day out."

Emma ran into the house for a moment, dropped off her things and brought a second chair back out with her. She sat it down next to Lillian and said, "Work was fine, then the bank, the market and the post office. Oh, we're at forty-seven now."

Lillian was aghast. "That postman again?"

Emma laughed. "Oh, no, I believe he's finally given up hope. This was the banker." Emma appeared pleased, if only for the entertainment value.

Indignant, Lillian asked, "Mr. Hayes? He's as old as I am."

Emma, now a bit more clinical, straightened her skirt and said, "This one was unique, I will say."

"How so?"

"Well, truth be told, it wasn't as much a proposal of marriage as it was a merger. He said that I wouldn't have any obligations as his wife other than to take his name. He doesn't want to die without someone to leave his estate to."

There was a silence and then Lillian asked carefully, "What did you say?"

It took a moment for the point of the question to register but then Emma said with a fair amount of disdain for even the mention of such a notion, "I refused him, of course."

Lillian was cautious in pressing the issue. "Perhaps you should at least consider this one, Emma."

Emma was hurt. "And marry for money? They have a word for that."

"Now, dear, it's not good for a woman to be alone without means."

"I have means of my own, thank you. I don't need a man to take care of me."

"Do you want to end up alone? You must consider such things at your age."

Emma took a second but then stiffened her back and asked intractably, "And give up my name, my reputation and any hope of..." She stopped herself before she mentioned her stubborn hope of Archie coming for her, but Lillian caught it anyway. Emma continued, "I thanked him for his generous offer and wished him well."

Lillian lowered the boom. "It's been sixteen years. Archie isn't coming for you, dear."

Emma softened her posture and voice. "There is no statute of limitations on a promise."

Lillian looked at her with equal parts admiration and pity. "Could there ever be a love truer than yours?"

Emma took Archie's handkerchief from her pocket and wiped her eyes a bit. "I tell myself to move on, but I can't. He's so much a part of me that to try to love another man would be to commit adultery in my heart."

"That thought has kept me alone for forty years."

Emma grabbed her hand. "You have me."

"That I do." Lillian pulled the handkerchief from her sleeve and dabbed her own eyes a bit.

"Lillian, I'm tired." Emma whispered with tears in her eyes.

"Tired of waiting for him?"

Emma sighed. "I'm tired of carrying this for the both of us." Indeed the new life that their love had birthed, "Them," was at death's door and only Emma's tenacious hope was keeping it alive.

They sat with their handkerchiefs to their faces for a moment and then Emma said, "We're silly girls, aren't we?"

As butterflies flitted from one of Emma's peonies to the next, Mrs. Harrison looked out on her front yard and said, "I suppose we are."

Taylor thought for a moment, began to say something and then stopped herself.

"What's on your mind, punkin?"

Taylor reacted viscerally to her second grade nickname, but went on. "Is that kind of love... healthy?"

He shook his head. "I don't know. What do you think?"

She thought a second. "Well, it sounds romantic and noble and all, but that's easy to say because we know it worked out. What if it didn't?"

Grandpa repeated himself, "I don't know."

She turned to him with a little mock derision, "You're supposed to have all the answers."

"Why is that?"

"Because you're old."

Grandpa snickered, "Age doesn't give you the answers. It just changes the questions." The crowd behind the plate cheered as the pitcher gave up another free pass. "Like why on earth is that kid still pitching?"

Taylor asked, "How many is that now?"

Grandpa looked at his scorecard and said, "I show it's fourteen to eight."

"You think we have a chance?" Taylor had a little spark in her voice.

Grandpa understood she wasn't talking about the game. "Anything's possible."

30
The American Giant

Archie and his new best friends were relieved to discover that there were no pirate proas following the Magellan, so they snuck back on board and grabbed whatever supplies they could find. They had no chance of piloting such a large vessel with just the four of them, so they piled all the food, water, bandages, maps and anything else of use into the landing craft, set the Magellan ablaze, and headed for land.

Archie had lost a good deal of weight during their imprisonment but was still strong enough to man the oars. In fact, the other man who was charged with rowing with him could scarcely keep his oars in the water. In twenty minutes they had reached the shore - but what shore? Where were they?

Exhausted from their ordeal and two of them nursing significant wounds, they decided to hide the boat in a small cove and make camp a few hundred yards inland. They expected that the pirates would be back at any moment, but as the Magellan sank slowly into the sea, they felt more and more at ease. As soon as the last of the mast was under water the pirates wouldn't have as easy of a time finding them, but for all they knew they might have just landed on Moro soil. They took turns at watch and slept as well as could be expected.

In the morning they studied the captain's maps and discovered that they had been traveling in circles for the last few months and were only a few miles from Iloilo City. When they reached the city a couple of days later one of the two injured men was in no condition to continue. He and the other injured man decided to stay in Iloilo for the time being. The third survivor was relatively healthy and fluent in Spanish so he quickly latched onto the crew of a Spanish warship. He tried to get Archie a spot, but Archie was in no mood to go into battle again and declined. He figured there had to be an American or British ship arriving soon that he could attach himself to, but the wait was a long one. Western shipping companies had heard about the resurgence in pirate activity in the area and were avoiding the Sulu when they could at all help it.

Isolation had become such a consistent theme in Archie's life that he didn't think twice about making the journey home alone, but this was a special kind of isolation. Being alone is one thing, being alone amidst thousands of people who can all speak to each other but not to you is quite another. Archie had experienced depression before and when the days of waiting turned into weeks and the weeks turned into months he knew he had to do something to keep himself from losing his mind. He had avoided it for years, but this called for desperate measures so he succumbed; he started writing letters to Emma again.

Archie began his trek back home in the fall of 1879, but he didn't reach New London until January of 1882. That twenty-eight month journey tested him in every way a man could be tested and, to Archie's way of thinking, he failed more often than he succeeded.

Just the task of staying fed, clothed and sheltered in a foreign land when you started with nothing was a huge challenge, but when you add to that the need to accumulate enough resources to get passage on the various vessels necessary to make progress toward home, it strained every bit of Archie's ability. He learned quickly that being a foot taller and a hundred pounds heavier than virtually anyone he came in contact with was a commodity in and of itself. Getting hired onto dock crews and other labor-intensive projects was easy, and he eventually learned to negotiate his wages after working unknowingly for the equivalent of pennies a day for a while.

One day he was working on the docks when a fight broke out

amongst some of the men. Archie went to break it up but one of the combatants took exception and came after Archie with a knife. With his left hand Archie grabbed the knife wielding arm and with one twist snapped it in two places and then hit the man with a right uppercut so devastating that it lifted the poor fellow a couple of feet in the air before it deposited him in a wooden crate nearby. Those that had been supporting the knife wielder ran in several different directions as a hush came over the crowd that had gathered. Archie went to the crate to see if the man was still breathing and to Archie's relief he was okay. His jaw was shattered and his arm looked a mile of mountain road but he'd live.

Archie yanked him out of the crate and the man limped away as the crowd began to cheer. In an odd way, this event in Archie's life led to his eventual rescue from the islands and funded his journey home. Every man in town with less sense than strength wanted to challenge Archie's skill, and it wasn't long before he had found an enterprising fellow willing to arrange the fisticuff matches and charge admission. How ironic that Archie had become a circus act at the very same time that Barnum and Bailey were hitting the circuit in the United States.

For more than six months Archie worked on the docks every day and beat the living daylights out of a half a dozen feeble-minded louts two or three nights a week. At first he made about four dollars a day on the docks and about fifteen dollars at night, but after a while his moonlighting was rewarded with nearly fifty dollars an evening, sometimes more on a good night. He soon decided to quit his day job altogether.

It became a badge of honor in town to have survived going toe to toe with the "American Giant" and then show off the bruises to prove it. Archie had learned how to not hurt them severely while still putting on a good show, but every week or so a fellow would land a punch and then get pretty badly flattened. Eventually, no one even tried to hit him. It was safer that way.

About five months into Archie's show business career he was

challenged by a man his own size. *Hmm, I may have to actually earn my money tonight*. A couple of minutes in, it became clear to all concerned that this big fellow had no business being in a ring. Today we would have an adroit diagnostic term for the man's condition but Archie just knew that he was fighting a child in a man's body and called it off. The crowd booed him mercilessly, but he pacified them by announcing that he would fight three men at once. He beat all three of them senseless, of course. That stunt turned out to be quite popular, and for the next few weeks he took on multiple men at least once a night; the crowds grew. Archie was saving the bulk of his money, and after he'd collected $2,000 he began the serious task of figuring out a way home.

In spring of 1881, an Australian passenger ship stopped in Iloilo to repair some damage and refuel on its way to Hong Kong, so Archie bid the circus life goodbye and bought his way on board. Once he got to Hong Kong, he knew what to do. He caught a British ship to Japan, an American steamer to San Francisco and then the railroad across the U.S. toward home.

When he finally boarded the Union Pacific Railway in San Francisco, he still had enough money to pay for first-class passage to Council Bluffs, Iowa and he got the first real rest he could remember in three years. With time to hear his own thoughts, he started to take stock of the man he had become. He wrote "Emma" letters questioning whether he was still the same man she had fallen in love with ten years earlier. The answer was a resounding "No," but the issue was more of whether or not he was a better man.

On the plus side of the ledger, he felt as though his temper, while not completely corrected, was at least under control. On the island he had learned to fight with restraint, unless he had been drinking - then all bets were off. To the extent that alcohol and getting into fights tended to be close companions, even if the other man was the only one drinking, he resolved to eliminate his newly found penchant for adult beverages in hopes that he could solve both problems at once. He knew Emma would be happy about that.

On the downside, he had considerable guilt about injuring people for a living, and still struggled with killing the men he had during his escape, but he declared that chapter of his life over. He and God had not been on speaking terms for years, at least not like they had been. Sure, they tended to have a heart to heart whenever Archie found himself in big trouble, but there was no evidence to point to of anything like a regular friendship. Emma would not be pleased by that at all. Archie acknowledged that it was only by Providence that he was still breathing, much less almost home, but it was by that same Providence that he had lost the love of his life. He wasn't sure which side God was really on.

As he pulled into Council Bluffs he had a choice to make. Should he take the northern route through Chicago or the more southern route that would take him through St. Louis? Since it was December it made much more sense to go south but south would take him past southern Indiana where he might be tempted to take a detour to Cambridge. *Chicago here we come.*

When the Magellan didn't return as scheduled in 1879, the shipping company stopped making payments to Eleanor, and the family was soon in deep trouble again. It was assumed that all hands were lost at sea, but nothing more was known until Archie stepped off the train. Eleanor refused to have a service for Archie despite urgings from John and Fred, and frankly burying an empty casket was a pointless and expensive proposition. By the time Archie, now thirty years old, returned, the family had moved twice more, finally landing at 12 Franklin Street. It was just Eleanor, John and Fred by this time, but when Archie finally found them and walked through the door, he still received a hero's welcome. For the family it was as if he had returned from the dead.

Archie got his machinist job back, and John (23) and Fred (17) were working as clerks in stores in town, so they were able to move to a better location. Their final home as a family in New London would be at 40 Broad Street, back down by St. James again only a few hundred yards away from their first New London location.

Archie settled back into normal New England life, but he would never be the same. The scars that he carried with him were immense; we'd call it PTSD today, but there was no one to talk to - no one to confide in. So back to his letters he went. It was another rabbit hole he couldn't dig out of, and now he didn't even bother trying.

31
Opportunity Brother!

In 1887 a new rail line had just been completed all the way through to Los Angeles, and the southwest was booming. Little towns on the outskirts of Los Angeles like Monrovia, South Pasadena and Pomona started popping up all over.

Archie's brother John was now twenty-eight and had saved up enough money from various business ventures to move out west; his entrepreneurial instincts were itching. He had asked Archie repeatedly to go with him, but Archie always refused. With his departure date only a week away, John decided to give it one last try.

Since Archie, now thirty-six, had been back from the Orient, he had readopted his secluded spot at the burial grounds, though it wasn't quite as secluded as it had once been. John found him there and snuck up behind him. "Archie?"

Archie about jumped out of his skin. It might not be fair to describe what John did as sneaking, but when one is engrossed in letter writing they tend to not notice their own surroundings. Archie quickly folded up his letter and put it in his pocket.

"Archie, who are you writing?"

"It's nothing."

John was worried for his big brother. "Are you still writing her every day?"

Archie tried to justify it somehow but couldn't. "I prefer to think of it more as a journal, but yes."

John sat down next to him. "Have you ever sent one?"

Archie shook his head slowly. "No. I couldn't do that to her. She's likely very happily married and I... just couldn't."

John was blunt, if not tactless. "What if she isn't? What if she's just as sad and alone and as miserable to be around as you are?"

Archie couldn't exactly be mad at him, he was correct after all. "Well then I wouldn't want to add to her sorrow now would I? What brings you up here?"

"I came to ask you one last time to come with me."

Archie groaned, "California again? I don't know why you see so much promise in that place. You've missed the gold rush."

John could hardly contain his excitement. "Opportunity, brother! Now that the railroad's finished, people are moving there right and left. They're gonna need all sorts of things and someone to sell it to em!"

For all of Archie's brotherly affection, he had to agree with everyone else who had ever met him that, to be kind, John could be a bit of a handful. Even John knew that. "I'm not going to go into business with you, John."

No offense was taken. "You don't have to. With all those new people in Los Angeles I'm sure they'll need machinists there too. Look, I hate to see you mopin' around all the time, wastin' your life in New London."

Archie stretched his neck back and forth. "I'm needed here."

"For what? Everyone's all grown up. You were gone for years and we all got along, no offense."

Archie thought for a moment for a reason to stay. "There's Jack."

"With his wife and how many children is it now?" John turned to him and looked him in the eye. "Archie, staying here isn't going to fix it. We could stop in Indiana on the way, maybe drop off a letter..."

"Wouldn't that be fun. Maybe I should invite myself to dinner and introduce myself to her husband and children."

"Okay, there are other ways of getting there."

Archie looked out over the river and thought for a bit and said, "I can't think of anything I want to do less than travel across country again, but a change of scenery might be helpful."

John saw a glimmer of hope. "Then you'll consider it?"

Archie was able to fend off his brother's nagging and stayed in New London, but no sooner had John left than Eleanor, now sixty, announced that she was moving to Pennsylvania to live with her sister, and Fred announced his engagement, so there was no longer any reason to stay – real or imagined.

Archie took the northern route again and arrived in Los Angeles in the spring of 1888. John had opened up a poultry supply business, and Archie helped him for a while, but it certainly wasn't something he wanted to do for long.

One day he was walking home from the shop when a bar fight spilled out into the street. It was an ugly affair and three officers from the new L.A.P.D. were doing their best to break it up. One of them got clocked with a stool and Archie came to his aid. When the dust had cleared the three constables and Archie were standing over a pile of bruised warriors. Patrolman Auble thanked Archie for his assistance and mentioned that the force was looking for some new men. "You're a Republican aren't you?"

Archie thought that was odd but replied, "Yes."

"Good," said Auble. "Come up to the station and talk to my captain, and I'll put a word in for you. We can always use a man who can handle himself in a fight."

As it turned out, the force had been having some racially driven problems with some of its officers. Back then the Democratic Party was still the home of the KKK and other racist groups, and the police force was made up almost entirely of Democrats. Los Angeles was home to many blacks who had left the south after the Civil War and, of course, had a significant Latino population. Having an almost exclusively Democrat rank and file wasn't working out very well, so half of the Democrats were let go and the force was hiring Republicans to replace them. Archie had impeccable Republican credentials in every way imaginable and even spoke a little Spanish; he was hired.

Grandpa and Taylor were on their feet cheering on Nick's team.

"Atta boy, Jacob! Good eye!" Grandpa bellowed.

Taylor asked, "Is that fourteen to eleven now?"

"Sure is!" Then Grandpa saw it coming. "Oh, drat. Here comes the manager to change pitchers."

The other team's manager started the slow walk to the mound, bent down to talk with his pitcher, patted him on the back and then banished him to left field and brought the left fielder in to pitch.

Taylor sighed, "So much for that."

"Don't lose hope. If this kid was any good they would have brought him in sooner."

They sat back down and as soon as they hit their seats Taylor asked, "We have a while. Can we finish it?"

"Sure." Grandpa leaned into his favorite part of the story. "So, Archie was given badge number eleven. Back then the police force was mostly a brute squad that broke up fights in saloons in the worst parts of town. On the side, a group of them they called the Strongmen put on shows with bare knuckle boxing and feats of strength. At thirty-eight, Archie was the oldest man on the force, but he could still deliver a blow with the best of them."

Taylor laughed. "I guess being a pirate and a circus act had some benefits after all. What about Emma?"

32

Let's Stick Our Feet in it!

The 1880's aren't known historically as a tumultuous decade, but that's largely because modern historians didn't live through them. In addition to losing a President, the clashes between the U.S. cavalry and the Indian nations intensified and then wound down with the defeats of Sitting Bull and Geronimo. Race relations in the south got even worse as lynchings of African-Americans increased, and the winter of 1888 was, yet again, one of the worst ever recorded in the plains states where cattle carcasses littered ranches by the hundreds of thousands.

Technology advanced rapidly as the electric light, automobile, submarine, dry cell battery, radio transmitter and receiver, phonograph and drinking straw were all either invented or became available commercially. The Prohibition movement was gaining ground all over the country which led to invention of a "liquor-free" or "soft" drink called Coca-Cola.

Emma was twenty-four when the 80's began and as they ended she looked back at what she considered a lost decade. As 1890 dawned she was a thirty-something spinster living as a servant in someone else's house. She had reunited with her family, in a way, but all of her siblings were married and off on their own.

Emma's relationship with Archie's memory had been on again, off again. She still remembered to pray for him at eight o'clock each night, but there were times when that was a pleasure and times when it was a drudgery. She was still deeply in love with him, but she was also deeply in mad at him. There was a time in the late seventies and early eighties when she felt the Lord impress upon her the necessity of praying for his safety and well-being but most times she just prayed for his happiness and that of his wife and children. Those were hard prayers to pray.

The 1890's didn't start off any better for her. In October of '90 Emma noticed a lump on her sister Lily's neck while they were doing dishes one evening. Emma urged her to have it looked at by a doctor, and it turned out that it was cancer. The lump grew until it was the size of a grapefruit and in July '92 it was decided that it had to be removed. With her husband a successful businessman, Lily was afforded the best care available, but still died at home a few weeks later as a result of an infection she contracted during the procedure.

The whole family was shattered; the baby isn't supposed to go first. Their mother was a wreck for months. The one tiny silver lining in her sister's death was a thaw in Emma's relationship with her father. Not to say they became close, but they at least crossed over the threshold of cordiality.

In February of '94, Emma and her sister Mary Ina stopped by their parents' house one morning to help their mother clean up the remnants of a family dinner the night before. A large contingent of Susannah's side of the family from Ohio had made the trip to Richmond and had stayed at the Williams' for a few days. It had been exhausting for Susannah and her daughters had pity on her and were off to the rescue.

When they entered the house they called out for her but got no reply. Emma trotted upstairs to check for her and Mary Ina looked in the kitchen. Emma heard a scream from downstairs and ran down to the kitchen to find Mary Ina leaning over their mother who was sprawled on the kitchen floor. The newspapers reported that Susannah Williams, "a large fleshy woman," had died suddenly of apparent heart failure. She was sixty-two.

Emma had become accustomed to grief, but the death of her mother was worse than anything she had experienced, save losing Archie. *But why?* Her mother wasn't a young woman, and she had been having trouble breathing recently so it shouldn't have come as a surprise.

And yes, she was close to her mother, but that didn't seem to be the cause either. As the days went by, it became clear to Emma that losing her mother made her the matriarch of the family so to speak - the unmarried, childless matriarch of the family. As much as Emma liked to think of herself as an independent, working woman of means and holder of a patent, she would prefer to be dependent on a husband and depended on by children tugging at her apron. Her mother's death painted in more vivid colors her personal sense of emptiness at not having achieved any of her most cherished life goals.

Then, just to add injury to injury, Mrs. Harrison came down with the flu in June of that same year and passed away on July 3rd. Emma was more prepared for this loss, in fact she had been bracing for it any day for the last twenty-two years, but still… Mrs. Harrison had made Emma the executrix of her estate so the next few weeks were filled with many duties and they at least occupied her mind.

Emma was all alone in the world. Susan and Luna, neither of whom married, moved back to Richmond in the late seventies and lived across town, but then Susan moved west when the railroads were completed and finally settled in Southern California in 1893.

"What part of California? Do we know where that was?" Taylor was seeing the light at the end of the tunnel.

Grandpa liked this part too. "Sure. You've been there. They call it the Arboretum now."

Taylor gasped, "In Arcadia? On Baldwin Avenue! That's her cousin?"

Grandpa nodded, "Yep, Lucky Baldwin was a distant cousin. We think she stayed in the guest house they use in all the movies. You remember Fantasy Island? 'Ze plane! 'Ze plane!'" Taylor had no clue what he was talking about. "Never mind. Anyway, Susan heard what had happened in Richmond and sent word that Emma should come and visit."

After Mrs. Harrison died, Luna became concerned about Emma and dropped by one Saturday to keep Emma company. They chatted on Mrs. Harrison's porch for hours as they watched the butterflies flit about from flower to flower in the garden. In truth, it was Emma's flower garden, porch and house now as Mrs. Harrison left them to her in the will along with most everything in the house and five thousand dollars; the rest of her estate went to charity. That, coupled with the eleven thousand Emma had saved while working and living rent free for twenty-two years, meant that she had no need to work any longer. Sixteen thousand dollars in 1894 was a virtual fortune when the value of her five bedroom house and two acres of land was assessed at $3,500.

She had so many options now that she had no real responsibilities. She could take up painting or more gardening, she could travel, or she could create church and school programs for children like she always wanted. Maybe she could do it all. But even Luna could see the emptiness in her eyes, the eyes of a woman who had little to live for. She suggested that they travel out to California to visit Susan.

Emma tried to be polite. "That's a very nice offer, Luna, but it's a very long trip."

Luna squealed, "That's the fun of it. We can see the sights; St. Louis, Yellowstone, the Grand Canyon..."

"Luna, Yellowstone isn't on the way."

"Well, I was never very good at geometry." Luna was a little confused but she was used to it. "And besides, you've never even been out of Indiana."

"I've been to Ohio."

Luna apologized, "I forgot. But that's what, a mile and a half?"

"It would be very expensive."

"You're the richest woman I know."

Emma waved her off. "Oh, I am not."

"You've been working for twenty years and haven't spent a penny. Now you have all this."

"Who will take care of the house?"

"Well, Little Miss Money Bags will just have to hire someone."

Emma was running out of excuses. "I don't know."

Luna flashed that toothy grin. "You'd be with me."

Emma turned to her with one raised eyebrow and they both had a good laugh. Finally, Emma sighed and admitted, "I have always wanted to see an ocean."

"I think they have one of those!"

"Yes, Luna, it's called the Pacific."

"Who cares what they call it. Let's just go and stick our feet in it."

Emma thought for a moment. "That would be fun."

Luna held out her hand to shake on it. "Then you'll go?"

Emma had a lot of work to do to get ready for her trip. The plan was for the ladies to leave Richmond in early October and stay in California at least through the winter. That meant her new home needed caretakers for up to six months.

That task felt quite peculiar to her. Twenty-two years ago she had answered an ad for a maid at this same address and then added gardener to her resume as the time went on. Now she was in the odd place of standing on the other side of the same door as other young people came calling to answer her own ad.

She found two suitable candidates and set on the next task of acquiring the proper travel accessories for the long trip. She'd never gone anywhere so she needed suitcases, traveling attire and whatever else traveling people needed. The research into such things was nearly a full-time job on its own. After asking around, she was told that one indispensable element for the long journey would be reading material.

Emma intended to buy a newspaper at every stop along the way. Luna didn't read much, but she bought a copy of the October edition of every magazine she could get her hands on.

They agreed that they would limit themselves to two suitcases each and that each of the bags needed to be light enough that they could be lifted onto a carriage by the two of them without help. That limited them to one hat each of course, and that would have to be worn on the trip.

Finally, the big day arrived. Emma's furniture was dutifully covered with sheets, instructions were given to her caretakers and the carriage to the train station arrived right on time.

By the time they arrived in St. Louis and the first leg of the journey had been completed, Luna had already perused all of the pictures in her magazines. As they set off toward Kansas City the next day she figured she might try reading them to pass the time and came across a very familiar name in her copy of Harper's Bazar.

"Emma, isn't your cousin Alice's married name Brotherton?"

That was certainly out of left-field, even for Luna. "Yes. Why do you ask?"

Luna was trying to put the pieces together. "When did you see her last?"

Emma thought for a moment. "I suppose it was at her wedding."

"When was that?"

"I'm going to say it was in seventy-five. No, it was fall of seventy-six because I had to get excused from work to make the trip to Cincinnati and I had just started in July at the bicentennial celebration. That's a long time ago. Why do you ask?"

"How are you related again? She's your father's niece?"

Emma reacted to Luna's scrunched up nose. "Yes, Uncle Alfred is my father's only sibling that lived and she is his only child. I'm afraid it's all up to Garr to carry on the Williams name." She laughed and then asked again, "At the risk of repeating myself, why do you ask?"

Luna was getting a little excited. "Did I hear that she was a writer?"

Emma was getting a bit frustrated at Luna's non-answer answers. "She certainly had the knack for it. I heard something about her writing poetry for the Atlantic Monthly but I've never read anything she's written."

Luna got a big toothy grin on her face and giggled conspiratorially, "Would you like to?" She pointed to the article in Harper's and handed it to Emma.

Emma's eyes lit up as she saw the article. As she started to read she realized that Alice was writing about their grandmother Rebecca. Tears streamed down her face as she read.

Harper's Bazar
Saturday, October 6, 1894
On the Porch
By Alice Williams Brotherton

Twas too far to walk to Meeting
And the horses had to plough
John won't take them from the furrow
For the Fourth-day Meeting now

So I've had to give up going
But I always come out here
To keep the hour of Meeting
An' to feel the Presence near

I know I'm growing feeble
An' Maria is quite right;
Though I hadn't been sick in Meeting
Yet 'most any time I might

So I tidy frock and apron
And put on my sheerest cap
And sit out on the side porch
With the Bible on my lap

I'll put the hard thoughts from my heart
And in the stillness wait
For the comfort an' the message
To all who meditate

The Book falls open at the text
"I will lift up mine eyes
Unto the hills, whence cometh help"
Why! That is a surprise!

Why, all the livelong morning
I've been thinking of the hills
I was born an' raised among 'em
How that mock-bird's carol trills!

There was one beside the spring house
When Josiah came to me
Where I stood a-churning butter
On that day in Tennessee

His father was a minister
Had preached for Friends, First-day
In Lost Creek Meetin'-house
An' they had mount' to ride away

ARCHIE AND EMMA

When Josiah, from the stirrup,
Turned back to get a drink
From the old spring by the dairy
With the moss upon its brink

I can see his eyes n-twinkle
As I held the dripping gourd
"Thee is like Rebekah at the Well
Now, does thee mind the word

Which Eliezer brought her?"
And I felt my hot cheek blush.
It was then the mock-bird's treble
Broke the early morning hush

"Will thee come with me, Rebecca?"
Said Josiah, in my ear.
"I've an inward drawing to thee.
Will thee be my wife, my dear?"

A "Yes," a kiss, and then he went
We met no more at all
Till the week that we were wedded
At Friend's Meeting, in the fall.

Tut, tut! This is too foolish!
Let me think upon the Word;
Not let my thoughts go drifting off
At carol of a bird

"I will lift mine eyes unto the hills"
Th' flat country looked strange
From my father's porch we looked
Right up to the old Smoky range

I could see him as he journeyed
Up the mountain road they went
To attend a Monthly Meeting
Up to Pine Creek Settlement

We came 'way out to Ohio
While I was yet a bride
Were living here nigh forty year
An' then Josiah died

"I will lift mine eyes" at evening
When the clouds mass in the west
They look like the hills of heaven
Nigh the City of the Blest

"Whence cometh help!" I like to think
The call will come to me
Josiah's self the messenger
"Come up; we wait for thee."

Oh, there must be hills in heaven!
He will come down from the heights
And we'll climb up from the valley
Till we see the heavenly lights

Ah, the weary years of waiting!
But "the time will seem not long"
When we hear the mock-bird's carol
Mingle with the angels' song

Emma had been wonderfully reunited in verse with her beloved grandmother after twenty-six years. Rebecca's stories of her whirlwind romance with Hezekiah had been so beautifully and faithfully recounted by her cousin that all of those blessed times they shared together rushed back through her heart. Alice was eight years older than Emma and had moved to Cincinnati before Emma was old enough to know her, but she had evidently spent a good deal of time with Grandma Becky too. Emma resolved to write to her and compare stories to see if there were any more nuggets she could gather.

The rest of the trip was spent reminiscing about Grandmother and virtually memorizing the poem. But for all of the wonderful memories it conjured up it also reminded Emma of the many losses in her life: Rebecca, her mother, her sister, Mrs. Harrison and, of course, her own whirlwind romance. As they headed for Los Angeles with only the rhythm of the rails as a soundtrack, Emma allowed herself to imagine for the first time in a long time what it would be like to see him just once more.

33

I Used My Head, Coach

The Cub's new pitcher was no better than the last one and, with the score now 14-13 in the bottom of the sixth and final inning, the bases were still loaded with one out and a 3-2 count on the batter. Grandpa and Taylor were on their feet cheering for good old what's-his-name, number eight.

"C'mon kid! You can do it." Grandpa shouted.

"What's his name?" Taylor yelled at Grandpa.

Grandpa grunted, "I don't know."

So Taylor shouted, "C'mon number eight!"

The pitcher stared in at the catcher for the sign. Evidently the sign the catcher gave him roughly translated to "Throw a strike, you moron!" That didn't exactly help his confidence. Tentatively, he wound up and aimed the ball like he was shooting darts and the ball bounced two feet in front of the plate. The umpire barked, "Take your base!" and Nick's side of the grandstands erupted in celebration.

Taylor yelled, "Good going kid!"

Grandpa was beside himself. "They did it! I knew they'd do it!"

Taylor, the voice of reason, tried to dampen his enthusiasm, "It's just a tie, Grandpa."

"Sure, but they've never done that before!"

Then like dark storm clouds appearing overhead, threatening to turn celebration into mourning, Nick stepped into the on deck circle.

"Is that Nick with a bat?" Taylor shrieked. "He already struck out once. Does he have to do it again? This next kid is pretty good isn't he? I mean Nick won't have to bat again, will he?"

Taylor was beginning to hyperventilate a little. The only thing worse than being the least talented player on the team would be striking out to end the best chance the team would have all season of earning a victory.

Grandpa assessed the situation. "There's only one out so unless there's a double play or this kid wins it right now, Nick will bat."

Alex, number twelve, was one of the bigger kids on the team, and one of its best hitters. You could forgive him for being a little excited. This was the first time all year he had a chance to win a game. This was his time. He promised his coach that he'd "get 'er done" as he walked to the plate. He had to do this himself, what with the worst hitter in the history of baseball on deck.

Now an older, more seasoned player would recognize that all of the pressure to throw strikes was on the pitcher, who at this point would have a hard time hitting the floor with his hat. Wisdom would say that Alex should take a few pitches and make the boy prove he could throw the ball over the plate; after all, another walk would end the game. Even just solid contact anywhere on the field would win the game, but baseball brings out the dreamer in all of us and Alex could already see in his mind's eye his triumphal trot around the bases after he sent the first pitch screaming over the scoreboard in left field.

Alex dug into the batter's box and with a confident smile he stared out at the pitcher, daring him to throw one by him. The boy on the mound was shaking in his cleats. He was positive that he was about to lose the game and incur the wrath of his teammates and coach, who had all strangely ceased shouting words of encouragement his way.

The pitcher wound up and hurled a fast ball right down the heart of the plate. Alex reared back and swung with all of his might and sent the ball screaming - straight up. The Cubs fans cheered and called out to the catcher to catch the ball, as if that wasn't his plan all along. He got himself into position to make the catch but made one important error; he forgot to take off his mask. Catchers are taught to take off their masks and fling them some distance away on a pop up so they can see the ball better and so they won't trip over the mask. If the mask is still on your face you certainly won't trip over it but you may lose sight of the ball as it crosses through the bars on your face.

The catcher looked straight up for the ball, held his glove up over his head, and lost sight of it. He signaled to teammates that he couldn't see it and just then the ball hit him flush in the face. It was a good thing he was wearing a mask. But what happened next was a first for nearly everyone present; the ball stuck in the boy's mask.

The pitcher fished the ball out of the mask and held it up for the umpire who bellowed, "Yer out!" The crowds on both sides were stunned. One side cheered when the ball was struck, the other side cheered when it went straight up, the first side cheered again when it hit him in the face and the second cheered when it stuck in his mask.

After all of the commotion had died down, Grandpa leaned over to Taylor and said, "Now two out, bases loaded, tie score and here comes Nick. That's every young boy's dream."

"Or nightmare," Taylor said while biting her recently manicured nails. Then she yelled, "Come on, Nick! You can do it!"

"Come on, Nicky!" Grandpa screamed.

Now Nick wasn't really the worst hitter baseball had ever seen; in fact back in a younger division when the coach still pitched to his team, he batted over .400 and made an all-star team, but as the pitching sped up his vision problems made it more and more difficult to keep up. He really couldn't see the ball until it was past him. He often said he'd be better off closing his eyes and listening for it.

But what he lacked in skill, he more than made up for in smarts, and he had a plan. Unlike Alex, Nick had no delusions of grandeur about getting a game-winning hit; he was up there to get a game-winning walk. He figured that with a pitcher that lacked both experience and confidence he'd trick him into walking him by making the plate move on him.

As he stepped into the box the crowds on both sides were going wild, but Nick couldn't hear a thing; he was focused on the plan. For the first pitch he stood as far away from the plate as he legally could. He was so far away that a pitch six inches inside would be out of reach, but in the heat of the moment both the pitcher and the catcher adjusted to Nick rather than the plate, and the first pitch came whizzing in a foot inside off the dish.

"Ball one!" yelled the man in blue.

The coach screamed at his pitcher to throw the ball over the plate, but Nick had now moved as far back in the box and as close to the catcher as he could. He hoped this would make the plate look further away to the novice pitcher. When the boy threw his pitch, it was high when it crossed the plate. *Mission accomplished.*

"Ball two!"

The coach was tearing what was left of his hair out and signaled to the umpire that he was going to the mound. Only the coach, catcher and pitcher know what was said in that meeting, but from the look on the young pitcher's face it didn't appear to be particularly helpful for his psyche.

Nick moved way up toward the mound to give the pitcher another look to deal with. The third pitch came inside and Nick tried to get his hands out of the way, but the ball hit the bat and trickled down the first base line. Nick started to run, but by the time he got out of the box the ball had rolled foul.

"Two and one!"

As he walked back to the plate it occurred to him that a walk wasn't the only way to get on; getting hit would do the trick as well. He picked up his bat and stood as close to the plate as he possibly could and get away with it. Then he told himself that if the ball came inside instead of getting out of the way he'd back up toward the catcher. This way he would appear to be avoiding the ball but still get hit. It's the strategy that people use when running with the bulls in Pamplona. Instead of turning right or left when given the chance, they try to outrun the bulls. It's just as dumb to try to outrun a baseball, but it would be a winning strategy in this case.

The pitcher wound up and threw the next pitch into the dirt, and it got behind the catcher a little bit. Nick quickly held up his hand to tell the runner on third not to try to score, which was wise.

"Three and one!"

Now Nick wasn't going to swing no matter what. He dug into the box right up on top of the plate again and braced for impact. The pitcher wound up and threw one right down Broadway.

"Count's full!"

The whole field was in chaos, everyone was yelling and cheering, but it came down to two little boys with two different jobs to do: the pitcher had to throw the ball over the plate, and the hitter couldn't let him.

Taylor screamed, "Come on, Nicky!"

Nick dug in again. This time he had to at least foul off any pitch that might be a strike and not swing at anything that wasn't; a tall order when you can't really see it.

The pitcher started his wind up and the whole field went silent. The ball hurtled toward Nick and then something happened that hadn't happened all season; he saw the ball clearly; because it was about to hit him in the face. At the last second he turned his head just enough for the ball to hit his helmet's earflap. It slammed into him with a thud. It struck him with such force that it knocked the helmet right off his head and he fell face first into the dirt.

The crowd on Nick's side went crazy for a second and then quickly quieted down as they realized that the child might be injured. Nick stayed sprawled in the dirt as his coach ran out to tend to him. He got down on his hands and knees and spoke softly to Nick, "Are you all right, son?"

Nick was doing a little inventory silently to himself, *Okay, I can hear. Can I see?* He opened his eyes for a moment and confirmed they were still operational. With everything functioning properly he turned his head slightly toward his coach and said, "I used my head, Coach."

The coach breathed a huge sigh of relief and Nick started to sit up. Reflexively, the whole crowd cheered and then one half of the crowd continued their interrupted celebration, except for Nick's mother of course who had already hopped a fence and was racing toward home plate. She arrived just as Nick was hoisted up on the shoulders of some of his teammates. They began shouting his name. "Nick! Nick! Nick!" The coach yelled for them to come over to the dugout to start the cheer for the other team. Unfortunately, they forgot for a moment that Nick was perched on their shoulders and promptly dropped him on his head. Baseball is a lot like life that way. One moment you're on top of the world and in the next you're face first in the dirt.

Grandpa and Taylor rejoined the celebration themselves and then Taylor sighed with satisfaction and said, "Wow! That was a great game!"

Grandpa was equally pleased. "It sure was. It's never over 'til it's over." Then he gave Taylor a little look and said, "Glad I kept score." He started to collect his things. "Suppose we should pack up."

Taylor started to join him for a moment and then stopped in her tracks. "Wait a minute! We're not leaving until you finish the story!"

With a wry smile he objected, "But the game's over."

Taylor looked him right in the eye and in a voice that made no bones about who was now in charge she said, "Sit!" and pointed him to his chair. So they sat.

Grandpa picked up where he left off. "Where were we? Ah yes, Luna convinced Emma to go visit Susan in California with her. They stayed at Lucky Baldwin's ranch and one day they decided to take a sightseeing trip to Los Angeles."

"How old were they now, Grandpa?"

He answered, "Emma was thirty-eight and Archie was forty-three."

34

Ring Fingers and Tar Pits

December 22, 1894

By 1894, Archie had called Los Angeles home for six years and had watched it transform before his eyes from a sleepy cow town to a bustling city. Los Angeles was experiencing a bit of a boom. In the 1890 census approximately fifty thousand people claimed the City of the Angels as their home, but by 1900 the total of Angelinos had doubled, in part due to the discovery of oil in 1892 near Chavez Ravine - what is now Dodger Stadium.

It was December 22nd, 1894 and the L.A.P.D. was out in force assisting the citizenry as they negotiated their Christmas shopping. Archie was assigned that crisp Saturday morning day to direct traffic on his usual beat at the intersection of First and Main streets. To modern ears that might not seem like much of a task given that the automobile was still in its fledgling stages and hadn't reached the west coast yet. Cars would surely make Archie's life more difficult in later years, but he still had plenty to contend with.

In addition to the unusually heavy foot traffic for the Christmas season, bicycles were the new rage. Being that they were a relatively new addition to the roadways, enthusiasm for the new toys was much more advanced than either operator skill or any corresponding traffic laws. There were also the usual horse and buggy operators trotting past, and the real danger; the horseless streetcar. There were many rail companies vying for business in those days and crossing Archie's path at First and Main were both a cable line and a new electric operation. Archie's task was to keep the pedestrians from getting run over by bicycles, the pedestrians and bicycles from getting hit by horse drawn carriages and all of them from being hit by streetcars. He had his hands full.

Adding to his headache, First and Main was a very busy corner. Today it is the site of the L.A. City Hall, but even then it was the center of the city. Just a couple of blocks up Main Street, where it forked into Spring Street, was a major shopping district, including the First National Bank and the Farmers and Merchant Bank. Then a block closer was the U.S. Hotel. Down the other direction on Second and Main was St. Vibiana's Cathedral and the Westminster Hotel. Archie was flanked on his corner by the Grand Opera House and The Natick House, a swanky new hotel. If daily mass at St. Vibiana's got out at the same time as an opera, the streets looked like a modern day Times Square at lunchtime.

Little did Archie know as he stood there waving his arms at the oncoming traffic that from that day on his life and the life of his family four generations hence would be tied to that very plot of ground. John's poultry supply store was just down the street, but in 1901 he would move into the Natick House and become the Natick Hotel Bookstore. The business would pass to Archie's son and stay in the Natick House until 1950 when the hotel was demolished. Grandpa started working for his father when he was in high school and helped move it to Fourth and Spring that year. He took it over and ran "Natick Store" in that location until the 80's when his son joined the firm. When the game winning centerfielder was born, he was raised in the store's final location in Monrovia until the turn of the millennium. The store finally closed its doors in the late 2000's after more than 120 years in operation.

Archie's relationship with Emma's memory was on again, off again. He had remembered to pray for her every night, for the most part, and most often prayed for her happiness and that of her husband and children. He felt in a strange way that her children were somehow his and hoped that he'd get to meet them some day. In '92 he had an odd sense that he should double his efforts in praying for her and her parents, so he did. Praying for her was always painful, but it was the only way he could be involved in her life.

Susan was thrilled when Emma and Luna arrived just before Thanksgiving. She had tired of her cousin Lucky Baldwin, a recurring theme in his life, and looked forward to reuniting with real family. The grounds of the Baldwin property weren't as lush and cultivated as they are in their current state as the Los Angeles County Arboretum and Botanical Garden, but still a sight to see. They stayed in the Queen Ann Cottage, then known as "Baldwin's Belvedere," perched on the shore of horseshoe-shaped Baldwin Lake. The women became quite enamored with sitting on the porch and watching the aquatic birds and peacocks frolic in this little desert oasis.

She had only been in California for a month, but Emma was already falling in love. After growing up in the cold of the Midwest, December mornings in the mid-seventies seemed like living in paradise. The weather, the dry air and the beauty of the surrounding mountains made Emma seriously consider staying on a while, if she could find the right excuse.

It wasn't until mid-December that Susan convinced Emma to take a trip into the big city to see the sights. Luna was especially excited to see the La Brea Tar Pits and wanted to watch the University of Southern California Methodists play football; they weren't called the Trojans until 1912. Emma offered to pay for their trip and lodging, though she wasn't aware that the "quaint little house" that Susan had picked out, the U.S. Hotel, was among the more expensive accommodations in the city.

They arrived in Los Angeles by train the afternoon of Wednesday the 19th and spent that evening settling into their hotel. None of them had ever been any place quite like it. They were treated like royalty with a footman to attend to their bags and even an elevator man to work the hand-cranked contraption.

They settled on visiting USC on Friday and spent Thursday exploring the downtown area and getting their own Christmas shopping done. The stores in Los Angeles were a veritable wonderland compared to Richmond. Siegel, under the Nadeau Hotel at First and Spring, was the largest clothing store Emma had ever seen, and just next door Edward T. Cook the bookseller was having a sale on Bibles that drew Emma in. In the early 1880's, the new English Revised Version of the Bible had been published as the first serious competitor to the traditional King James Version. Few of the booksellers in Richmond were carrying it, so she thought she'd take a look at it. She bought six. Then they stopped at the Meyberg Brothers, Desmond's and J.T. Sheward's and toted away more bags than they could handle.

While they were out, Emma picked up a Los Angeles Herald and saw an ad for a Saturday matinee showing of the Merchant of Venice at the new Los Angeles Theater, but her cousins wanted no part of it. Then she noticed an article saying that General William Booth, founder of the Salvation Army, was arriving in town on Saturday and there would be a parade down Grand Street. They all agreed that they would take the day to see the Tar Pits and then come back and hear General Booth at the Salvation Army barracks at 8 P.M. He would be speaking on his social work project "The Darkest England Social Scheme."

That Saturday morning the ladies wandered up Main Street from their hotel trying to find a rail line that would take them out to Rancho La Brea. Luna's map said the closest intersection was First and Main.

Luna turned the map around a couple of times and declared, "The train stop should be right here somewhere."

By this time Susan had remembered why she left Indiana. "It won't be a catastrophe if we don't see the tar pits today, Luna."

Luna said, "Where's your spirit of adventure?"

Emma was already pretty tired and answered, "I traveled two thousand miles with you. It's probably somewhere between St. Louis and Albuquerque."

Susan had an idea. "Why don't we just sit down for a bit and have a snack?"

Emma agreed, "We must have walked five miles yesterday; my feet still hurt. I could use a rest."

Luna was concerned. "You're not giving up on me are you?"

Susan calmed her fears. "We're just taking a break. Let's ask someone where a good place to eat would be."

Luna pointed into the building in front of them. "I'm sure the Natick House has a restaurant."

Emma waved her off. "No, I'm tired of hotel food. I'll just ask this policeman."

She walked a couple of yards over to the corner and reached way up to tap the giant police officer on the shoulder. "Excuse me, sir. We're from out of town. Would you know where we could get a quick bite to eat?"

Archie whipped around like he had heard a ghost. Though decades had passed, he recognized that voice as if they had never been apart. He looked down at her and saw a slightly older, slightly larger version of the girl who had haunted his dreams night after night for twenty-two years. His pulse started to pound. He tried to speak, but his heart was in his throat. All he could muster was a faint, "Emma?"

His sudden movement had startled her. When she got her feet back under her and looked up at him again she recognized him immediately. He was every bit as handsome as the day he left, but even in just a glance she could see in his face a man who had known the harshest of sorrows. She could barely breathe. "Archie?"

He couldn't help the silly, boyish grin that was taking over his face, but he didn't care; the world was again spinning in its proper orbit.

Her whole life before she lost him flashed before her eyes until the joy that she once knew daily was washing over her again for the first time.

They were both completely lost in this moment of truly historic proportions.

How was this even possible? How could they lose each other for so long and then run into each other at random thousands of miles away? This accidental encounter seemed more like design.

Suddenly they woke from their mutual fog and realized that they were no longer children and that the other must have a real life. They backed away a bit in embarrassment.

Susan and Luna recognized him too and made their way over to the corner. Luna, ever the pragmatist, took a not-so-subtle peek at Archie's left hand. Archie laughed uncomfortably and held it up to show off his naked ring finger.

Emma fainted dead away.

35
How Many Times?

Emma landed in a heap at Luna's feet and Susan dove to the ground to keep her head from hitting the cement sidewalk. Archie didn't know what to do, but her reaction to seeing him gave reason for hope.

They were drawing a crowd, so Susan did her best to wake Emma and then slowly brought her to her feet in a few moments as she saw Emma's eyes start to clear. She whispered, "He's real, sweetheart. He's really here."

As Emma stood and tried to regain her composure Archie blurted out, "You're just as lovely as I imagined you."

Emma was afraid that if she tried to speak she'd hit the pavement again, so she took Susan's hand and gestured for her to do the talking as she had when she and Archie had met again for the first time so many years ago. Another advantage of this arrangement was that if Susan did the talking Emma wouldn't have to take her eyes off Archie.

Susan tried to start a conversation. "When did you come to Los Angeles, Archie?"

Archie replied succinctly, "In '88." Evidently, his skill in repartee had not developed much further in twenty years. The truth was he couldn't take his eyes off Emma either; not much had changed.

Archie's face had been thoroughly burned into Emma's mind's eye, but that had been so long ago that her memory was filling in the blanks with this new image. She noticed several new features; the most concerning to her being a scar over his right eye. That had to have a story behind it.

Susan tried again. "And you never married?"

Archie could see the sadness in Emma's eyes as they welled up. His enduring picture of her was that dreadful day on the street corner in Cambridge as she tried to hold back the floodgates. Here they were all over again. All he could say was, "No."

This wasn't going anywhere, so Luna blurted out, "Neither did Emma!"

Susan laughed a little, and Archie's heart nearly stopped.

Luna continued, "Not that she didn't have offers. She was proposed to fifty-two times."

Susan corrected her, "Fifty-four."

"I'm sorry, fifty-four times."

Archie was dumbfounded. "Why did you not accept them?"

Emma reached into her dress pocket and pulled out his handkerchief with the monogram and showed it to him as Susan explained, "You can't marry a man when you're still in love with another."

"So you've really stayed single all these years?" He caught himself, realizing that he was being far too forward, and tried to backpedal. "That is, uh, well, I mean to say..."

Susan jumped in to save him. "Yes, she has."

With a little indignation Luna carped, "She's been waiting for you for twenty-two years! You're very late!"

They all, even Emma, had a good laugh that broke the tension.

Archie felt like nothing at all had changed and then asked his most difficult question, "And the Society?"

Susan was happy to answer. "Emma's been attending the Presbyterian Church for years."

Emma tilted her head and looked deep into his eyes in a way that communicated all he needed to know.

He straightened his jacket and said, "Then we've wasted enough time." With that he dropped to a knee, removed his hat, and placed it under one arm.

Luna and Susan squealed and backed away to leave them alone, which sent Emma reeling. She could barely stand but Archie grabbed her hand and steadied her. As their hands touched, chills went through each of them and time stopped for a moment as they both stared at their hands finding their proper place after all of these years. Her hand disappeared into his just like it had that evening at the opera house.

Archie regained his composure and began, "Emma, I once asked what I would ever do without you. Well, I found out, and it was no good." Archie's voice cracked. He pulled himself back together for a moment but the rest of his speech sounded like it was being delivered by an adolescent going through the change. "I have been through terrible days when the only thing that kept me going, I'm embarrassed to say, was the thought that you might still love me. That thought saved my life more times than I can count. I don't want to ever be without you again. Will you marry me?"

Emma couldn't respond. She was numb. All of her years of loneliness, the misery she had committed herself to, and the doubts that had taunted her day and night started to depart her like dark spirits at an exorcism. She looked at the hankie in her hand that represented all of those wasted years and then threw it to the ground and said forcefully, "How many times do I need to say yes?"

Archie began to weep. "Then you will?"

She dropped to her knees right there on the street corner, grabbed his giant face in her hands and pressed her lips to his. What ensued was the most passionate kiss in the history of kisses. It may have only lasted a moment or two but both of them seemed to be trapped in a timeless state. Though they were kneeling on a crowded street corner the only thing that mattered, really the only thing that existed, were the two of them and this new creation that had just been brought back into being, "Them."

As this embrace continued it became quite the spectacle; this was

1894 after all and this kind of thing didn't happen in public. Susan became more and more embarrassed until she muttered under her breath, "Oh my."

Then Luna asked Susan with concern, "What do you think her answer will be?"

36

The Way You Deserve

Taylor sat back in her chair and sighed like she had just taken a bite of one of Grandma's famous Christmas cookies. "That should put me in a good mood for a month."

Grandpa had a rather satisfied look on his face too. He never got tired of telling that story, but he wasn't quite done with Taylor yet. "That was December 22nd. They were married on New Year's Day."

Taylor started doing the math. "That's like…"

Like a man trying to catch a train Grandpa interrupted, "Ten days later, yes."

Taylor smiled. "I guess he was right when he said he didn't want to waste any more time."

"My dad was born in '96; she named him Archie, of course, and gave him the middle name George after her brother. Then my aunt was born in '99 and she named her Mary Ina after her sister."

Taylor started to get up from her chair and bent down to give Grandpa a hug. "That story was so wonderful, Grandpa. Thank you for telling it to me."

Grandpa said, "Well, we're not quite done."

Taylor dove back into her chair. "More?"

Grandpa leaned in conspiratorially, "Maybe the best part. Emma's relationship with her father had never truly recovered, though they had learned to be cordial, especially when her mother passed, but she wrote to tell him about the wedding… and he showed up. In fact, he showed up and never left. He stayed with them until his death in '98."

Taylor scrunched up her nose a bit. "He stayed with them? Like, in their house?"

"Well back then families tended to stay together. Her sister Mary Ina and her new husband came to live with them not long after as well."

Taylor seemed a bit relieved. "I love happily-ever-afters."

They started to get up and break down their chairs and gather up their belongings. Grandpa had one eye on Taylor and then after a silent debate with himself he asked, "So, do you take anything else away from this story?"

"You mean like a moral, Grandpa?"

"Yes."

Taylor stopped what she was doing and looked to the sky as she thought out loud, "Well, I guess there's a lot of 'em. What do you think it is?"

Grandpa was ready with his answer. "That you're the fairest and purest creature God has ever created and you don't need to waste your time with punks who aren't capable of loving you the way you deserve." There, he said it.

Taylor had been hit right where she lived, but she couldn't help loving Grandpa for it. She looked to the ground, smiled and said, "I didn't get that from the story."

"I may have added a little of my own."

Taylor curled up her nose in frustration and said, "You're right, Grandpa. Carter is a punk."

"What do you see in him?" Grandpa asked.

"I don't know." In a moment of clarity Taylor diagnosed her own issue. "I guess he's...there, you know?"

Grandpa took her hand and looked her right in the eye. "Do you think so little of yourself that he's the best you can do?"

Speaking for teenage girls everywhere, Taylor said, "Don't we all?"

Grandpa had an idea. "Do you want me to call him for you?"

"No, that's okay, Grandpa."

"It's no trouble, sweetheart."

"Really..."

"It would give me great pleasure."

Grandpa laughed in a way that Taylor thought might have bordered on the maniacal. "I'm sure it would but I'll call him when I get home. Thank you, Grandpa, for everything."

"You're welcome, sweetheart."

They gathered the rest of their things and started their way up the hill to the street. Then Taylor asked, "How come my dad never told me that story?"

"He's a bum." Grandpa said with a chuckle. Imagining a look on Taylor's face that wasn't there he added, "J.K."

Taylor was still focused on the story. "So how long did they have together?"

Grandpa knew this was going to be hard to hear so he stopped walking and looked her in the eye. "Well, not long I'm afraid. Archie died of a heart attack in 1907, so they only had twelve years together."

Taylor fought back tears.

Grandpa said, "Well, honey, God only promises us forever, not tomorrow."

"How long was she alone?"

"Grandma lived until 1927, so she was without him again for another twenty years." He saw that she was losing the point of the story so he explained, "You know, sweetheart, it's a very different thing to lose the love of your life when you don't know if you'll ever see them again than to lose your love when you know you'll see them real soon."

37

November 15, 1927

Thirty-one-year-old Archibald George Mercer headed home at noontime to check on his mother and make her some lunch. Seventy-one-year-old Emma was living with her son these days and had been feeling a little under the weather for a week or two. Archie was beginning to worry about her a bit.

He left Natick Store on First and Main and grabbed a Yellow Car, the new electric train system, and headed for home down Pico Boulevard. When he walked in he found Emma right where he'd left her that morning, in her chair facing the front window sifting through a box of old letters and clippings she had asked him to get down from the attic late the previous week.

"Hello Momma. How are you feeling?"

Emma took off her reading glasses and said, "Oh, the same as usual. Old."

Archie headed toward the kitchen. "I came home to make you some lunch."

Emma called him back. "Before you do that, look at what I found." She pulled out an old newspaper clipping.

Archie took it from her and scanned the yellowing fragment. "Pop's obituary?"

"Not really," Emma said, "It's the announcement of his passing. Page two in the Sunday paper. It was a wonderful tribute. They mention you and your sister."

Archie started to read,

Los Angeles Herald
Sunday Morning, May 26, 1907

PATROLMAN DIES OF
HEART DISEASE

FALLS DEAD TALKING
TO A FRIEND

Had Been Member of Force
Since 1889
and Was Favorite with Supe-
rior Officers and Fel-
low Police

Patrolman Archie Mercer of the local police force dropped dead from heart disease in front of his new house, 1052 Dewey avenue, at 2:15 yesterday afternoon.

Mercer had been telling John T. Buchanan, one of his old friends, how he wanted alterations made in his house. They walked out to the sidewalk and began joshing about a fishing trip which they intended taking. Mercer suddenly reeled and said, "Oh, John!" and fell dead before his friend. The body was taken to Pierce Bros' undertaking parlors.

Mercer was 56 years of age and lived with his family at 1238 Dewey avenue. For some time he had been suffering from pleural asthma, but seemed to have recovered and expected to return to his old beat on North Spring and Main streets.

Mercer was one of the oldest men in service. He was first appointed on May 15, 1889, when he was given star No. 11.

Was Popular Officer

In all the years he has been on the force he made many friends and was known as a man of the highest integrity. He was liked by all his fellow officers and by his superiors for his quiet, unassuming manner.

Mercer leaves a wife and two children, the eldest of which is a boy 10 years old and the younger a girl 6 years old. His family will receive $1000 from the police relief fund. This is supposed to be the only insurance Mercer carried.

A touching incident occurred when Captain Auble went to the place to get the body of his old friend. Mercer's little daughter, a tot of 6 years, went to the garden and picked a bunch of simple flowers. She went up to the officer and gave them to him saying: "Please put these on papa, won't you?"

Emma said, "That is my favorite picture of him. He always looked so handsome in that uniform."

"Are you well, Momma?"

Emma took her handkerchief from her pocket and dabbed her eyes a bit. "I just miss him today more than the ordinary."

"Let me run and get you a sandwich. What else would you like?"

"A cup of tea would be nice. I have a chill."

As she waited for Archie, she pulled a stack of letters from the box and started to pick through them to find her favorite. Since the year he passed, she'd maintained a ritual each fall and winter of reading every one of the letters Archie had kept. During spring cleaning, they went back up in the attic so she could focus on cheerier things, but the letters helped her not feel so alone during the holiday season.

Being a single mother of two small children for many years had kept her so busy that she didn't have time to reflect on all that life had thrown her way, but after Archie and Ina had left the house she grew rather nostalgic. She knew it was impractical at her age, but she still had dreams of visiting Cambridge and Richmond again. She wanted to lay flowers on her parents' graves – her father would have turned one hundred this year – and perhaps see her beloved hill. If anyone was inclined to believe the impossible it was she. After all, who could have ever dreamed that she would have earned a patent, become a mother at forty, voted in four presidential elections or spent twelve glorious years with the love of her life? She had much to be thankful for. When she looked back, all she saw were the green pastures and still waters. The valleys of the shadow of death were no longer visible.

She still set Archie's place at the dinner table every night and was frequently caught speaking to him out loud, though Archie and Ina had long ago learned not to worry about her or question her about her devotion to him. He had died when they were so young that most of the memories they had of him were hers. And the stories... oh the stories... The stories she told about him and their life together filled the room so vividly that they could almost hear his voice. He had been gone for twenty years but he never left.

Archie returned with her lunch and set it on the little table next to her chair. "Here you go, Momma. I have to run back to the store. Is there anything else I can fetch you?"

"How about a hug? Can you do that for your old mother?" Archie leaned over and gave her a big hug and she whispered in his ear, "I love you, Archie."

"I love you too, Momma. Now be good."

"Oh, you know me."

"Yes, I do know you, so be good." And with that he hopped out the door and darted down the street headed for the train stop.

Emma watched him go and took a sip of her tea. She found her favorite letter, put her handkerchief to her face and breathed him in again as she read.

Somewhere in the Philippine Islands
20th of January, 1881

My Dearest, Darling Emma:

As I sit underneath our moon tonight I am struck by how important this little ritual of mine has become for my own health and state of mind. Many is the day that just the thought of you has kept me going when circumstances have urged me to give up. My one glimmer of hope and consolation through the many tests I have encountered is that someday we will be reunited, whether in this world or the next.

Won't that be a glorious day, that day of all days, when finally our sorrows have ended and our tears have been wiped once and for all from our eyes! "And there shall be no more death, neither sorrow, nor crying, neither shall there be any more pain: for the former things are passed away." "For now we see through a glass, darkly; but then face to face."

She held the letter to her chest and took a deep, halting breath. Then she closed her eyes and they were reunited one last time.

Epilogue

As Eric Metaxas says in his beautiful biography of William Wilberforce, "Inside the small eternity of the book the subject is once again brought to life."

The pure joy I have experienced in facilitating the rebirth of my great-grandparents on these few hundred pages has been perhaps the most rewarding of my career. But it is tempered by the necessity of allowing them to leave us once again at novel's end.

If you have found yourself caught up in their story and shed a tear or two in the last few minutes, then you might understand why I felt it necessary to include this epilogue, if only for personal, therapeutic reasons.

It has not been without the sincerest trepidation that I have endeavored to tell the story of two people I never had the privilege to meet. I hope that they would not only be pleased, but at least recognize themselves just a little bit in my characterizations.

The journey to re-tell their story has taken me to their "former haunts" and transported me back in time to "breathe them in more fully." The tears shed as we toured the Mercer Houses in Cambridge City and New London, stood on Emma's Hill, or sat in what we can only imagine were Archie's sacred places in Connecticut, were a tip of the cap to the profound good that their story has done for my family and those who have allowed us to share it. For their story reminds us once again of the goodness and mercy of our Creator and how, "His eye is on the sparrow and I know He watches me."

As I sit here at my computer with little Thomas' pewter cup sitting on my desk, which has since been inscribed with my name as well as those of my grandfather, father, and soon my son, tears trickle down my face as I try to figure out how to say goodbye.

Perhaps the best way was captured by their daughter, my great-aunt Ina, as she memorialized them on their tombstone, now on display at Rosedale Cemetery in Los Angeles. I leave you with what she wrote:

SAFE IN JESUS

FATHER
ARCHIBALD MERCER
BORN MAR. 23, 1851
DIED MAY 25, 1907
ASLEEP IN JESUS
JOHN 3:16. FOR GOD SO
LOVED THE WORLD, THAT
HE GAVE HIS ONLY
BEGOTTEN SON, THAT
WHOSOEVER BELIEVETH
IN HIM SHOULD NOT
PERISH, BUT HAVE
EVERLASTING LIFE.
SO SHALL WE EVER
BE WITH THE LORD

MOTHER
EMMA F. WILLIAMS
BORN FEB. 22, 1856
DIED NOV. 15, 1927
ASLEEP IN JESUS
I THESS. 4:13 TO 18
FOR IF WE BELIEVE

THAT JESUS DIED
AND ROSE AGAIN,
EVEN SO THEM ALSO
WHICH SLEEP IN JESUS
WILL GOD BRING
WITH HIM.
WHEREFORE COMFORT
ONE ANOTHER
WITH THESE WORDS

Modern Day Slavery

As this book went to press, the Islamist terrorist organization known as ISIS was engaged in the murder of reportedly thousands of men and the kidnapping and enslavement of many more women and children. This is nothing new.

Estimates are that somewhere between twenty and thirty million people today are living in slavery around the world. My guess is that those estimates are conservative. At best, that's about double the number of the Africans who were kidnapped and sold into slavery during the entire two hundred plus years of the African slave trade. Of those enslaved about 75% are in forced labor while the other 25% are sex slaves; over a quarter of these are children.

Children are often sold into slavery by their own parents who can't meet their basic needs. These precious souls around the world need our help.

There are many fine organizations dedicated to fighting this scourge, but I have been a supporter of one of them for the past thirty years and can attest to the profound impact that Compassion International has had on the lives of millions of children worldwide.

Compassion's ministry is focused on the child and his or her physical, medical, educational and spiritual needs with the goal of releasing them from the cycle of poverty in Jesus' name.

I can't recommend them highly enough for their effectiveness and financial integrity. They are an organization worthy of your support. So please join me in the struggle to abolish modern day slavery by visiting www.compassion.com.

Acknowledgements

When my father, or as you know him, Grandpa, told us the foundation of this story at Christmas a number of years ago, my jaw about hit the ground. I had heard a few things from my great-aunt Ina near the end of her life, but in her state I wasn't completely sure what was truth and fiction. If my dad hadn't passed the story along to us that night it might have been lost forever.

I immediately went to work researching the tale and re-telling it in theatrical form. We produced the stage play in 2008 at Azusa Pacific University, and then I started on the book to go with it. During research for the novel I made many new discoveries and rewrote the play for the Telemachus Society production of it in 2011. It has since been re-written again for a touring version of the show, and with the completion of the novel I will likely take yet another crack at it.

The book has inspired the play and the play and its players have inspired the book. I would be remiss to not acknowledge the fine work of the actors and technicians who have made this story come to life on stage over the years and how they have significantly informed the final product you hold in your hands.

At the risk of omitting someone, I am indebted to the following artists; Andrea, Allie, Gabrielle, Jennifer C., Michaele, Ashley, Bri, Ethan, Kaylee, Jessica, Sarah, Charmaine, Scott, Jennifer H., Mark H., Heather, Chris, Mark K., Jesse, Gretchen, Ryan, Mark L., Daniel, Nathan, Carol, John, Nick, Laura, Kyle, Karen, Kendra, Kevin, Zak, Aaron, Mikael, Jeff, Susanna, Rachel, Victoria and Alicia. Thank you for believing in this story and breathing life into it.

The process of researching and writing this book took more than six years and could not have been accomplished without the help of a great many people, including my volunteer copy editors Leah, Linda, Heather, Kiersti and Sue.

First and foremost, thanks go to the many family members who have faithfully kept records, saved newspaper clippings and photos, written genealogies and shared these stories orally: those still with us would include my parents, John and Carol Mercer, and my cousins Harold and Phil Groschwitz.

I've also had a number of people go out of their way to help me obtain scraps of information, point me in the right direction, take me on tours or just sit and chat. These would include: Constance Kristofnik of the New London Historical Society; St. James Episcopal Church in New London; Daniel Horgan Esq., current owner of 111 Huntington Street; Brian Rodgers, of the New London Custom House; David Goff, Pastor of the Lost Creek Friends Church; Mary Jo Slonaker, current owner of the Mercer house in Cambridge; and the Los Angeles Police Historical Society, just to name a few.

But no one was more helpful in this process than my friend Leah Huddleston. I wrote a letter several years ago to the Western Wayne County Historical Society asking for help and I got more than I could have ever dreamed of: I got Leah. She took on the task of researching my family and made it her own cause. When we visited Cambridge City in 2011, she acted as our tour guide and has continued to find tidbits as I completed the manuscript. I could not have done it without her.

CPSIA information can be obtained at www.ICGtesting.com
Printed in the USA
BVOW02s2133251015

423947BV00001B/28/P